ALL THE LIES

A DCI Will Blake Thriller

J.E. Mayhew

Obolus Books

ISBN-13: 978-1-9998407-8-5

Cover design by: Meg Cowley

To Cousin Angela,
who seems to read all my nonsense
and is kind enough to say she enjoys it!

Although the story is set on the Wirral, the names of some establishments and roads have been fictionalised to protect the unloved and godless... but you can have fun guessing...

JON MAYHEW

A truth that's told with bad intent
Beats all the lies you can invent.

WILLIAM BLAKE.

CHAPTER 1

The whole forest had turned on him. It felt like it was fighting him and trying to stop him from getting away. The earth beneath his feet had actually tilted and become a slick mudslide. Every tree lurched into his path, so that he smacked painfully into each gnarled trunk. Branches clawed at his eyes and brambles pulled his legs from under him. Soon he was no longer running but rolling down the hillside. Even then, roots took a swipe at his temple, sending sparks of pain shuddering through him.

He couldn't feel the wound in his stomach. The pain of that had just become a part of the agony that engulfed his entire body as he pitched down the hill through the trees. The warm wetness of the blood had been lost in the icy soaking from bushes he'd tumbled through. He knew it was deep and he knew he was in serious trouble.

A tree stump stopped his fall abruptly, cracking a rib and punching the breath from his body. He howled silently and lay still for a second, gasping for breath.

He couldn't rest, though. Higher up the hill, the snapping of twigs told him that he was still being chased.

Hunted.

The lights of the big house flickered through the canopy of the forest. He wasn't far away from safety, but it seemed like miles. Groaning, he pulled himself to his feet. For a second, a few stars glittered through the branches, then swirled around. He blinked and steadied himself, then leaned forward and vomited onto the needle-coated forest floor.

Another twig snapped back in the depths of the forest and he launched off, like a startled deer. But the ground betrayed him again, sending him plummeting through the undergrowth; pitching and hurtling like a deranged acrobat, bouncing off rocks and wood as though he'd been flung. And then he was there on the edge of the big house's front courtyard.

He tried to call out, but his throat was dry and clogged with blood and dirt. His breath came out in short, strangled gasps and every shuffling step towards the light of the windows sent needles of pain up his legs. The lights in the house swayed. Footsteps scrunched on the gravel behind him, but he heard voices crying out from the house and the front door unlocking. Then the light grew brighter and whiter until he had to close his eyes and let gravity take him.

*****

In all her born years, Duana Lambert had never

seen so much blood. It covered the poor boy and stained the gravel beneath him. Even on this cloudy night where the moon only occasionally broke through to shed a cold blue light, she could see the dark liquid soaked into his clothes. More shocking, somehow, was the sight of Rosie standing over him with a large knife in her trembling hands. Streaks of red smeared her cheek, her hands, even her apron.

She looked at Duana, wide-eyed. "Phone my brother. Phone Will Blake."

CHAPTER 2

Quite how Detective Chief Inspector Will Blake ended up with the responsibility of a cat and a small dog was a constant wonder to him. It was a duty that weighed more heavily on him than his job sometimes, maybe because of his job, with its long and unpredictable hours. He'd reluctantly inherited both animals but wouldn't part with either of them now. He sat in his neighbour, Ian Youde's, kitchen, cradling Charlie, his Jack Russell.

Although Youde lived alone in a big house, he kept it immaculate, something that shamed Blake often. Youde's kitchen was spotless and smelt of home baking even this early in the day. The stack of dishes in Blake's own sink was at least two weeks old and he was running out of plates and cutlery.

"I know you're not a big fan of cats, Ian, but it'd only be for a couple of days. I'll take Charlie with me but Serafina has to stay here," Blake said, scratching Charlie behind his ear as he snuffled under Blake's chin. He'd fleetingly considered a cattery but, knowing Serafina, he realised that would be asking for trouble. Serafina had an aptitude for causing chaos. It was a good job she and Charlie had taken to each other. They'd been rivals at first but Serafina had developed a kind of possessive tolerance of the dog. She put up with him most of the time and might even show him some affection but if anyone else went near him, she growled like a tiger.

"Charlie is fine with me, too, you know, Will," Youde said. He was a mean-looking man with cropped, silver hair, a suntanned face, and narrow, suspicious eyes. Blake hadn't liked Youde at first and had assumed he was as grudging and curmudgeonly as he looked. But Youde had saved his life since then and proved himself to be a good neighbour and a friend.

"I know, Ian," Blake said. "But he may prove useful. I'm hoping if Laura sees him, it might help her think about coming back..."

Youde looked pained. "You think emotional blackmail is goin' to work, Will? She ran away to escape from a criminal gang, not because she felt like a change."

"I know," Will said, stroking the dog, absent-mindedly, "but she'd be safe here and she must be lost without her animals. I know it. Charlie will remind her of who she really is, not who she was in the past."

"Well, good luck with that, Will. And you think you've tracked her down?"

"Possibly," Blake said. "Her mobile phone was used in Andover..."

"You've been tracking her? Is that even allowed?"

"A colleague of mine is trying to trace her as part of the case," Blake said, not meeting Youde's gaze. "Somebody ran off with a lot of money, Ian, but there's no solid evidence that it was Laura." He almost believed the lie himself, but Laura had phoned him. She'd told him that she'd done terrible things, that he wasn't to look for her but what else could he do?

"And what if she doesn't want to come back, Will? What if you travel all that way to find her and she runs away again?"

Blake shrugged. "I'll cross that bridge when I come to it. Right now, I'm heading down to Andover. That's all I know."

*****

The phone call that changed everything came as Blake was hurtling down the M56 in his 1988 Opel Manta. It had been his father's pride and joy, the first brand new car he'd bought, and he'd kept it going long past the time it should have been scrapped. For that reason alone, Blake had a fanatical attachment to the car, even though he hadn't been as skilled as his dad at keeping the car in tiptop condition. Blake had worried about making such a long journey in the car but hiring another vehicle seemed like a betrayal. A cradle stuck to the windscreen held his phone and let him see Google Maps. It all looked a little Heath Robinson but seemed to do the trick. Until the phone rang.

Charlie lay in his puppy carrier, safely strapped into the passenger seat and the roar of the car's engine had sent him into a deep slumber. When the phone began to ring, Charlie leapt up inside the cushioned crate and started yapping wildly. Blake stabbed his finger at the screen to answer the call, accidentally closing the map of where he was going. He stabbed at it again and managed to put it on speaker, before the whole lot fell off the windscreen onto the floor.

"Will?" It was a woman's voice, but Charlie's yapping was making it difficult to hear.

"Laura?" Will said. "Is that you? Are you okay? Charlie, be quiet!"

"Will? It's me, Rosie..."

"Oh," Blake shouted, trying not to sound disappointed. "Hi, Rosie, long time no..."

"Will, you've got to help me. I'm in big trouble," she said. The line broke up and Blake couldn't work out what she said next.

"What kind of trouble Rosie?"

"I need you up here now..." Her voice dropped out again.

"I can't do that, Rosie, I'm on my way down south. I'm sort of on a case. It's important..."

Blake glanced in the mirror, wondering how long ago he'd passed junction 10. Junction 9 was the turn-off for the M6 and if he missed it, then he'd have to double back. "Where are you?"

"The police station..." The signal broke up again. Blake saw the junction ahead and pulled the Manta into the lane for the M6 heading south.

"The police station? Rosie what's going on?"

"It's murder, Will... I've murdered...someone!"

The lanes taking traffic north and south were about to split. "Sod it," Blake muttered and swerved the Manta into the North lane. Horns blared behind him, but he'd made the decision. He'd have to search for Laura another day.

CHAPTER 3

As static caravans abandoned in a farmyard went, it was quite classy, Laura Vexley thought. But she'd stayed in some terrible places and was setting the bar low. In fact, she was probably digging a hole and burying the bar. The place smelt vaguely fungal, like the inside of an old training shoe and black mould spotted the corners and windows frames. Yellowed net curtains hung limply in front of the filthy windows. One end of the caravan had a seating area and a chipboard table that looked like a Pitbull had bitten chunks out of it. The other end housed a cramped bedroom and a toilet. Washing, it seemed was to take place in the tiny sink by the gas cooker.

A dog barked furiously at something she couldn't see in the total darkness. Laura looked down at the suitcase full of money and knew it wasn't worth it. She had known that when she'd run. The money would be something to live on. Cash opened doors that would otherwise stay shut and it left no trail. She looked around, concluding that some doors just didn't need opening. But this would do for now. She was just passing through anyway.

When she had arrived in Ludlow station, she'd

walked to the town's centre and entered the first pub she could find. That way, there would be no taxi driver to remember her at the station. A quick search on her phone found her the static caravan at the back of Sourwater Farm. The name sounded forbidding enough. Even better, it had a string of condemnations on Trip Advisor: shabby, run down, isolated, inconveniently situated for any tourist sights. The last one was 2017. It sounded perfect. She wanted to lie low for a while before she made any decisions about the future. After a swift glass of cider and a bite to eat, Laura had stocked up on snacks and fast food from a convenience store. This crap food was going to kill her, she knew that but needs must. Once she was stocked up, she called for a taxi to take her to the farm.

Even though the taxi driver was chatty and friendly, Laura had kept as tight-lipped as possible. With a psychopath like Kyle Quinlan waiting to pounce on her, she couldn't afford to make any mistakes. Quinlan was her ex-husband, a cruel, violent man. She'd stolen money from him and he had disappeared, only to return with wealth, power and a desire to make her his own. When she rejected him, he turned against her. In his own twisted way, he thought he was doing her a favour by letting her run for it and giving her a head start. She'd been moving from town to town since November, staying in cheap B&Bs

and avoiding anywhere that involved using a credit card or anything that might give her whereabouts away. She had spent Christmas in a motel near Peterborough, watching the crackly television wondering what Blake was doing and desperately resisting the urge to call him. Quinlan would be watching, she knew it. If Blake came to find her, then Quinlan wouldn't be far behind.

Shadows were growing longer by the time Laura had reached Gilmore Farm. The taxi driver had taken several wrong turns and had to double back on himself twice before they found it. The farmhouse stood on the junction of two narrow lanes, hemmed in by a high, straggly thorn hedge The old building loomed above it, a Victorian dwelling with crumbling brickwork and peeling paint. She checked the farm out first, sneaking round the back of the dilapidated farmhouse. The muddy yard looked fairly orderly; a tractor sat in the shelter of a dutch barn. Big round bales of hay filled one side and a trailer was parked in the other. A few empty steel drums stood sentry outside an old wooden shed. A brindled terrier strained at its chain, flecks of spit flying from its jaws as it barked. That was what had brought the farmer himself to the back door.

He was a big man, with close cut black hair and a tall, square frame. With his chiselled jaw and sharp, intelligent eyes, he reminded Laura of

Blake. But it was less to do with his looks than an air of vulnerability that the man had. He wore a faded denim shirt under a ragged set of overalls. "Can I help you?" he had said, ignoring the dog as it carried on barking and testing the length of its chain.

"You the owner?"

"I am," he had said in a slow, gentle voice. "Steve Gilmore. Can I help you?"

"I believe you have a caravan to rent. I've come to look at it," Laura had held Gilmore's gaze until he coughed and looked away.

"I haven't had many takers recently," he muttered, scratching his head. "It's over there. I normally charge forty quid a week..."

Laura glanced over at the dirty green box squatting in the corner of the yard. "I'll give you thirty and you'll throw in some bleach and cleaning products. If it's as manky on the inside as it is on the outside, I'll need to disinfect it, won't I?"

Gilmore had grinned, his blue eyes twinkling. "Fair enough, miss...?" He left the question of her name hanging in the air.

"Stacy," Laura said. "Stacy Smith."

"You a scouser, Stacy?"

"Sort of," Laura said. There was no point trying to hide her accent.

Gilmore narrowed his eyes. "If you could give me that rent upfront, that would help. I've had people do a flit without paying in the past. How long are you thinking of staying?"

Laura had encountered this before. Some people just didn't like the accent or had preconceived ideas about scousers. Personally, she blamed newspapers who had demonised people from Liverpool and the surrounding area repeatedly over the years. "A couple of weeks at the most. Here," she said, stuffing sixty pounds into Gilmore's huge palm.

He pocketed the money. "Thanks," he said, with an embarrassed grin. "It's quiet out here if that's what you're looking for. Just me."

An involuntary shiver ran through Laura and she glanced up at the house. It looked tall and forbidding. A light glowed in the bedroom window. "Great," she said.

"The caravan's open; the lock doesn't work, I'm afraid," Gilmore said, giving her a sheepish smile. "But like I said, nothing ever happens here."

"Okay," Laura had muttered and watched Gilmore limp back to his house.

Now, sitting in the flimsy, old caravan, with the dog barking in the background, she suddenly felt vulnerable. Her hand strayed to the pay-as-you-go mobile in her pocket and, yet again, she considered calling Will Blake. No. Quinlan had said he'd be watching Will, too. The moment Will came to her, he would be followed, bringing Quinlan or one of his cronies close behind him. Despite being the great policeman, Will Blake couldn't keep her safe now. Besides, it was probably best for Will's career if he wasn't burdened with a criminal as a girlfriend. She pulled back the crispy net curtain and looked at the farmhouse. It was tall and narrow, the gables sharp and pointed. A weak light still shone in the upstairs window, and Gilmore's huge silhouette framed in it as he stared out at her.

She dropped the curtain and sat down again, listening to the dog barking. Her work at the cat sanctuary and as a pet behaviourist seemed like another time completely. It was something she had chosen because of her love of animals first and foremost. But there was also a feeling that all creatures deserved a chance at redemption. Dogs and cats weren't savage by nature; often they had been taught to be scared or wary of people. They attacked when they felt threatened. Most crazy pets were the product of lazy or ignorant owners. Or cruel ones. But with a little effort and compassion, most animals could be helped. She believed that about people, too. She had to.

Old habits died hard, though, and, rummaging in her bag, Laura found a dog chew and a ball. She opened the door and went out into the muddy yard. The dog threw itself to the limit of its chain but Laura sidled closer and sat just out of range, sitting low and throwing the dog chew into its reach. The dog pounced on the chew and began to destroy it. Laura squatted there in the cold, not making eye contact. It looked well enough from what she could see, glossy coat, not underweight.

"What're you doing?" Gilmore said, appearing behind her, suddenly.

Laura gave a start and jumped up, but the dog didn't start barking, it was too intent on finishing off the chew. "The dog was barking. I thought I'd give it a treat and introduce myself...What's his name?"

"Archie," Gilmore sighed, shaking his head. "He never shuts up, these days."

"Maybe he's bored. Or wants to come inside," Laura said.

"He's always lived in the kennel. He's been like this since my dad passed away a few months ago."

"I'm sorry," Laura said. "He could be missing your dad, too. Just wants a bit of company." Archie stood silently, staring at them. Laura threw the ball and he leapt up to catch it. "I could take him for a walk tomorrow, if you you're okay with that."

Gilmore frowned at her. "Why would you do that?"

"I dunno," Laura said. "I've got nothing much else to do."

"I don't see why not. You can if you want."

Archie had scurried over, keeping low and wagging his tail. Laura grinned and scratched him behind his ear. "See you're just a soft old pudding, aren't you? He can come in the caravan with me if you don't mind."

Gilmore looked troubled and glanced around the dark yard. "No. He needs to be outside to keep guard."

"I thought you said nothing ever happens round here."

"It's quiet but that doesn't mean there aren't thieves," Gilmore looked round again. "Or others up to no good. No keep him out. You never know who's out there.

CHAPTER 4

A sleety rain rattled on the hood of Blake's jacket as he watched Charlie squatting on the grass by the side of the carpark at Teebay services. He'd tried to ring Rosie back but with no success. Moments of uncertainty like this tormented Blake. He hated them. It was the same on a case; those first few hours when a body was discovered and there was nothing; no clue as to how the poor victim had ended up dead, if they had died violently or not, it put him on edge. Every time. This felt worse because he was choosing between an attempt to save Laura and a garbled message from his sister. He'd wrestled with this feeling for the last hour and a half as he hurtled up the motorway.

He looked down at the shivering puppy. "What d'you reckon, Charlie? Is blood thicker than water? You don't reckon, do you?"

He stooped and tried his best to collect the rather slimy deposit that the dog had left, grimacing as the plastic of the poo bag slid between the blades of grass. The rain and sleet would wash away the residue soon enough. "Not my favourite job, mate," he said to Charlie, who wagged his tail as a thank you.

In his heart, Blake knew he couldn't ignore Rosie's call for help, but even now, a big part of him wanted to turn around and head back south. Picking Charlie up, he went back to the car. As soon as they were inside, Charlie gave himself a huge shake, spraying water everywhere. "Thanks, mate. If I give you a snack now, you promise not to dump or fart in the car?"

The look Charlie gave Blake was certainly laced with a heavy dose of, 'no promises.'

The phone rang again and Blake poked it with his finger so hard, he almost knocked it out of its cradle again.

"Will?" Rosie sounded small and frightened. It reminded him of a time when they were kids and she'd stumbled into his and Jeff's bedroom after a terrible nightmare. She sounded as disorientated and bewildered now.

"Rosie, are you okay. What's happening?"

The mobile reception was still glitchy. "Yes. They've taken me to Dumfries to a custody suite..." Blake could tell the word sounded alien to her. The call continued to drop in and out. "... interview me... legal..."

"Rosie? I can't hear you properly. Don't say anything unless you've got a solicitor to advise you, okay?"

"You're telling me not to help the police?"

"No... yes... I suppose... it's always best to have someone there who knows the ropes. Innocent people have been convicted of murder before now. I'm nearly there..." He ended the call and frowned at the phone, wondering if he should call his younger brother, Jeff. They didn't always get on for a whole host of reasons, but he should let him know. Jeff would only bitch about it later on if he didn't. Quite what he'd do with the information apart from fret and worry that it was stopping him from writing, Blake wasn't sure. Jeff always seemed to have an excuse about why he hadn't finished his latest work. There was always some distraction or 'complicated' woman making his life too hard to make up a story. "Pot, kettle, black," Blake snorted. His own love life was hardly simple at the moment. But Jeff was such a drama queen. Blake tapped the contact button and soon the phone was buzzing again.

Annoyingly, Jeff's line couldn't have been more crystal clear. He was as alarmed as Blake had expected. "Why? What did she do? Who? That's impossible. It's ridiculous! Rosie wouldn't harm a fly..."

"Woah, Jeff. I didn't arrest her, you know. I couldn't make out much detail, it was such a bad line. I just thought I'd keep you in the picture. As soon as I have more details, I'll let you know."

"Right," Jeff murmured. He sounded surly and

preoccupied. "Just make sure you do. If there's anything I can help with let me know, right?"

"What's that meant to mean?"

"Well, you know what you're like, charging off and trying to solve every problem yourself. Just ask for help if you need it."

"Okay. I'll let you know," Blake said. This wasn't the time to have an argument. They were both stressed, and Jeff had only just received the news. He hung up and started the car.

The Paradise Found Community, the commune where Rosie Blake lived was in the Southern Uplands of Scotland, a small, deep valley lost somewhere in between the rolling hills. Rosie had spent much of her adult life north of the border, living in various communes and groups. At one point, Blake's parents, convinced she'd been brainwashed by a cult, were really worried about her but she'd proved herself to be independent minded. A restless soul, she rarely settled anywhere for long. This commune had been the longest place she'd stayed put since leaving home.

The traffic was quiet, but the sleet didn't let up. Heavy droplets splattered onto his windscreen and rattled on the roof. For once, Blake was thankful that he'd thrown all his outdoor gear into the boot of the car, just as though he was going out to work. He had thick boots and wellingtons in the back along with a heavy coat and waterproof trousers.

Question after question tumbled over in his head as he drove. If Rosie had killed somebody, then it must have been by accident, possibly even self-defence. He couldn't think of anyone he knew who was less offensive than Rosie. He'd thought this last time she'd been home for their mother's funeral just before Christmas. She was Vegan and had always held very strong pacifist views. He couldn't imagine her getting angry enough to lash out at anyone.

It was only early afternoon by the time he arrived at Dumfries although the dark clouds and lashing rain made it feel like twilight already. The town looked like a grim oil painting in the dim light. He remembered that he had stayed here once long ago on holiday but the place seemed bigger now and the one way system flummoxed him. As towns went, it didn't strike him as much different from any in Northern England, with all the usual high street outlets and a mix of coffee shops, charity stores and tea rooms. At first, he'd called into the Dumfries and Galloway Headquarters and caused some confusion as it was the wrong station. Once he'd shown his warrant card and explained his predicament, they directed him to the station with a custody suite.

The police station was on a main road. After

some driving around, Blake managed to find a carpark behind it. Blake parked, cracked a window open for Charlie and walked along the road. The cold air bit into him and he was glad of the coat to keep the sheets of rain that bounced off the pavement. It struck Blake that the old station had been extended fairly recently. The first half of the huge building was made of large sandstone blocks, but the main entrance was wide and modern, a mix of glass, steel, and newer brickwork. It looked imposing and took up most of one side of the street. Bracing himself, Blake stepped through the sliding doors, welcoming the rush of warm air that enveloped him.

Inside, Blake felt at home, straight away. A small waiting area and a pin board full of notices, a few chairs against one side of the wall, a line of chipped paint and plaster where the backs of them had rubbed. A glass screen separated the receptionist from the public space. She was a little older than Blake, with dyed black hair held back from her face with a flowery band. Her sharp features and watchful eyes told Blake that she was an old hand at this game and could assess punters the moment they stepped through the door. She wore a blue jumper and white blouse, but Blake knew she wasn't an officer. Her eyes narrowed a little as he approached the counter then she blushed, and a smile fluttered across her mouth. Her name badge told Blake she was called Kirsty Allan.

"Mr Blake," she said, grinning again. "We've been expecting you. Can I just say, it's a pleasure to meet you? I used to love Searchlight!"

"Thanks" Blake said, blushing. He never got used to being recognised. Years ago, in what seemed like another life now, Blake had been seconded to the television programme. It dealt with unsolved crimes and Blake had a minor part asking for the public's help in identifying various criminals caught on CCTV. Even though his slot on Searchlight was relatively small, he had quite a fanbase, largely female. His bosses at the time had suggested he take the role because he was 'easy on the eye.' "It was some time ago, now, though..."

"Oh, I know but, all the same..." Kirsty Allan glanced around and then slid a pen and a piece of notepaper across the counter. "You couldn't just..."

"Kirsty!" a voice snapped, making both her and Blake start.

CHAPTER 5

A small, stocky man in his late forties, or early fifties stood at the door to the main body of the station. He wore a brown suit, and his stout frame tested the limits of its seams. Blake wondered if it was muscle or fat; it was hard to tell. He seemed like he'd been poured into the suit. His red hair was threaded with silver and cropped into a flat top. A rash of stubble made it look as though it was migrating around his chin and neck. A pair of fierce, dark eyes glowered over a button nose and Blake couldn't shake the comparison with an angry terrier. He shuffled forward.

"I hope you're not bothering our honoured guest, Kirsty," he said, throwing his hand out as though he was going to karate chop Blake. "Detective Sergeant Luckie, sir." Blake couldn't help but notice the way he said, 'sir' almost through gritted teeth.

He shook the proffered hand, warily. "Will Blake. Is my sister...?"

Luckie held onto Blake's hand. "We'll come to her in a moment, sir. I just want to make something very clear. I know all about you, sir. And I've spoken to your Superintendent..."

"You have?" Blake said, pulling his hand away. "That seems like a massive breach of confidence if you don't mind me saying so."

"Given your ability to make headline news wherever you go and the seeming carnage that is left in your wake. I'm concerned for the safety of this case."

"Carnage?" Blake said. "I'm sorry, you've lost me…"

"All I'm saying is that we have our ways of doing things here and if you step out of line, then I won't make any exceptions or let you off the hook, sir. You might be a minor Scouse celeb in your part of the world, but I don't want you coming here and messing things up…"

Blake straightened up and looked down on the man, silencing him. "I think you'll find, Detective Sergeant, that what my colleagues appreciate is my thoroughness and attention to detail. Now, I'm sure you're all generally very professional up here, but I don't appreciate you swinging your dick around the moment we've met. I got a call from my sister. Apparently, she's in trouble. I'm going to help her if I can. Can I see her please?"

Luckie pursed his lips. "Right you are. But I'm just saying, sir…"

"You've said enough, Detective Sergeant. Where's my sister?"

DS Luckie reddened and cleared his throat. "You'll have to sign in first."

"Thanks. Oh, and I'm not a scouser. I'm from the Wirral."

"Same place..."

"No. There's a world of difference. I'll educate you some time."

Blake turned back to the counter and signed in, then signed Kirsty's slip of paper, looking up and winking at her as he did. She suppressed a smirk and took the autograph back. DS Luckie gave an impatient snort and led Blake into the main body of the station.

Rosie sat in a featureless interview room that, like the rest of the building, could be anywhere. It hadn't been that long since Will had seen his sister, but she had changed. She was tall, like him and their brother Jeffrey, but right now, she looked tiny and abandoned. Her greying, blonde hair was plaited and hung down over one shoulder. She reminded Blake of his mother and to see her so upset, broke his heart. She looked old, Blake thought, but being accused of murder and then being questioned by police for hours can do that to you.

A young man sat next to her, presumably her brief. His suit looked sharp and expensive. He wasn't some market town solicitor. Clearly, The Community could afford the best.

She jumped out of her seat and hugged onto Blake as soon as he entered the room. “Will, thank God,” she said. “I don’t know what to do. I feel so helpless. They keep asking me questions.” She glanced back at the young solicitor. “Simon has told me not to say anything, but it feels so dishonest and unhelpful…”

“Okay, Rosie, take it easy, I’m here. Sit down and tell me everything.”

*****

Detective Inspector Kath Cryer sat at her desk, in the office at Merseyside Police HQ, trying to steel herself for a day of report writing and catching up with paperwork. Around her, other colleagues seemed to be facing a similar struggle. It was a cold, grey day at the time of year when you got up to go to work and came home in the dark. No let-up in either the weather or the inventive ways the criminals of Merseyside devised to evade the law. Currently, she was musing over whether to use the word ‘backside’ or ‘anus.’ She was trying to describe how a local lowlife had filled the plastic capsule from a Kinder Egg with drugs before stuffing it up his rear passage when he was approached by Kath and a uniformed officer. Unfortunately, during a hospital strip search, the egg had popped out with violent force, hitting a member of the medical team in the eye.

Despite this gross image, she stared down at the bar of Fruit and Nut that she had promised herself she wouldn't buy on the way into work. It was a habit that had developed after Christmas and she needed to break it if she was ever to get her weight back down from its post-festive peak. She had never been a great one for diets and setting resolutions to get into shape for summer, but she'd almost screamed when she went on the bathroom scales last night. The chocolate bar sat there, twinkling on her desktop. "Eat me, eat me," it whispered.

Maybe she could give it to DC Kinnear, sitting opposite her. He had even less willpower than she did. She glanced over the desk at him munching on a Jammy Dodger.

"Where did you get that, from?"

Kinnear looked up, like a kid who'd just been caught stealing from a charity box. "Where did I get what?" he said, spraying crumbs across the desk.

"Bloody hell, Kinnear, could you be any less couth?"

"Sorry..." Kinnear spluttered covering his mouth to contain the fallout. "Madge from Reception brought them up. Apparently, there was a meeting and these were left behind. I mean, who in their right mind leaves a Jammy Dodger on the plate?"

Kath gave a tart smile. “Don’t you mean Marge from Reception?”

“No. There’s a Marge and there’s a Madge, they both work on Reception and they both seem intent on bringing me biscuits. I mean why do women of a certain age do that, Guv?”

“Do what?”

“You know, feed up young men like me? Is it an empty nest thing? Why do they keep giving me stuff to eat?”

Kath unwrapped the chocolate bar. “I dunno, Andrew. Personally, I wouldn’t waste good biscuits on you.” She broke off a chunk and popped it into her mouth. “So, which one’s Madge? Is she the one with the dyed auburn hair and the chunky gold necklace?”

“They’ve both got dyed auburn hair and chunky necklaces,” Andrew Kinnear said. “One looks a bit sterner than the other and Madge has got a mole just by her ear.”

“I’ll just check their lanyards, I think,” Kath said, smoothing out the chocolate wrapper.

“Easy for you. If I did that, it looks like I’m staring at their boobs,” Kinnear said.

Kath looked puzzled. “But you’re gay…” she began but then stopped and suddenly looked fascinated by a file in front of her.

Kinnear didn’t notice but carried on. “So? I can

hardly squint at Marge's name badge and then say, 'it's okay, luv, I'm not staring at your boobs, I'm gay!' Can I?" Kinnear had put on a really camp voice and was waving his arms around.

"Are you all right, Andrew?" Superintendent Martin said, from behind Kinnear, who went bright red and gave a squeak of alarm. "Yes. Yes, sir. Just... just discussing office... office etiquette with Kath..."

Martin raised one eyebrow. He was a hawkish-looking man, lean and severe but he was not without a wry sense of humour. His withering one-liners were feared throughout the force. He looked preoccupied today, though. "Good. Well done. Has Will Blake been in touch with either of you two?"

"No, sir," Kath said, glancing over to Kinnear. "I thought he'd taken a few days off. He said something about going down south."

Martin nodded and scratched his chin. "He has but I've just had a call from a Detective Sergeant up in Scotland saying he's got himself involved with an investigation up there. His sister has been accused of murder, apparently. He hasn't contacted you at all?"

"No, sir."

Martin glanced around the office and lowered his voice. "Then keep this quiet, okay? I know you're very loyal to Will but let me know if he calls. I don't want this department being dragged into any kind of fracas with Police Scotland. Okay?"

"Okay, sir," Kath said. Kinnear nodded. They watched Martin stalk off between the desks. As soon as he was out of earshot, Kath pulled her mobile out of her bag.

"What are you doing?"

"Texting Blakey to let him know we're here if he needs any help."

CHAPTER 6

Rosie Blake stared at the tabletop in front of her and shook her head in disbelief. It was a feeling that Will shared. How did he come to be sitting opposite his own sister in a police interview room asking her about the murder she'd been accused of? It was madness. There was no way she was capable of harming anyone. Simon Carver, the brief had moved to the side of the room and scribbled notes.

"So just tell me, in your own words what happened, Rosie," Blake said. Leaning forward. "Just take your time."

"It was quite late, about ten o'clock. I was preparing some vegetables for a soup and I heard a noise outside," Rosie said.

"What kind of noise?"

"Like a groan. It sounded horrible. I thought someone might have hurt themselves, so I went outside and that's when I saw Jonah..."

"Jonah?"

"Yeah, Jonah Huxley. He's been a member of the Paradise Found Community since he was a kid. He comes and goes. He was lying on the ground. I ran over to him." She stopped and put a hand to her mouth. "God, I've never seen so much blood, Will. It was everywhere. I tried to bring him round, but he must have been dead already. I was covered in his blood. Then everyone came out and saw me there, with the knife..."

Blake rubbed his face. "What knife?"

"The one I'd been chopping veg with," Rosie said. "I still had it in my hand when I went outside."

"Ten o'clock is quite late to be preparing vegetables, Rosie," Blake said. "How come?"

"Well, I was doing a big batch of soup. I was going to freeze some but I wanted get it ready for the next day. Sometimes there's a lot of us to feed. I'd nearly finished."

"So, you took the knife out with you when you saw Jonah laying on the ground?"

"Yes," Rosie said. "I think I must have," she said and shivered.

Blake took a breath. "You don't sound very certain, Rosie. This is a difficult question for me, but I have to ask it. Did you kill Jonah Huxley?"

Rosie said, her face creased up. "I - I don't know."

"What do you mean, you don't know? You just told me you went out and there was blood everywhere..."

"I know but I passed out. It's all a bit hazy, if I'm honest. I remember going out and seeing Jonah but then it's a blur. But Duana says..."

"Who's Duana?"

"Duana Lambert, she's sort of the head of The Community, as far as we have anyone in charge. She says we all killed Jonah."

"What does she mean by that?"

Rosie shrugged. "Collective responsibility. Jonah was one of ours and we let him get hurt."

"That's bollocks," Blake said. "Somebody killed this man and it wasn't you. Did you have any reason to harm Jonah Huxley?"

"No. He was a bit of a pain. A smart Alec, you know a bit lippy but he never bothered me. I grew up with a pair of lippy smart Alecs." She gave a lost smile.

Blake smiled back and squeezed her hand. "Don't worry, Rosie, we'll figure this out. Is there anything else you can remember?"

"Not really. It's just like some horrible dream. You could go and talk to Duana," Rosie said, hopefully. "She might be able to explain what happened better."

"I can do that. Will you be okay?" he turned to the young man. "I presume you're staying to represent her, Simon?"

"As long as I can. I think DS Luckie wants to detain her but I'm keeping a close eye on the clock. Unless they're going to charge her, I'll have her out of here within twenty-four hours."

Rosie nodded. "Duana called Simon the moment they arrested me."

"Good. Do what he says. Keep schtum for now, especially if you're going to say things like you don't know what happened. People do end up being convicted for things they didn't do, Rosie. You need to think hard and get your story straight. In the meantime, I'll go and see this Duana and report back if I find anything new. Do you have a postcode for the Community?"

Rosie scribbled down the address with shaking hands. "It's a fair drive from here, Will. An hour or so. You can stay over in my room if you need to."

"I think your room will be a crime scene, Rosie," Blake said quietly. "They'll be searching through it for any clues."

"Oh," Rosie said, her face falling. "God, how did all this happen? I always thought the Universe would provide if I did no harm..."

Blake bit his lip. He'd seen plenty of harmless people wronged by life. His job, as he saw it sometimes was to stop harmful people from thriving at their expense; a battle he often felt he was losing. "Don't worry, Rosie. We'll get to the bottom of this. One thing I do believe is that the truth can't be hidden."

Rosie nodded and gave Blake a look as though she was seeing him for the first time. Not as her brother but as a police officer who dealt with this kind of trauma every day. Now she was in the thick of it. "Duana will help you. She can be a bit prickly and defensive about The Community but she's a good person."

"Okay, then," Blake said, standing up. Rosie hugged him again. "Try and stay calm, Rosie. Don't say anything with or without Simon being present, okay? I'll be back later, and we'll sort this mess out." He gave her a playful punch on the shoulder, as only a brother could. "Do some of that hippy shit meditation or something, eh?"

Rosie gave a tight smile and nodded. Blake hated seeing her like this, clinging to him like a little child. He swore to himself he'd bring back that bright, independent woman if it was the last thing he did.

Outside in the corridor, DS Luckie leaned against the wall, with his arms folded. "She was covered in Huxley's blood," he said, without any provocation. "The knife had her prints all over it."

"Was that the knife used in the attack or the one she was chopping up carrots with just before she heard Huxley outside?"

"We're waiting for forensics to come back to us on that," Luckie admitted. "Look, sir, I'm not saying we've got our killer..."

"Damn right you haven't," Blake snapped. "My sister wouldn't harm a fly..."

Luckie raised an eyebrow. "And how many times have you heard that line yourself?"

"True," Blake said, reddening. He couldn't deny that often family members didn't really know what their siblings, children or even parents were capable of. "I'm heading over to Paradise Found to talk to Duana Lambert."

"Good luck with that. We've had officers grilling them for hours. They're all taking the blame. It's like fucking Spartacus over there."

Blake couldn't help but smile. "Well, I'll see for myself, won't I?"

"Just so you know," Luckie said, hitching up his trousers, "I meant what I said before. Don't screw up this investigation, sir."

"I'll be the soul of discretion, Luckie," Blake said.

"And I wouldn't spend too long there, either. It's starting to snow and there's a weather warning out. Last thing we need is for you to be stuck out there with all our witnesses, sir."

*****

Even though it was almost dark, Blake could still just about see the rugged landscape. Having been taken out walking in North Wales and the Lakes by his father, he loved this kind of countryside. There was something about it that cleared your thoughts and cleansed your soul. Not that he would be able to see much of it soon as thick flakes began sticking to his windscreen. The wipers struggled to keep up with the flurry as it worsened, and Blake squinted through the storm for the turning that his phone said was imminent.

"Not great weather for a country stroll, mate," he said to Charlie, who stared at him from the padded travel crate.

A dark track flashed by and Blake slammed on the brakes. Surely that wasn't the lane into the Paradise Found Community. It looked more like a bridleway or a wide footpath tracking up the hill. He wondered about the wisdom of driving up there but the idea of walking in the growing blizzard was insane. Muttering a short prayer for the underside of the Manta, Blake reversed and turned into the lane.

According to the phone, the Community lay two miles up this lane, deep in a small valley. The snow clung to his windscreen now in huge clumps, making the wipers groan as one layer of white replaced the last just wiped away. Blake leaned over the steering wheel, grimacing at the restricted view. At first, his car climbed to the top of a hill where the wind buffeted him and the snow blew in horizontal lines across the moors. Then, he crested the hill and plunged down the other side in a sharp descent towards the valley floor. Bushes and trees closed in on him on either side of the lane and soon the world was just the small cone of light from the headlights.

"I'm not sure about this, Charlie," Blake muttered. The little dog gave a whine as if in agreement. Branches scraped the side of the car and a number of ominous clunks from the underside of his car made Blake dab his brakes constantly. He imagined his exhaust lying in the snow somewhere behind him and winced. Was he just driving into a wood? Had he taken the wrong turn? Maybe he shouldn't have trusted the map on his phone. The number of times he'd heard stories of lorries and cars stranded up mountains or on railway tracks because they blindly followed their satnavs. The trouble with this was it was more than embarrassing, he could end up in serious trouble if he was stranded in this snow.

Despite his caution, the car speeded up, slithering on the icy track. It grew darker and the lane snaked around a bend, taking Blake by surprise. He slammed on the brakes and wrestled with the wheel. The back of the Manta slewed to the right, hitting something hard and straightening out. This was insanity. He should have stayed in

Moffat with Rosie.

He had his foot firmly on the brake now, but the car picked up speed, sliding on the slush and mud beneath the locked wheels. Something scraped the roof of the car, making Blake glance up. His wing mirror vanished, and it sounded like a rear bumper had broken off as the car tried to turn sideways in the narrow lane. Blake cursed and dragged the wheel to the left.

Charlie barked and something bleached white and uncertain in the glare of the lights and the swirl of the snow leapt up from the ground. It could have been a barn owl or an old carrier bag. For one mad second, Blake thought he saw a pale arm and a white, screaming face. Instinctively, he dragged the wheel to the left to steer away from the thing. The trunk of a huge oak tree loomed before him, white in the car headlights. Blake braced himself, struggling desperately to keep the car on the road.

It wasn't a head-on collision; the Manta had swung sideways again but its rear didn't correct itself in time and the passenger door slammed hard into the tree. Charlie yelped and Blake was thrown against the side of the car, his head clipping the window. The Manta bounced back from the tree and rolled onto its side, sliding further down the lane until coming to rest in a cloud of smoke and steam.

CHAPTER 7

The phrase 'no comment' was used so often when Luckie talked to people that it sounded strange if anyone replied with some kind of variant. So, when Rosie Blake kept saying, 'Sorry, no comment' Luckie almost replied that it wasn't a problem. He bit his tongue. He didn't like the smarmy city boy sitting next to her. He and Blake had obviously told her to keep quiet. In fact, there was something incongruously slick about him, as far as Luckie was concerned. He reeked of wealth and privilege. The kind of fella who might get a Premier League footballer off a speeding fine or something. How did a guy like this get to be representing some long-haired hippy with plaits and a cheesecloth dress who weaves her own yoghurt for breakfast?

"There's no need to apologise, Ms Blake," Luckie said. "If you feel bad about not helping me with my enquiries, you can remedy that by answering my questions. You've nothing to hide, after all."

"No comment," Rosie said. "Sorry."

Luckie gave a sidelong glance to DC Harris who sat, filling the chair next to him, scribbling furiously in his notebook. God knows what the giant of a man was writing. Luckie was afraid he might stick his tongue out, he seemed to be concentrating so much. Luckie would have to talk to him about that. He just prayed he wasn't doodling. Harris spent far too much time doodling.

Luckie leaned forward. "D'you think your famous brother is going to come back from the glen with the real killer? Is that it?"

Rosie flinched and Luckie actually felt a twinge of guilt. This was like kicking a puppy. "I don't know," she said in a small voice, then glanced over at Mr Smarmy Suit. "I mean no comment. Sorry."

"So you say you were preparing food in the kitchen..."

"Chopping carrots," DC Harris said, suddenly.

Luckie glowered at him and he went back to his notepad. "When you heard Huxley outside. Groaning."

Rosie Blake opened her mouth to answer and then remembered. "No comment."

"To my mind, groaning isn't a very loud sound. If Huxley was shouting, I'd buy it, but groaning? Naw. I don't buy it. Too quiet."

Harris made a rumbling noise in his throat as though he was going to demonstrate a groan but caught Luckie's eye just in time.

"I'm sorry. I can't help you..."

“It’s all free love and open relationships down in the glen, isn’t it?” Luckie said. Harris looked up, startled, and then scribbled a note down.

Rosie scowled. “It’s not orgies every night, if that’s what you’re implying.” She clamped her mouth shut, straight away.

Luckie kept his face straight. This woman wasn’t a seasoned liar, and she could be teased out of her silence by playing on her loyalty to The Community. “Isn’t it?”

“Isn’t it?” Harris repeated, his voice laced with disappointment.

“What happened? Did someone else fall for Huxley, is that it? A love triangle? Jealousy? You wouldn’t be the first woman to have killed over a younger man…”

“I…” Rosie began to say but her brief put a hand on her arm. “No comment.”

Luckie turned off the recorder. “You aren’t helping matters, Rosie,” he said. “We’ll get to the bottom of this, trust me.”

*****

Duana Lambert lowered the receiver back into the cradle of the old telephone and sighed. It had seemed so bright and futuristic when it had first been installed. A trimphone it was called. She remembered being so excited about it and the promise of a bright future it held. It was so old now. Superseded by mobile versions that Duana could never have imagined when she was a little girl. Somehow, that phone had become a symbol of everything that had gone wrong, every disappointment and every heartache that this place had brought. This would soon pass, though. In the many years of living in the glen and running The Community, the police had come and gone. They'd leave again once this blew over. She ran her long fingers through her thick red hair and sighed. Something shifted in the shadows of the big hall and she froze.

Freya Finley emerged from the darkness. "Was that about Rosie?"

"Yes," Duana said, relaxing, slightly. "Her brother is coming over, apparently."

"Shit!" Freya spat.

"Just relax. We'll get through this. We're all responsible for Jonah's death, remember?"

"If the little bastard hadn't been nosing around, trying to cause trouble, then maybe he wouldn't have ended up dead."

"We let that happen. We could have stopped it years ago, but we didn't. Now we mustn't let it disrupt things, okay?"

"There's too much going on. What about Rosie? What if this brother of hers goes poking his nose too far?"

Duana shivered and wrapped her cardigan tighter around herself. "We just have to stay calm, that's all. If Mr Blake proves to be too inquisitive, then we'll have to deal with him. But we'll cross that bridge if we come to it. Right now, we have to carry on as normal."

Freya stared at Duana. "As normal? There's nothing normal about any of this, Duana. It just brings back bad memories. I'm not sure I can cope."

"Stay calm, Freya. The Community looks after its own. Nobody gets in the way of that. Nobody."

*****

An icy twilight filled the inside of the car. Blake could smell something chemical, which troubled him. His head throbbed and his temple felt wet. It was blood. He shivered. Why was he lying on his side? He looked down and marvelled at the glittering diamonds that covered his body, wondering where they came from. Through the fog in his head, he remembered what had happened. It was glass from the shattered windscreen and windows. His eyes widened. The smell was oil and petrol. He couldn't stay in the car.

"Charlie? You okay boy?"

The little pup whined but the crate seemed to have protected him. He poked his head out of the side, looking forlornly at Blake.

Fumbling with his seat belt, Blake groaned as he unclipped himself and eased himself out of the driving seat. The car was on its side and he lay on what was now the floor. His body throbbed with pain, but it burnt most around his ribcage. Gasping, he pulled at the passenger door handle. It clicked uselessly and Blake cursed. Gritting his teeth, he dragged his legs from under the wheel and managed to ease himself into a standing position. Fragments of broken glass cascaded from his clothes. His head popped out into the cold air. A good two inches of snow had already formed on the side of the car around the window. The wind blew it into Blake's eyes, and he slipped back down inside the car. Not that it offered him much protection; snow whipped down the narrow lane and through the shattered windows, filling the rear parcel shelf and the back seat but not reaching Charlie's crate. He twisted round to open the crate door and a jolt of pain shot through him. The door was open though and Charlie scrambled out.

Again, Blake stood up, trying to ignore the pain in his ribs. He lifted the little dog onto the side of the car. Bracing himself against the tempest and the agony that lanced though his body, he wriggled out through the window himself, soaking his clothes. He lay, panting and unable to move for a second, Charlie whimpered and licked his face. Groaning, he dragged himself to his feet and staggered around to the back of the car. The boot had popped partly open and his gear lay tumbled in one corner. He dragged the heavy, waterproof jacket from the boot and got it on. Then he ripped his soaking trainers and socks off and pushed his damp feet into dry ones, sinking his feet into his stout walking boots. Each movement was torture, but he needed to change, or he'd never make it down the lane. Behind him was two or three miles of snow-clogged lane, up to the main road and he hadn't passed a house for several miles before the turn off. His only hope of survival now was to get to The Community.

The pack with his dry clothes in felt ridiculously heavy but he managed to hook it onto one shoulder. He tucked Charlie into the front of his coat and zipped it up as tightly as possible. The heat blossomed across his chest. Maybe they'd keep each other warm and alive.

"Right, Will Blake," he muttered. "One foot in front of the other. Move." He stepped away from the car and his foot sank deep into the snow, sending him rolling down the lane. Charlie howled and something hard clipped Blake's shoulder. At last, he came to rest at the foot of a tall pine tree. Pulling himself up again, he checked the little pup and stepped gingerly onto the lane once more. The snow was falling thick and fast, filling his vision and freezing his face. Blake trudged on, hoping he wasn't too far away from the Paradise Found Community and help.

He wondered where Laura was and if she was thinking of him. This hadn't been what he thought he'd be doing when he set off this morning, that was for sure. He tried to focus on Rosie as he fought through the snow, but the pain stopped any sensible thoughts dead. Cold bit at his fingertips and gnawed at his joints. As he stumbled along, Blake began to feel detached from the world. His feet were numb and the pain in his chest throbbed constantly, but it was as though they were happening to someone else. Like feeling a pulse. Even the warmth of Charlie seemed to be fading. Blake's legs began to feel heavy as though he was wading through sucking mud, not snow. He felt like should just rest. Find somewhere sheltered, curl up in a ball and sleep.

A pair of rusty, iron gates emerged from the blinding whiteness. They were tall and held up by two imposing stone gateposts. It looked like the entrance to a country home. Beyond the gates, a small lodge huddled under the trees. A light glowed in the front window. With the last traces of his strength, Blake heaved the gates open and shuffled towards the front door. He raised his hand to bang on it, but the door swung open and Blake slumped forward, letting exhaustion take him.

CHAPTER 8

A fire crackled and Blake was wrapped in a luxurious warmth. Something pressed down on him, trapping the heat. Blake's eyelids felt heavy as he dragged them open and stared at shadows dancing on a yellowed, cracked ceiling. He lay in a huge bed, with blankets and quilts pinning him down. Pushing them down, Blake tried to sit up, wincing at the pain in his ribs.

It was a small room, lit by the fire in the hearth. Charlie lay curled up on a folded blanket, soaking up the heat from the fire. Heavy curtains covered the windows, so Blake had no idea whether it was day or night or how long he'd slept. A dark oak wardrobe filled one wall and a matching dresser squeezed in at the foot of his bed. Shelves lined the walls, cluttered with books, jars of coins, ornaments. At the end of one shelf, a couple of stuffed weasels snarled at each other in a glass cabinet. Sitting in the corner of the room sat an old man, half in shadow, half illuminated by the dancing fire. He had a shotgun across his knees.

"So, you're alive," he said in a reedy voice. "I thought for a while that you and your little dog were done for. What were you thinking of stumbling around in that storm?"

Blake grimaced and settled himself into a sitting position. "Is there a reason you have a gun with you?"

"You may not know it, sonny, but there's been a murder in the valley. You could be anyone. I'm not taking any chances." Blake could see the old man more clearly now. He was small and pinched-looking with pronounced cheek bones. His baggy sweater hung off him, but Blake could see a certain power in the man's body, as though a life on the hills had given him a strength that belied his years.

"And you didn't think to look in my wallet in my coat pocket?" Blake said. "Have a look there. My name is Will Blake. I'm a police officer."

"You're the Polis?" the man said. He glanced down at Charlie. "He doesn't look like much of a Police dog."

"Have a look." Blake pointed to where his coat hung on the back of the door.

The man narrowed his eyes. "If you're thinking to trick me..."

"I'm Rosie Blake's brother. I've come to find out what's going on here. I crashed my car in the lane. I think I've cracked my ribs. I'm no threat to you, trust me."

The man slowly stood up and leaned the gun against the wall. Never taking his eyes from

Blake, he rummaged in the pockets and pulled out the wallet. "Heh," he muttered, relaxing as he read the warrant card. "William Blake. Did your parents have a thing for the poet, then? Tyger Tyger and all that?"

Blake rolled his eyes. "I think if they'd known, they would have called me Stanley or something. I don't know your name, though."

"Thomas Irving," he said. "Rightful heir to the Devil's Glen."

"I'm sorry, you've lost me. I thought this was the Paradise Found Community…"

Irving's lip curled, revealing yellowed teeth. "That bunch of hippies and perverts? No. They live in the big house down in the valley. This is the old lodge. Should all be mine, though, by rights. They've been trying to get rid of me for years but I'm not going anywhere."

"Right," Blake said. "Well, thank you Thomas, I think you might have saved my life and I'm very grateful…"

"Well, you turned up on my doorstep, didn't you? I could hardly leave you lying there, cluttering my front door up and then there was this little fella…" Charlie had woken up at the sound of Blake's voice and stood wagging his tail. Irving scratched the dog behind his ear. "He swung it for you."

Blake grinned at the man's wry humour. "How long have I been out?"

"A few hours," Irving said. "Ideally, I'd have got you into a hot bath, but you were in a mess, with that cut on your head and, you're right, it looks like you've cracked a couple of ribs. Where did you say you crashed the car?"

"Not far away, I don't think," Blake said, touching his forehead and feeling a large plaster on his brow. "I lost control and hit a tree."

"Aye, you're not the first, Will," Thomas said. "It's a steep hill and treacherous in this kind of weather. I used to taboggan down it when I was a bairn, but I wouldn't recommend it in a car."

Blake nodded. "Well thanks again, but I need to get down to the big house. My sister has been accused of that murder..." It felt as though someone had punched him in the gut. Blake fell back groaning.

Thomas chuckled, mirthlessly. "It's the middle of the night. You won't be welcome right now. Rest and wait until the morning."

"Looks like I don't have much choice," Blake muttered. "So you've lived here all your life, Thomas?"

"Aye," Thomas Irving said, his face darkening. "It's a dour place, cursed too, but it's my home..."

"Cursed?"

"There's a lot of bad things have happened here, Will Blake. This murder is just one in a long history of tragedies and outrages. There'll be more, too, of that I'm certain."

Thomas Irving stared into the firelight and listened to the crackling flames before starting. "The Devil's Glen has always had a bad reputation, Will. Stories of the wee folk and bogles tricking people in this valley go way back. It is said that during the reign of Edward II, English soldiers were stranded in this valley and forced to resort to cannibalism to survive. Centuries later, Jacobite soldiers were hanged from the oldest oaks in the bottom of the valley. This place is full of ghosts."

"Not a happy history, then," Blake said, letting the story wash over him. There was nothing he could do to help Rosie right now and maybe Irving would give him some background. Maybe he'd fall asleep.

"Nobody owned the Glen, nobody wanted it. Until my great, great grandfather, Ramsey Reid, bought it. His mills had made him a small fortune and he had a reputation as a cruel and heartless landlord. He built the big house and this lodge in the hope of building some kind of legacy. His sons were wild and abused the tenants terribly. That's where my line of the family comes from. My great grandmother fell pregnant after encountering Robin, Ramsey's eldest son."

"And I don't suppose Ramsey Reid ever acknowledged the paternity," Blake murmured.

"Not until he was drawing his final breath and, in a rare fit of remorse, he bequeathed this house to my family." Silence fell over the room and it felt as though the very fabric of the house was listening to Thomas' story. The fire cracked and spat, and something scraped at the windowpane behind the curtains. "Hear that?"

Blake nodded.

Thomas' voice dropped. "One hard, cold winter, not unlike this, a cottage up on the top of the valley caught fire. A family of six, mother, father and bairns died in that blaze, but one small boy managed to escape. Desperate, he staggered down into the valley to the big house for help. But Ramsey Reid forbade his servants from letting the poor child in, threatening them with dismissal and worse. He sat by his fire drinking port and listening to the begging boy scratch at the window. They found the poor wee bairn frozen to death the next morning, his fingertips stuck to the glass."

Blake gave a nervous laugh, but he shivered, listening to the scraping behind the curtain. "That's just a tree branch," he said, feeling foolish the moment he said it. He considered telling Irving about what he'd seen just before he crashed but thought better of it.

"Anyway," Thomas Irving said, tutting loudly. "Listen to me going on. You need your rest. I'll leave you in peace." He stood up and headed for the door.

"Thanks," Blake said, easing himself under the covers but wondering if he would be able to sleep again thinking about that scratching on the window.

*****

Detective Sergeant Neil Luckie stared at the almost empty room and shook his head. He'd stayed late at the office, reading through the interviews and files on the murder without looking up. He hadn't even noticed when his colleagues started leaving. Nor did he really take in their comments about the weather. Sometimes such absorption wasn't a bad thing; it had earned him a reputation for doggedness and dedication. When he did look out of the window, he wished he'd been rather less preoccupied with the murder and more interested in the snow that fell in thick flakes, burying everything. "Shit," he muttered.

It dawned on him then that he wouldn't be going home tonight. His car was probably sitting under a snow drift already. He'd need a shovel just to get into it and then the roads would be blocked. He wasn't going anywhere. Luckie wasn't any stranger to throwing an all-nighter, far from it, but he worried how this weather would affect the investigation.

They had gathered as much of the evidence that they could on the day but now the crime scene would be left unattended. Getting back into the glen would become a mammoth task, even if the snow melted as fast at it had arrived. And everything would be delayed, the post-mortem, any follow-up interviews, forensic analysis of samples taken from the scene. Luckie had often been teased about his name, especially when things went wrong but today, he genuinely wondered if the fates were laughing at him up there, somewhere. Because if they wanted to throw a spanner in the works, this was one of the biggest they could find in their cosmic toolbox. That and Will Blake, of course.

CHAPTER 9

Luckie had pushed a couple of chairs together and made a makeshift bed. That gave him a few hours uncomfortable sleep and a stiff back. He woke up groaning and tried to go back to sleep but, after half an hour of shifting awkwardly, and cursing as the chairs slid apart, dumping him on the floor he decided to stay awake. He looked through what they had already gleaned from the crime scene. It was scant little.

After hours of poring through files and rereading reports, Luckie sat glowering at the picture of Rosie Blake. His instincts were telling him that she wasn't capable of killing the young lad, but he could only go on the evidence. That brother of hers needed to pull the broom handle out of his backside, Luckie was sure of that. "Shit," he said again as it dawned on him that Blake was probably stuck in the valley with the witnesses. Blake's senior officer had sounded less than impressed about Blake getting involved when Luckie had called him. "He's one of my best officers," Martin had said, but Luckie noticed that he hadn't added anything like 'a safe pair of hands' or 'I expect you to extend your full cooperation.' Instead, he'd muttered something about Blake's past association with Searchlight and suggested that Luckie alert the media officer as soon as possible. It was hinted at that Blake courted spectacle and headlines. Superintendent Martin hadn't said it in so many words, but he'd implied it.

Luckie stared out at the dense curtain of white that fell outside. He didn't think the media would be doorstepping anyone today other than kids on sledges making the most of the fact that school was closed. That was something to be thankful for, anyway.

DC Ashleigh Clarke leaned over his shoulder, making him start. "Anything interesting?"

"D'you have to sneak up on people like that, Ashleigh?" Luckie said, picking up the file again with trembling hands. "Have you been here all night?"

Ashleigh nodded. "Sure," she said and leaned in close. "I slept in the medical room. There's a bed there."

Luckie shook his head. "I wish I'd thought of that..."

She raised a perfectly plucked eyebrow. "I don't think we'd both have fitted on, Luckie," she said, with a grin. DS Luckie died a little inside. At thirty, she was young enough to be his daughter and sometimes, when he spoke to her, he felt he'd come from another planet. Or maybe just another time. She made references to films and TV programmes he'd never heard of and was always banging on about new social media accounts. Luckie had just about got to grips with Facebook and then given it up as a waste of time. He even suspected her of making some up just to make him feel even older. She had long dark hair, and deep brown eyes that sparkled with intelligence and mischief. It was obvious that she worked out and kept herself in shape. Some of the younger officers had underestimated her when she first arrived but she quickly put them in their place. "Is that Huxley's file?"

Luckie cleared his throat. "Yeah. I just can't get my head round it. Why would all those people down at The Community claim to have killed him?"

"Collective responsibility," Ashleigh said. "Huxley grew up in the Community. He was effectively orphaned when his father died. The Community became a surrogate parent. In some weird way, they feel responsible for him."

"It's bullshit, though, isn't it? They aren't helping find out what happened to him, they're protecting another in their group. All they're doing is muddying the waters so we can't pin down who the actual killer is."

"Isn't she the one we've got, Sarge? The one who was leaning over him with the big knife? Seems like a good candidate..."

"But we're not just looking for the best candidate, are we, Ashleigh? We're trying to get to the truth about what happened to this young lad."

"I got the impression from the notes that he wasn't the most popular character down in the glen..."

"Then why defend his killer? What are they hiding?"

Ashleigh shrugged. "According to the file, Huxley had a history of drug abuse and petty crime. He's been pulled for a bit of burglary, a bit of possession. Maybe he just fell in with the wrong crowd, got too deep into something and it bit him on the arse."

"What like?"

"I dunno. Maybe he owed money, or just gave the wrong person some lip and they came after him. You know, it's so easy to fall into trouble when you're living like Huxley was."

Luckie disagreed. "If it was something like that, it would have to be big for them to trek out to Devil's Glen and hunt him down. Plus, evidence points to him being up in the woods which would suggest some kind of meet-up. No, I'm convinced the answer lies within The Community."

Ashleigh typed Huxley's name into the computer. "There's a whole list of known associates we could check through, but I don't think we'll be knocking on doors today. Not with all this snow."

"We can make a few phone calls. After all, if we're trapped inside, so are they," Luckie said, giving her a sly smile. "They might be glad to hear from us..."

"Really? It's six o'clock in the morning..."

"Judging by the interviews, Huxley's mates are all twenty-four hour party people. I bet they haven't gone to bed yet. They'll still be raving."

A smile quirked Ashleigh's mouth. "Raving? What does that mean?"

"You know," Luckie wobbled in his chair, waving his fists around. "Raving..."

"Looks like feeble dad dancing to me, Sarge. Tell you what, then, you pop the kettle on, and I'll get started with the phone calls."

"Right," Luckie said, his voice hoarse.

By the time he returned with two steaming mugs, Ashleigh had just concluded her first call. "Well, he wasn't so happy to hear from the polis. Rearrange this popular sentence: 'effing time, effing, know, effing, what you, effing it is, effing do..."

"Got that far? Well done," Luckie said, plonking Ashleigh's mug down on her desk. "That all right for you?"

"Wet, warm and made by someone else," Ashleigh said, cradling the mug. "What's not to like?"

"Well, that could apply to many liquids, not all of them even beverages..."

"Really, sarge?" Ashleigh said staring up at him. "You had to go there?"

"Well, I'm just saying, standards have to be maintained. If your tea's weak as pish, it may as well be..."

Ashleigh turned back to the phone. "I'll make the next call..."

"Aye," Luckie said and scanned down the list of associates. "Hello, hello," he said, his finger stopping at an Andrew Kean. "I know this one of old. He never sleeps."

"A friend of yours?" Ashleigh said.

"Our paths have crossed," Luckie said. "Small time dealer. Amphetamines and uppers, mainly. He's a talkative soul, too. Can't help himself. Let's hope I catch him at the right time."

The phone rang for what seemed like an age and Luckie thought it was going to voice messaging when it was answered. "Hell, yeah, baby! What can I do you for?"

"Erm who is this?"

"It's me, Andy. Kean as mustard and ready to do

your bidding, oh master..."

"Hi Andy, it's Detective Sergeant Luckie..."

"Bugger," Kean snapped and Luckie heard a scrabbling sound as though the young man was gathering up his belongings.

"Andy! I just want a quick word that's all."

"Where are you?"

"What do you mean where am I?"

"Like, where are you? Outside my door or in your car or what?"

Luckie grinned and savoured the idea of telling Kean he was just outside and then hearing him flush all his wares down the toilet. It was almost too much to resist but he had bigger fish to fry and he needed Kean's goodwill. "What's this Andy? D'you think I phoned you for kicks? Are you going to ask me what colour underwear I've got on next? Where d'you think I am in weather like this? I'm in the office at Dumfries Polis Station."

The line crackled with Kean's sigh of relief. "Thank God..."

"Are you all right, Andy? You sound a wee bit stressed. I could come round if you want me to. It'd be no trouble..."

"No! Look what d'you want, Luckie?"

"Jonah Huxley."

"What about him?"

Luckie weighed up his next words carefully. Huxley had no real next of kin; The Community was about as close to family as he could get. So Luckie had no real worries about putting the news of Huxley's death into the public realm and upsetting a family member. On the other hand, you just never knew what other cases Huxley's death might be tangential to. Revealing that he was dead might start a chain of events that could cause trouble somewhere else. Some officers would err on the side of caution but Luckie came from the 'say, 'fuck it' and see' school of thought. "He's dead Andy. Killed up at Devil's Glen. Would you know anything about that?"

The line went dead. Luckie phoned the number again and this time he did get put onto voice message. He took a breath. "We seem to have been cut off there, Andy. Must be the snow. Call me back straight away or I *will* come round, and I'll flush your head down the bog after your stash of drugs." He killed the call and rattled the phone onto his desk, sitting back.

Ashleigh looked at him from her desk. "Do you think he'll..."

The phone rang and Luckie smiled. "Excuse me, DC Clarke. I have a call." He answered. "Hell, yeah, Andy! What can I do for you?"

Kean sounded glum. "I don't know nothing about Jonah's death. How did it happen?"

"Looks very much like murder, Andy. We're not sure yet because we're waiting on the post-mortem, but he was found lying in a pool of his own blood. Big hole in his side. Can you help me?"

"I've not seen him for weeks, Luckie. And I've been at home the last few nights what with it being so rainy an' all."

"I'm not accusing you of anything, Andy. What was he like last time you saw him?"

"Come to think of it, he was acting like he'd won the lottery or something. He came round with a load of bevvies. Goin' on about how he was gonna be rich or something."

"Did he say what was going to make him rich?"

"I dunno. It's all a bit hazy, to be honest with you. He was cagey about the details, but he said he knew something. 'Knowledge is power,' that's what he kept saying. He was pointing at his head and saying that. Whatever he knew, he thought it was going to make him rich.

CHAPTER 10

A bitter cold nipped at Blake's nose, which was the only part of him that poked out of the covers. The fire was dead, and an icy light crept from between the thick curtains. Charlie was nowhere to be seen but the tantalising smell of frying bacon drifted in from the hall and Blake could hear the clinking of cutlery. His stomach growled.

Blake didn't want to move. At that moment, he felt no pain, but he knew that when he shifted, all hell would break loose throughout his body. But he needed food and a coffee. Several in fact. He braced himself and slowly sat up in bed, grimacing at the pain. Somehow the cold air took the edge off it. He lowered himself onto the floor, feeling his legs complain. His ankle was blue and purple.

Blake shuffled over to his pack and unzipped it, rummaging around for clean clothes that would keep him warm. Maybe he could get a bath or a shower over at the big house.

Once dressed, Blake opened his bedroom door and limped out into a cold hall with stone walls and a flagged floor. The smell of coffee and bacon made his stomach rumble again. Following his nose, he found Irving in a steamy, warm kitchen where his coat hung over an antique Aga. It looked to be pretty much dry. Charlie sat at Irving's feet staring intently at the bacon sandwich in the man's hand, just waiting for a drop of fat or even a chunk of meat to fall. If Laura was here, she'd probably say something about not encouraging the little dog to beg from the table but right now, if it was the only way to get some bacon, he'd have squatted next to Charlie.

"You're awake then," Irving said and took a bite out of the huge sandwich. The much hoped for string of rind tumbled from between the slices and into Charlie's waiting jaws. The old man waved a bony finger at a plate full of toast and fried bacon, sausage, and egg.

Blake sat down and slapped three rashers between two thick slices of bread. He nodded wordlessly in appreciation to Irving, whose face wrinkled into a grin. The old man poured a mug of coffee and slid it over the table to Blake. They chewed and drank in silence for a while, Blake relishing the warm, filling breakfast.

"So," Irving said. "You're heading over to the big house today."

Blake nodded. "I know you don't think much of them, Thomas," he said. "How long have they been there?"

"The Lamberts have been in that house since

the early Seventies. Her dad was Eric Lambert, the rock star. You won't have heard of Abaddon's Confessor, I don't think."

Blake shook his head.

Irving plonked his mug down and chased a rogue piece of bacon from between his teeth with his little finger. "They were a rock band. A bit like that Black Sabbath, you might say. Terrible racket they made. Not my cup of tea at all. Anyway, he bought it in the Seventies and filled it with hippies and misfits. His daughter carried the tradition on."

"My sister's one of those misfits," Blake muttered. He didn't want to be ungrateful, but Irving seemed to paint all the residents of the Paradise Found Community with the same brush. On the other hand, how many times had he and his brother Jeff shook their heads in despair at Rosie's seemingly naïve and bizarre take on the way of the world?

"Seriously, Will," Irving said. "I'm sure your sister is a lovely girl, but that house has a history of evil. The Lamberts drove my parents to an early grave with their carrying on..."

"What do you mean?"

Irving stared over Blake's head as though looking onto the past. "Wild parties, Satanic rituals, drugs. I'm not joking. Lambert bought the house because of its reputation and he added to it.

D'you know when you look into someone's eyes and you just know there's something dark lurking inside them?"

Blake nodded. He'd seen plenty of twisted individuals in his time. Josh Gambles, a serial killer he'd recently brought to justice sprang to mind straight away. "I do."

"Some of the people who came to stay were like that. Lambert certainly was. He had cold, black eyes. A bairn went missing from the village up the road. The Polis never found out who took her or where her body lay but suspicion rested heavily on Lambert and his entourage."

"Did you ever feel in danger yourself?"

"All the time. They were at the other end of the valley, but it still affected us. Lambert's dogs would run wild and kill our sheep. Sometimes, we weren't sure if it was his dogs doing the savaging or his house guests. Some nights, we'd hear footsteps around the house. Fingers trying the windows. My father slept with his shotgun by the bed, in the end. But the worry of it saw them off. I was left alone here to look after the place and keep it going. It was me sleeping with the shotgun, then. Things improved when Lambert died but his daughter's 'Community' has had its fair share of problems, too."

"Such as?"

"Places like that attract freeloaders and

troublemakers. Jonah Huxley was one of many messed-up kids who passed through here with their equally messed-up parents. He was one of the worst, though. He was into drugs and all sorts. In and out of prison, too. He broke in here a few times and took money."

"You can't have taken too kindly to that."

"I phoned the polis but Duana Lambert always managed a sob story for them and sent them packing. Oh, she's got the gift of the gab all right."

"Did he cause trouble amongst the residents of the Community?"

Irving shrugged. "I can't imagine him not rubbing someone up the wrong way, no matter how forgiving they pretend to be up there."

"When did you first find out that Jonah Huxley had been murdered?"

"When the polis cars and the ambulance came screaming down the lane. I knew something serious had happened, so I took a stroll up the valley. I saw Jonah being loaded into the ambulance and of course, our delightful Detective Sergeant Luckie wanted to ask me a thousand and one questions."

"Yeah, I've met him," Blake said, giving a brief grin. "Do you know of anyone in the Community who might have wanted to kill Huxley?"

Irving shook his head. “No,” he said.

“How about you, Thomas? Would you want to kill him?”

Irving looked levelly at Blake, “You’re a good judge of character, Will. I might have topped the wee shit. But I wouldn’t have stabbed him, I’d have blown his head off. I didn’t do it, Will. Believe you me, that so called Paradise Found is far from perfect.”

“Well, I’ll see for myself, I suppose,” Blake said. “I need to get my car down here, too. Wouldn’t want it blocking the lane…” He stopped and looked at Irving who smirked at his coffee.

“Have you looked outside, Will? The lane back to the main road is completely blocked with snow.”

“What?” Blake peered out of the window. The snow still fell in thick flakes, filling his vision. Everything was buried or rounded off into a weird snow sculpture.

“I should imagine that your car is buried by now. I’d better call the polis to warn them that there’s an obstacle in the lane, just in case the plough tries to get down. Not that it will. We’re the last to be dug out when this happens.”

Blake stared at Irving. “You mean we’re trapped down here?”

“Aye,” Irving said. “For a good while, I’d say.

Mind you, the good news is that if the killer is still in the glen, they aren't going anywhere, either. Or maybe that's bad news."

CHAPTER 11

A sense of disquiet gnawed at Jeff Blake's nerves as he sat in the prison visiting room, waiting for Josh Gambles to come for their weekly interviews. Jeff had learned to set aside the fact that Gambles was a serial killer. His brother, Will, had tried to shock Jeff by describing in graphic detail exactly what Gambles had done to his innocent victims and he had succeeded. But Jeff was writing the murderer's biography for his own personal reasons. Maybe one of those reasons was to wind up his big brother.

In the past, the two of them had been unnecessary rivals for their parents' affection and had taken different paths. If he was brutally honest with himself, Jeff had more or less failed as a novelist, peaking early with a bestselling literary work that had then sank without trace. Jeff's chances of getting back to that first pinnacle of success were slim but this book about Gambles might just swing things in his favour. Jeff had struggled financially ever since his second book flopped. He'd even had to borrow money from Will, which gave his brother a nice big stick with which to beat him. He had compounded his sins in Will's eyes by agreeing to write this biography. Gambles had an obsession with Will

Blake and the Searchlight programme which had complicated matters. If that wasn't enough, it turned out that Gambles had been with their mother in her final moments and, whilst he hadn't killed her, he had hidden her body from the family for two years, leaving them to wonder what had become of her.

Even though the biography was a thorny subject between them, it was the news that Rosie was in trouble that worried him. No, it wasn't just worry, it was a sense of irritation that she'd got herself in such a situation. One thing Will and Jeff shared was a sense of protective exasperation towards their sister. She wasn't a youngster anymore. None of them were and it was time she had found her place in the world. "Fine coming from me," Jeff muttered to himself, smirking and wondering if that was how Will saw *him*, too.

The other thing that irked Jeff was the fact that Rosie had called Will first. He knew that as a police officer, Will would probably be of more help than Jeff, but it highlighted Jeff's lack of practical skills. He felt useless.

The door to the visiting room opened and Gambles sauntered in flanked by two prison guards. He looked unkempt, his hair unbrushed and his dark beard, normally trimmed, had grown up his cheeks and down his neck. Normally slim, he looked scrawny as though he hadn't been eating. One eye was a swollen, thundercloud blue. His wrists were cuffed and there looked to be no prospect of them being unlocked.

"Trouble?" Jeff said as Gambles sat down with a sigh.

Gambles was clearly trying to summon his best enigmatic serial killer expression but instead, he just looked annoyed. "Just some of my fellow inmates deciding that there is a hierarchy of virtue, even in here. As though people who have beaten their wives to death or stolen from terrified, frail pensioners somehow have the moral high ground and can take it out on me."

"I see," Jeff said. "And there isn't?"

"I can see that someone might look at my work and think it barbaric, but it doesn't make them any better than me. If anything, it confirms their place at the bottom of the scale of ethics. Theirs is the code of the lynch mob. They'd hang anyone regardless of guilt or innocence if it took their mind off their own troubles for a moment. They're scum. Anyway, I gave as good as I got, I think. One of them is on the hospital wing and they've extended my time in solitary which suits me just fine."

"Right," Jeff said. He didn't know what else to add.

"Is something wrong, Jeffrey? You don't look

your usual chipper self, either. Has Will been yanking your chain again?" Gambles' one good eye glowed with excitement. He loved talking about Will and the difficult relationship between the two brothers. For a sociopath with no concern for the feelings of others, he had almost clinical observational skills when it came to analysing emotions. Maybe it was a bit like pulling the leg off a beetle and watching it writhe around on its back in agony. You can see its pain but you don't really care.

"No, it's my sister," Jeff said, cursing himself. He had vowed not to let Gambles pry into the Blake family life, but the man had a way of getting under your skin.

"Ah, Rosie," Gambles said. His brow furrowed as he dredged up the information from his mental archive of the Blake family. The psychopath had studied them for years because of his obsession with Will, he knew things about them that they'd forgotten. "She's up in Scotland, isn't she? In the Paradise Found Community, I believe. Have the wheels finally come off there? It was only a matter of time."

"How do you know about Rosie and the Community?"

"Information is power, Jeffrey, you know that." Gambles had recovered his old confidence for the moment. A crafty smile played about his lips, implying he knew much more than he was going to tell. “You know, at one point, I planned to go up there and join. Get close to Rosie. That would have been divine. Imagine, we could have all ended up round the same Christmas dinner table, pulling crackers and passing pleasantries.”

Jeff couldn’t help but grimace. “I suppose it would have been preferable to killing so many people, Josh…”

“But the idea repels you, doesn’t it? It would never have worked. Rosie is a vegan and I like my meat. Anyway, the key word here is, ‘planned.’ Planning means research. I looked into the Community and what I found surprised me.”

“In what way?” Jeff said, cursing himself for getting drawn in.

Gambles’ eyes glowed. “Have you ever heard of Eric Lambert, the rock singer?”

“Jeez,” Jeff said. “The mad guy from Abaddon’s Confessor?”

“The very same. Full marks, Jeffrey.”

“What can I say? I like my Seventies rock bands.”

“Hmm. Yes, not really my cup of tea,” Gambles said, dismissively. Jeff couldn’t help but feel a little piqued. After all, Gambles was the one whose idea of entertainment had been watching back-to-back episodes of Searchlight, just to catch Will asking for help to capture some petty criminal or other. "Lambert owned the property and passed it on to his daughter who set up Paradise Found when he passed on."

"Eric Lambert was a full-on Satanist, wasn't he? He mixed with all kinds of dubious characters. There was some talk of him meeting and corresponding with Charles Manson."

Gambles shrugged, seemingly put out by the mention of the much more famous murderer. "Yes, just talk, though, I think you'll find. Lambert was a Satanist and I suspect that if he was still alive, he'd be in prison for committing all kinds of perversions. The valley itself has a very dark history. My kind of place if it wasn't populated with a load of pompous idealists."

"But what did you mean when you said that it was only a matter of time before the wheels came off?"

"It was a metaphor, Jeffrey, I shouldn't have to explain that to an author," Gambles said, with a mocking smile.

"You know what I mean."

Sitting back, Gambles steepled his fingers. Jeff felt like cringing. Gambles was a melodramatic prick with no real self-awareness. It was obvious that he was a ham actor, playing a role at moments like this. "I did spend a few days up there, actually. It struck me that there's more going on than meets the eye."

Jeff shook his head. "What like?"

Gambles inclined his head as though he'd rather keep some things to himself, but Jeff had studied him long enough to realise that he didn't really know but was too proud to admit it. "I realised that staying there was a bad idea and left very quickly. But I was left wondering how a place like that could keep going. I mean, it was populated by a few, largely arty types who had never picked up a spade in their lives trying to grow enough food to live on. It's a steep learning curve. And yet The Community thrives..."

"Maybe Lambert made more money than he let on."

"No. He was broke when he died. He only had the property. But I do think there's something in that, Jeffrey. After all, Lambert was the Devil himself, so I've read, and they do say that the Devil looks after his own, don't they? I'd check out Duana Lambert, his daughter, if I was concerned about Rosie."

CHAPTER 12

Blake had never seen so much snow. Being in the shadow of the Snowdonia Mountains, and a peninsula, the Wirral had its own microclimate. There was rarely much snow; the last really bad snowfall had been around forty years ago. Here it buried everything, clinging to the trees and drifting in sparkling clouds as more fell. He knew he was in a deep, narrow valley but it was impossible to see beyond the first row of pines that lined the road to the big house. Even walking in the deep snow was a challenge and Blake's legs quickly became caked. Charlie was amused by it at first, jumping up and sinking into it but he quickly ended up stuck, so Blake picked him up and carried him. By the time Blake rounded the corner and stood in front of the big house, he was sweating and out of breath; his whole chest pulsed despite the painkillers that Irving had given him.

The first thing Blake saw was the crime scene tent, buckling under the coat of snow. It looked like an igloo or would have if one of the poles hadn't bent. He gave it a shake, sending a mini avalanche from its domed top.

The house could hardly be described as welcoming. A huge wooden door and two Greystone gables loomed over what Blake assumed would be a gravel courtyard. Right now, it was deep under a white blanket. Blake saw four upper windows reflecting the whiteout that surrounded him. If just one light burned in one window, the whole place would have changed. Instead, it seemed weighed down by the snow that gathered on the high roof. Blake shivered. He felt as though the house was watching him, daring him to come in. A crow landed on the chimney pots and complained loudly, its cry muffled. He noticed a human outline in one of the upper windows, looking out. Blake raised a hand and waved. The black figure didn't move, and, finally, Blake dragged his eyes away. He placed Charlie on the step and pushed at the huge oak door. It creaked open.

If anything, it felt colder inside, if that was possible. Blake looked around the hallway. The scrubbed grey flagstones looked bare and a worn carpet struggled to cover the stairs. A chilling white light shone through a huge feature window at the top of the stairs. Four closed doors led off the hall. It was silent apart from Charlie's claws clicking on the stone floor.

"Hello?" Blake called. He tried the nearest door but it was locked. Moving further into the house, he tried the next door and it opened. Warm air greeted him, and he heard a fire crackling. He poked his head round the door and was greeted with a stifled scream.

A small, dark woman, with short black hair jumped up from her armchair by the fire and grabbed the poker that stood nearby. "Who are you?"

"Will Blake, I'm Rosie's brother. It's okay!" Blake held his hands up.

The woman looked wary for a moment. "Rosie's brother?" she said. "The policeman?"

"That's me," Blake said, stepping closer to the warmth of the fire. Charlie wriggled between his legs and settled straight away to worshipping the heat. "I've come to sort out this mess and get Rosie out of trouble."

"How did you get here?" The woman didn't lower the poker.

Blake smiled. "That's a long story. Short version: I came over last night, crashed my car in the lane on the way in and woke up in Thomas Irving's house this morning. Look, just getting up the valley has done me in. Can I sit by the fire?"

The woman nodded and slowly lowered the poker as Blake eased himself into one of the threadbare armchairs that looked as though they should be chopped up and thrown on the roaring fire in the stone hearth. The room was large with a high ceiling, a total contrast to the thick-walls and tiny windows of Irving's cottage. What furniture there was looked as old and dark, as the house. Although thick, the curtains were faded and ragged at the bottom. A few dark portraits hung on the wall and an extremely foxed mirror.

"Are you okay?" the woman asked peering at Blake as he held his sides and settled into his seat. He felt like sleeping already.

Blake nodded. "I think I may have cracked a rib. Badly bruised at the least. Sorry, I don't know your name."

"Megan Yule," the woman said. Her nose and eyes were red from crying. "I do a lot of the cooking here, along with Rosie. I'm sorry I screamed. It's just that the murder and all the police activity has really shaken me."

"I'm not surprised," Blake said. "So, have you been here long, Megan?"

She shrugged. "A couple of months, I guess. I'm a newbie here. I arrived just before Christmas." She drew a breath and hugged herself. "Couldn't bear the idea of another one of those in the refuge..."

"I'm sorry," Blake said. "It must be terrible to find yourself in the middle of all this. Did you see what happened?"

Megan pulled a face. "I didn't see Jonah... die, if that's what you mean. I heard screaming and came outside to see Rosie holding a knife and covered in blood."

"Where were you?"

"In here, hugging the fire. This place is bloody freezing," she said and smiled, briefly. "If I'm not hugging the stove in the kitchen, you'll find me here."

"So, who else came out to see what the trouble was?"

"Everyone: Freya Finley, Grant Rothwell, Duana. The only people who weren't there were Patricia and Norris Evans, and I could see him up in the window, doing his meditation like he always does." She shivered.

Blake remembered looking up at the window just before and nodded. "So, given that almost all of the Community were on the scene nearly straight away, who do you think was responsible?"

"We were all responsible, Mr Blake," a voice said from behind them.

Charlie whined and Blake turned to see a tall woman, dressed in a green jumper dress, woolly tights, and knee boots, leaning against the door. It was hard to assess her age, late forties, early fifties, perhaps but she could easily have been younger. She was stunningly beautiful, Blake thought, with her almond-shaped, emerald eyes and full lips fixed in a teasing smile. Her thick red hair hung in a long plait over her shoulder and she held her head high as though posing for a photograph.

"Duana," Megan said, almost apologetically. "Mr Blake was just getting warm by the fire. He crashed his car last night and..."

"Stayed at Thomas Irving's, yes, I know. Have you come to solve our little mystery, Inspector Blake?"

"I've come to find out who murdered Jonah Huxley," Blake said, "Cos it sure as hell wasn't my sister."

Clearly not used to being answered so bluntly, Duana Lambert's face twitched slightly. "Jonah Huxley was a troubled soul. The Community should have done more to help him. I fear we just chased him away to a darker place. I fear we are all to blame."

"That's all very abstract and noble," Blake said, "but unless you all had hold of the blade that actually stabbed him or plotted to kill him together, then I'm afraid they're just words. At the moment, my sister is locked in a police cell accused of murder and I know for a fact that she didn't do it."

Duana Lambert smiled. "You have a memory and an image of your sister, but you don't know her. Not by a long chalk."

"I know her well enough to say she's not a killer."

"No, she isn't. None of us are," Duana said. "The police will realise that soon enough, once they analyse the wound and the knife that Rosie held, they'll see that they are different."

"You seem very sure of that. How come you know so much about the weapon used to kill Huxley?"

Duana Lambert shrugged. "I share your faith in Rosie. She didn't stab him, so Jonah must have been killed by another weapon."

"Well that's fine then," Blake muttered. "I suppose we can all just relax. Except someone here *did* kill that boy..."

"It's possible that it was an outsider who came looking for Jonah. There's no reason to suspect anyone in the Community..."

"So what's with the 'we are all responsible' routine, if not to confuse any investigation?"

"If it is a member of the Community, then their own conscience will punish them. It's not for us to judge or hunt them. Eventually, they will have to find peace and they will confess. It could be years from now but..."

Blake shook his head. "It doesn't work like that. You're allowing the person to roam free and kill again if somebody upsets or annoys them. Here's a thought, what if the person did it because they enjoyed it? What if they decide they want to kill again? Would you be so forgiving if it was an outsider? You're putting people at risk. Have you thought about that?"

Duana Lambert narrowed her cat-like eyes and, for a moment, Blake thought of Laura. "Rosie was right about you, William Blake; you're a vexatious soul, and relentless with it." Her voice held a hint of approval.

"Really? What else did she tell you about me?"

"That everything you try to hold close to you, slips through your fingers like sand. She must have some kind of faith to have called for you, though. Feel free to look around. Perhaps Megan will drag herself away from the fire long enough to guide you."

Megan gave an anxious look and huddled down into her armchair with a groan. "Do I have to, Duana? It's not safe out there."

Duana lifted her hand. "I'll leave that up to you, Megan. I'm not going to tell you what to do, am I? I'm sure Mr Blake will protect you from whatever danger you imagine is lurking in this house."

Blake looked at Megan, expectantly. "All right, then," she said at last. "Come on, I'll show you round."

CHAPTER 13

As she walked the dog the next morning, it struck Laura that she was probably less than a hundred miles away from the Wirral and Will Blake. Which also meant that she was the same distance from her tormentor, Kyle Quinlan. Laura often wondered what possessed her to take up with him. He was good-looking, could be funny and charming, true but he was brutal and callous, too. Maybe it was her upbringing that led her to have low expectations for herself. Girls off her estate didn't typically go on to become captains of industry or entrepreneurs. That wasn't to say they were all stereotypical teenage pram pushers, either. But when a young man like Quinlan rolled up in a flash car, waving cash around, it turned her head because she'd grown up thinking of that as the true measure of a man. She'd learnt so much in the time she'd been free of Quinlan, both academically and personally. But, like many of her friends, she'd been trapped and now her past life had come back to bite her.

Right here, that life seemed a million, not a hundred miles away. She had no worries about being spotted here. There was nobody about and a beautiful silence filled the air. Laura had moved around the country, not stopping anywhere for more than a few days. She flitted around the country at random, defying a pattern; Andover one week then back up here, near Ludlow. Not that she thought Quinlan was actively hunting her, but Will might be and Quinlan would be watching Blake. It was the ultimate cruelty; Quinlan couldn't have her, so she couldn't have Blake. And it told her that for all Quinlan protested to her that he'd changed, he was still the same, cruel and controlling egotist that he'd always been.

Archie's claws clicked on the rough tarmac and Laura breathed in the cold February air. The hedgerows rose up high on either side and Laura could barely see any landscape. When she came to a gateway, she paused for a moment, looking across the fields and drinking in the distance of the nearest buildings. A car engine broke the tranquillity and Laura saw a red van drawing towards her. It stopped and a young man lowered his window. He had an untidy mop of brown hair that hung out under a red baseball cap. His mate in the passenger seat had close cropped hair and a combat jacket on. Laura held her breath. They were probably just tradesmen on a house job and looking for directions.

"Right, darlin," the young man said, in a Welsh accent. "Nice dog you've got there. D'you want to sell him?"

Laura hardened her face. "No. What kind of a question is that?"

"I dunno, do I?" the young man said, with a crooked grin. "Any farms round here?"

"Wouldn't know," Laura said.

"Nah," the young man said, narrowing his eyes. "You're not from round here, are you? A Liverpool Judy, I'd say."

"Watch out for your wristwatch, Billy," the passenger said. "She'll have it."

"Bye," Laura said and started walking. She could feel her heart thumping.

The van's engine revved and he leaned out, singing, "Row, bullies row! Them Liverpool Judies have got us in tow!" He laughed and drove off, souring the air with diesel fumes.

Laura watched them disappear down the lane. It was always the accent that gave her away. As soon as she opened her mouth, people knew she wasn't local. For a fleeting moment, she wondered how much elocution lessons might be, then dismissed it. It was nothing, anyway, a couple of local woolly backs being obnoxious.

She squatted down and stroked Archie's head. "Who'd sell you, eh?" She hadn't liked that. They might have just been a couple of lads mouthing off, but something about the way they'd eyed the dog up made her gut twist. She hadn't been worried for herself but she'd heard of dog fighting gangs who stole animals to use as fodder to train their own dogs on. It was probably nothing but she thought she might warn Gilmore. He might know them.

Gilmore was sitting in his kitchen supping a mug of coffee when Laura arrived back at the farm. The kitchen looked like the yard, maintained but in a kind of stasis, not an absolute tip like Blake's used to be but verging on it. One plate, one bowl and cutlery for one sat on the draining board. Food and cereal packets lay stacked on the work top, pushed aside rather than tidied away. Everything looked as though it had been given a superficial wipe but was in need of a good deep clean. Archie came in with Laura and immediately started hoovering up scraps that had been dropped.

"Yeah, they've been round a couple of times, looking for work or to trade some dodgy bit of farm machinery," Gilmore said when Laura told him about the lads. "Not really from round here. They go baiting on the fields round here, sometimes..."

"Badger baiting?" Laura said in horror.

"Yeah. I've seen them over on the upper fields with their lights. They asked if they could come on my land but I said no."

"Did you call the police?"

"No," Gilmore said, looking down into his drink. "Anyway, by the time the police came, they'd be long gone."

"You should stop them..."

"They aren't on my land and there's more of them than me. Anyway, it's none of my business."

"I bet if you let off a shotgun over their heads one night and told them to bugger off, they wouldn't come back in a hurry. People like that are cowards."

"Maybe," Gilmore said, with a shrug. "I've heard tell they can be nasty, too. I'm not sure they'd just run away.

"Now I am worried about him being outside all on his own," Laura said, scratching Archie's ear. "I'd feel safer with him in the caravan with me."

"Go on then, he can stop with you. I think I should be more worried about you kidnapping him than anyone else," Gilmore said and grinned. Laura smiled back and saw a gentleness in the man's eyes. He held her gaze a little too long and blushed. "It's been a long time since there's been a woman on the farm," he said. "Not since Mam died."

Laura raised her eyebrows. "You haven't got a girlfriend? That surprises me, a good-looking fella like you."

Gilmore blushed and shrugged again. "The farm takes all my time and by the time I'm finished, I'm too knackered to think about socialising. It's a lonely job. Don't come across many eligible women…" his blush deepened.

"Isn't there some kind of dating app for agricultural workers? You know, FARMR or something?" Laura said, giving him a cheeky smile.

Gilmore laughed. "Maybe I should invent it and make a fortune. Do you want a coffee?"

"Sure," Laura said. "Then I'll give this place a good scrubbing…"

"No, really, it's fine," Gilmore said but Laura just gave him a look that told him it was going to happen. "Okay," he said. "Then let me make lunch and dinner for you. Archie can stay inside, too."

Laura had scrubbed and mopped all afternoon and now, she sat in the old armchair by the stove, supping another mug of coffee. A thick stew simmered, filling the room with a mouth-watering smell. She smiled. "I could get used to this," she said.

Gilmore gave her a sidelong glance. "You haven't seen the state of the living room yet and the bathroom would make you run screaming for the hills."

"You need to get some help in," Laura said.

"Is this something you do?" Gilmore said, smiling. "Go around the land fixing things like that guy on Highway to Heaven?"

"I must have missed that one."

"My dad had the DVDs it was about an angel who went around America with a detective solving mysteries and making things right."

Laura gave a tight smile. "I don't know quite how to take that," she said. "But seeing as how you just called me an angel, I'll be flattered."

Gilmore flushed red. "I'm sorry... I didn't mean to..."

Laura just laughed and clicked her fingers. "Come on, Archie, let's leave your boss dying of embarrassment and go and clean the caravan."

For the rest of the evening, Laura gave her caravan the same treatment as Gilmore's kitchen. It proved much harder and less satisfying. By the end of the day, she lay in her bed, reading a book she'd purloined from the farmhouse, but her eyelids were drooping. Archie lay at her feet snoring.

She awoke with a start to the sound of Archie's rumbling growl. Putting a reassuring hand on his head, she sat up in bed and strained her ears. There were low voices outside in the yard. Laura eased back the stiff curtain and peeked out, her eyes slowly adjusting to the darkness.

Three men dressed in combat jackets and ski masks that covered their faces stood right outside, shovels in their hands and terriers on leads at their feet. Laura held her breath and prayed they didn't see her. After a brief, muttered conversation, they moved off and Laura slipped out of bed and into her clothes.

CHAPTER 14

If the big house was Duana Lambert's idea of Paradise Found, then Blake had a few questions he wanted to ask. The first one was, 'hasn't anyone considered some kind of central heating?' Charlie had made a half-hearted attempt to drag himself away from the fire when Blake stood up, but when it became clear that Blake wasn't going outside, the little pup curled up and went to sleep. The whole house was freezing cold. Some windows had huge gaps in the frames or cracked windows that allowed a howling wind through. "Is it always this cold?"

"Even in Summer, apparently," Megan said. "It's like the walls have absorbed the ice from every winter in the last two hundred years and never thawed out. Duana and Freya talk as though some great refurb is going to happen any day, but I reckon that's a bit of a pipe dream."

"You don't sound too enamoured with the place," Blake observed.

"I'm not. First chance I get, I'm out of here. Duana knows that. She relies on people like me passing through to do all the skivvying. They can't complain because everyone knows they're getting free board and lodging, but they aren't committed to the place."

"But Rosie wasn't passing through."

Megan stopped beside a rather rusty and depleted suit of armour that stood guard outside one of the back rooms. She looked pinched and worried. "Rosie is probably the most kind-hearted and generous person I've ever met. But she's a sucker. The others take the piss. She does everything round here. I'm sorry she's mixed up in all this."

"I see," Blake murmured, it didn't chime with the woman he knew. Growing up with two brothers meant she had to be wise to all kinds of tricks and she was. "She'd know when people were taking advantage, though. Could she have come to resent it?"

"And done... done that to Jonah? No. Not Rosie. She knows that the others don't pull their weight. It just seems to spur her on to work harder. These rooms down here are meeting rooms, but they're never used."

She pushed one door open and the smell of mildew hit them. Blake poked his head round the door to see a dusty dining table surrounded by chairs. The wallpaper, faded but clearly once a wildly Seventies psychedelic, had started to slide off the plaster and there was a huge crack in the ceiling.

"This place is falling apart," he said, closing the

door.

"Apparently, there used to be more than thirty residents all looking after the place, but they left or died. Now there are seven and only me and Rosie seem capable of doing any work."

"That must breed a lot of bad feeling..."

Megan pursed her lips. "You think it was one of the Community who did that to Jonah, don't you?"

"In my experience, most murders happen within families. This strikes me as one big dysfunctional family, that's all. Now, it may be true that Huxley rubbed people up the wrong way so much that they pursued him over hills and dales to knife him, but you really have to go some to get that kind of attention. Plus, the outfit doing the killing needs to be organised enough to travel and get away."

"Could just be some random psycho..."

"Random psychos tend not to sit up in deserted woods waiting for their victims to come along. They go where people go, pubs, shops, college campuses, places where they can meet victims. No, believe me, Megan, the killer may still be with us."

"That's comforting," Megan said in a small voice.

"Who phoned the police that night, Megan?"

Megan Yule blinked and swallowed before answering. "I... I think Rosie did..."

"Really? But wasn't she in shock?"

"Well, yeah but when she had recovered a bit."

"But nobody else thought to call the police or an ambulance?"

"We all panicked. Duana was worried they'd close The Community and take us all away or something. We didn't know what to do. In the end, I think Rosie called them. You'd have to talk to Duana about that."

An awkward silence fell between them. Megan seemed scared. "Okay," he said at last, "what else is there to see?"

Megan led him upstairs, every step creaking ominously as they went. Blake wondered how this place had managed to stay upright for so long. "There are seven bedrooms but a number of them have been turned into studios. There are old stable blocks at the back that have been converted into workshops, bedrooms, and a bunk house. The Community hires out the bunk house in the summer to raise a bit of cash."

"Looks like it needs it," Blake said, looking at the threadbare carpets and motheaten wall hangings. Some of this stuff must have been original, maybe even worth something once but now beyond restoration. Other pieces of furniture were iconic sixties and Seventies chrome and plastic.

"Yeah, Freya's planning to make and sell a little bit of craft stuff, costume jewellery and the like to bring in some more money but I can't see it working myself. It'll take more than a few quid from trinkets to save this place."

A thump from behind one of the bedroom doors made Megan flinch and she stared at the door, nervously.

"Megan what is it?" Blake said in a low voice.

"Nobody uses that bedroom," she whispered. "It should be empty."

Blake gripped the handle and held his breath. Now he was close he could hear the bumping through the door. A brief chill ran through him. What if there was someone in the room? Was he in any fit state to confront the intruder? He twisted the handle and pushed the door open.

Something dark swooped down at his face and, instinctively, he threw his hands up. Feathers grazed his knuckles and he saw a huge black crow flapping around the room. He stumbled back, almost knocking Megan over. The crow landed on the dilapidated bed and cawed angrily at him.

"Jeez," he muttered.

"It must have got through that open window,"

Megan said, walking over to the sash which had been pulled up. "Don't know how long it's been like that," she said, looking down at the slush and snow that had piled in and soaked the carpet.

Blake poked his head out of the window and looked down onto the back of the house and the square of stable buildings that huddled around a central courtyard. Duana Lambert, stalking across the yard, looked up at Blake but said nothing.

The snow still fell thickly, shrouding the view beyond. It clung to the creepers and vines that wrapped themselves around the walls as if trying to strangle the house. "Well we can't shut it before that fella goes," he said, nodding at the crow. He sidled round the other side of the bed and the crow bounded away from him and up to the window. With one indignant croak, it flapped its great wings and vanished into the whiteout.

Megan slid the window shut. "The lock's broken. I'd better get a mop or something to soak up the worst of that before it soaks through the ceiling downstairs," she said.

"Do you want me to come with you?" Blake said.

Megan thought for a second then shook her head. "No, I'll be fine. The mop and bucket are just at the bottom of the stairs. I need to pull myself together," she said and hurried out of the room.

Blake stepped out into the corridor again. A dim light came from a door at the far end and cut through the shadows. Something rustled beyond the door, and a low, distant humming made the hairs on Blake's neck prickle. He inched forward, the creak of every floorboard sounding like a gunshot. The wind moaned in the eaves of the house and somewhere, something tapped on the windows. Blake thought of Irving's story about the frozen child and shivered. Once more, he wondered how anyone could see this as any kind of paradise. The door groaned on its hinges as Blake eased it open. The humming stopped.

This had once been a master bedroom, judging by its size but it had been cleared to accommodate its current occupants. Row after row of mute faces stared at Blake with blind eyes, many of them clowns with painted smiles. It took him a moment to process what he was looking at. They were life-size figures cut out of hardboard and painted in bright colours. Blake picked out a grenadier with a big busby hat and a sailor in blue but in amongst them were faces he recognised, too. Some were celebrities, Simon Cowell, there was a David Bowie and Boris Johnson, but others he didn't know. He guessed they were members of the Community; Duana stood, smiling with her hands on her hips and, with a start, he spotted Rosie staring out at him. But the eyes were blank and white, with no pupils. It made their smiles look sinister, threatening, even. The humming started again.

A breeze drifted around the room, making the figures wobble slightly. Blake tried to see beyond the crowd of cut-outs. He edged further into the room. "Hello? Is anybody in there?"

The humming stopped and he heard a metallic click.

"I just want to talk," he said, craning his neck to get a better view of the back of the room. The figures swayed again, as though someone moved quickly behind them. He grabbed one of the figures and started to lift it out of the way, but a deafening scream filled the room. The world became a frenzy of fists and nails. Blake fell back as a meaty arm hit the side of his head. The screaming was part anger and outrage, part terror.

Figures tumbled over as Blake stumbled away from his attacker. He could see her more clearly now. She was a big woman with a round red face and short, mousey hair cut in a bob. Her thick glasses were skewed on her face which was twisted into a snarl of pure hatred. Fist after fist rained down on Blake and he fended them off as best as he could, but he was weakening.

CHAPTER 15

The smell of disinfectant, polish and urine turned DS Luckie's stomach every time he came to this place but that wouldn't ever keep him away. Not even the snow kept him from here. There hadn't been a week in almost twenty years that he hadn't visited Our Lady of Lourdes Nursing Home. He'd walked over from the police station in the snow rather than miss his weekly appointment. Nobody else from the original team visited anymore. They'd all moved on, got promotion or died.

Luckie wondered why he hadn't got used to the smell, but he knew why. It was the same reason he felt that raw grief and rage every time he visited. Because he'd never accepted what had happened to Callum Bane. This was unfinished business.

Callum was lost in the huge wheelchair that propped him up. A bag of bones in stained sweatpants and an old grey top, he stared vacantly out of the window. A tube poked indiscreetly from under his top and Luckie wondered if it was for feeding or getting rid of the waste. Luckie followed his gaze out into the garden.

"In the summer," Luckie said, "that place is

a blaze of flowers. You wouldn't think it now, would you? And where are those squirrels, eh? Pesky wee bastards digging up the bulbs. They'll all be asleep now, I reckon." Callum gave a sigh and stared out, his throat clicking and a string of drool pooling on his jogging bottoms. "D'you know, I love the smell of the roses in the summer and listening to the bees in the Laburnum." He paused as though Callum was saying something. "I know, I know, I haven't gone soft on you. I'm just saying. That'll all come round, mate."

He looked out again. Now the garden was buried in white.

"Snow, eh, Callum? Reminds me of Feb 1984. Do you remember that? We were just out of college. Drunk as lords, eh? We came out of the pub and found ourselves in bloody Narnia," Luckie said, laughing. "You threw a snowball at that girl. What was her name, now? Hodges or Hedges or something like that? I always think of that when it snows. Did you get off with her soon after that? Happier times, eh?"

Callum's left index finger twitched on the armrest of the chair. Luckie knew it was a response to his voice but what it meant he didn't know. "We've got a new case today. Down in Devil's Glen. A poor young lad was stabbed. I say poor young lad, he sounds like a regular pain in the arse, but I don't reckon he needed stabbing. You'd be all over this one, mate. It's weird. Except, we can't get down there because of this snow. And we've got Merseyside's finest, DCI Will Blake on the scene now because his sister is a suspect. It's all..."

Luckie blathered on about the case, about DC Clarke, about anything just to fill the time and keep Callum amused and engaged. If he *was* amused or engaged; Luckie could never tell. The door creaked open and a big man in a Lady of Lourdes polo shirt and jeans peered round the door. "Sorry, am I disturbing you?"

"Naw, you're fine," Luckie said. "I've not seen you around before. You new?"

"Aye," the man said extending a hand. "My name's Pete..."

"I can see that from your name badge," Luckie said. "You working with Callum?"

Pete nodded. "Aye. He's been here a long time..."

"Twenty years. D'you know much about him?

"Not really I just came on shift. I've done the induction course and seen his care plan. I know how to do the tubes and such but as a person, I've not got to know him, yet." Pete scratched his beard and looked a bit awkward. "Are you family?"

"A friend. An old work colleague. This guy was the best copper in all of Scotland. He and I grew up together and ended up on the force together."

Pete looked troubled. "What happened? If you don't mind me asking."

"A routine job," Luckie said. "Suspected robbery at a betting shop."

Pete shook his head. "But it went wrong..."

"We answered the call. The three thieves were in a transit van, driving away from the scene as we arrived. I pulled up and Callum here, got out. They drove their van straight at him. It took the door off our car and sent him flying a hundred yards up the street. He was in a coma for weeks and then..." Luckie said, nodding at Callum.

"Did you ever catch the robbers?"

"Two of them. One's still on the loose. That was twenty years ago."

"And you keep coming here after all that time."

"Aye," Luckie said. "The least I can do. He's my best friend."

"I'll take good care of him," Pete said, looking deep into Luckie's eyes.

Luckie could see the pain and empathy in the man's gaze. Clearly he had a similar tale to tell. "You've served, haven't you?"

Pete nodded. "Aye. Black Watch. I was in Iraq. I know what it means to lose a mate and I've seen a fair few whose lives have changed like Callum's.

He's in good hands."

"He might have to be, Pete. Cos if I ever catch up with the man who did this to him, I swear I might just take a life."

Luckie shook Pete's hand, gave Callum a final pat on the shoulder and walked out of the home into the cold, hostile snow.

*****

The effort of keeping his arm up to shield himself was beginning to tell on Blake's ribs. He lowered his defence for a second and got a crack in the eye for his pains. The woman's face filled his vision and he could smell milk and sour breath.

"Please. I'm not here to harm you," Blake panted. Megan appeared at the door carrying a bucket and mop. Her eyes were wide in shock. She ran over, wrapping the woman in a tight embrace and pinning her arms.

"Patricia, stop!" she yelled.

"Window! Window!" Patricia moaned, wriggling against Megan. "Window!" Her struggles weakened and she slowly wrapped her huge arms around Megan's neck and began to sob. "Window!" Patricia moaned. Megan caught Blake's eye and nodded in the direction of the door.

Blake took the hint and crept back into the corridor. He stood panting and rubbing his bruised face while Megan soothed the crying woman. The door opposite Blake swung open and a wild-looking man in what looked like an off-white dressing gown stared at him. The man was a mass of hair; a long beard hung down his chest and a grey mane sprouted upwards and outwards from around his face. What you could see of his features were haggard and thin. "What's goin' on?" he said, in a thick scouse accent.

Blake blushed and pointed into the room. "I think I upset Patricia."

"Easily done," the man said, staring into the room full of weird effigies.

"Sorry, I didn't get your name," Blake said.

"What's it to you? You a bizzie?"

Blake extended his hand. "Yeah. I'm Rosie Blake's brother." The man looked at Blake's hand and vanished behind his bedroom door without a word. "Great," Blake muttered. "Pleased to meet you, too."

Megan came out and closed Patricia's door behind her. "You okay?"

"Might have a black eye," Blake said, testing the side of his face with his fingers. "I probably deserve it. I didn't realise..."

"She has a learning disability," she said. "Doesn't have many words. Her mum brought her here years ago, apparently, and then died. This is her home, now."

"Does she make all those creepy figures?"

Megan nodded. "Yep. Duana calls them Silent Companions. Duana says that in the olden days, all old houses had them, like cut-outs of servants and children. Maybe they were to make burglars think a house was occupied when it wasn't. Anyway, we had some old originals here and Patricia took a liking to them. She started making them herself."

Blake nodded. "They have those life-size pictures of policemen in pound shops to deter thieves. I suppose it's a similar thing."

"Patricia's made hundreds of them. Duana told me that every now and then, they sneak a few away and dump them. Especially ones of residents who have left." Megan looked worried. "She's been quite disturbed by the murder and all the police activity."

"It's bound to unsettle her," Blake said. "And who's the Charles Manson lookalike in the other room?"

"Norris," Megan said, scowling at the door. "Longest-standing resident apart from Duana. He doesn't say much or mix with the rest of us. Just sits up here meditating. We have to bring food up to him. Anyway, I refused, so Duana does it. Can you believe that? Ms High and Mighty brings him his food."

"You're not a fan, then?"

"I told you. I get treated like a skivvy. We're all meant to pull our weight. Quite what Norris brings to the Paradise Found party, I don't know."

"Well it's not his witty repartee, that's for sure," Blake said.

"No, and he's not making the soup for dinner either. But I am. I'd better go and get started. Can I leave you here without you getting into any more fights?"

Blake gave an embarrassed grin. "I'll follow you down and have a look outside."

"When you hear a dinner bell, come to the kitchen for some soup. I'd be quick though, it goes fast..."

CHAPTER 16

Although the crime scene tent offered some shelter from the wind and snow, its white interior made it feel even colder somehow. There wasn't much to see. The tent had been pitched on top of the gravel where the body fell, preserving a slight impression of where Jonah's body had been. There was a suggestion of blood on the small stones but it was barely noticeable and around that it had been churned up by numerous feet. Blake stood on the stepping plates and stared at the outline on the ground, trying to imagine what might have happened. The tent blocked any view of the house or surrounding area, so it was difficult to visualise. He stepped out of the tent and looked up at the house. Norris' silhouette filled the window up at the top. Megan had said she saw him up there when they found Huxley. The others were down at the front, apart from Patricia. She didn't seem a likely suspect. Her attack had been sudden and seemingly unprovoked, but it had no skill or focus to it. A fit young man like Huxley would have easily evaded Patricia.

Jonah had run out of the woods and any of them could have followed him out and stood, pretending to be a witness. In his mind, Blake drew a line from the side of the tent to the bushes at the edge of the wood. Any tracks from there had been smothered by the snow but he could still see where the undergrowth had been battered aside by Jonah. The trail led Blake's eye beyond and into the woods. He could just see that the ground rose steeply under the canopy of the trees and his body ached at the thought of climbing up there. He knew he would have to, though because, for some reason, Jonah had encountered somebody in those woods and then fled for his life back to the house. There might be answers up there.

Blake's feet crunched in the snow as he approached the bushes. Across the drive, a large woman with brown hair strode from behind the house. She was shouting something behind her. A burly man followed quickly, waving his arms in the air.

"Freya! Come back! Don't be like that!"

Freya stopped and turned on the man. "Like what?" she yelled. "You don't know. You don't understand. You don't have blood on your..." She stopped dead and followed the man's gaze as he stared directly at Blake. The pair of them lowered their gaze and hurried into the house without another word. Looking up at the figure of Norris in the window, Blake decided to investigate the woods after lunch. Instead, he made his way towards the back of the house.

The buildings at the rear were in a much better state of repair. They were modern barn conversions; some were one storey while others had windows in the roof which suggested an upper room. Everything looked double-glazed and weatherproof and Blake wondered why all the money they had seemed to have been channelled into this part of the property rather than the house itself.

He peered through a couple of windows and saw living rooms and bedrooms, beds, armchairs, and tables that all looked modern and in good repair. At one end of the courtyard, a large brick built barn filled that side. The small windows had blinds pulled down over them. Blake rattled the padlock on the large wooden doors.

A footfall behind Blake made him turn. Duana Lambert stood with her arms folded, a crease in her otherwise flawless brow. "Find anything?"

Blake shrugged. "Just getting the measure of the place."

"The Community isn't just bricks and mortar, Will, it's the people," she said. "They make it what it is."

"Is that why you were reluctant to call the police when Jonah lay stabbed to death outside your house?"

Duana looked as though Blake had slapped her. She wasn't used to being challenged, that was a weakness Blake could use. Eventually, she gathered herself. "We were going to call but we had to make sure we knew how to defend our Community first..."

"Defend," Blake repeated. "A curious word to use."

"The locals aren't renowned for being broad-minded, Blake, even if they think they are. They tend to judge our lifestyle and philosophy. Thomas Irving isn't the only one who has it in for us. There are people around here who would love this place to close down. They see us as a threat because we question their way of life simply by leading an alternative one."

"So what is your philosophy?"

Duana Lambert inclined her head. "Do you know much about your namesake, Will? The poet and artist."

"A little. People like to quote his poetry to me..."

"To see a World in a Grain of Sand, And a Heaven in a Wild Flower..."

"That kind of thing but it's usually something to do with tigers with a 'Y'"

Duana smirked. "Blake believed that the divine was in everything and we can see it if we use our childlike imagination. When they come to live here, we encourage people to find their own path to the divine, through any medium, Art, Poetry or Dance. It doesn't matter. There are no rules."

"Sounds lovely. I could spend my life making model Spitfires," Blake said. "Wouldn't get much done though, would it?"

"Most people don't have a problem with that, once they uncouple themselves from the humdrum of everyday life. Blake believed in the joy of physical union, too. We don't have permanent partners here. Would that suit you?"

Blake thought of Laura and felt himself reddening. "I think I'm a one-woman man," he muttered.

"One at a time or is there just one for life?" Duana's smile was playful, almost teasing him.

Blake cleared his throat, wondering why the hell he'd gone down this line of conversation. There was something about Duana that invited, almost demanded, confidence. "One at a time, once but now? Life I think. Yeah."

"The poet, Blake had one special person, too. They were devoted to each other. Most marriages in his time were purely for financial considerations. But she was poor; he married for pure love."

"Very romantic."

"It worked for them but I think theirs is a rare case. Just be sure that the person you love feels the same or you'll suffer."

"So, was Jonah into this free love thing?"

Duana gave an impatient sigh. "You make it sound so superficial, Will. If we choose to share our bodies with another adult, it's still an important undertaking. It's a joyous thing, yes but there's a responsibility involved too."

"A young man like Jonah Huxley might have seen it differently. I know that at that age, I'd have jumped at the chance to..."

"I take your point. And, yes, Jonah could be flippant with some of his relationships. We did lose a couple of members that way but none of us are possessions. We don't own other people and nor do they own us."

"But a jealous lover, somebody who knows the Community could have come back to get even with him. It's a possibility."

"It is but the people we attract are peaceful. They're like your sister. We try to make Heaven on Earth by doing no harm to anyone or anything. 'Kill not the Moth nor Butterfly, for the Last Judgment draweth nigh,' as your namesake would say."

"People change. You said yourself that some of your residents found they weren't suited to your philosophy. You must have attracted your fair share of dubious or unstable characters over the years."

Duana's eyebrows shot up, as though the thought hadn't occurred to her before. "Very true. Which would support my initial assertion when we first met, that an outsider did this and left."

"In the pitch dark? And where would they go? Back up that lane? Through the woods and up onto the moorlands? That seems unlikely to me. This place has quite a reputation, hasn't it?"

"The Valley? Myth and superstition surround it, yes. That was probably why my father chose to live here."

"Its dark past suited his image, you mean?"

Duana's voice went flat. "My father followed the wrong path. I hope I've made a better go of it."

"Well somebody here doesn't share your ambitions."

She pursed her lips. "There is nobody here capable of killing another human being." Before Blake could reply, the bell for lunch rang. Duana relaxed a little. "Come and break bread with us. You'll see for yourself how civilised we are."

The kitchen was the one part of the big house that seemed well-kept and furnished. A big range cooker sat next to an Aga on one side of the room and cupboards lined the rest apart from an enormous sink and drainer under the window. A huge scrubbed-pine table filled the centre of the room. Despite the space being large, it was warm, and Blake got the impression that it stayed warm all the time. He sensed Rosie's hand here. Although shelves and cupboards were cluttered, it felt homely and there was a smell of cooking that permeated everything. He could imagine her stirring soups and baking bread.

Megan bustled around the table with a handful of spoons, making sure everyone was equipped. The residents looked lost at the big table and Blake got a hint of how big The Community must have been at its height. Freya sat staring at the huge pot of soup while the man next to her glared at the tabletop. Patricia wobbled her spoon between her fingers looking intently at the light reflecting off it and Megan settled herself next to her. Blake and Duana sat down, making the party up to six.

"This is Rosie's brother," Duana said. "He's a policeman."

Silence greeted this announcement. Then the clicking of claws on stone interrupted it and Patricia's face lit up. "Doggy!" she said, climbing out of her chair and crouching over Charlie. The pup went berserk at the attention, licking and chewing at Patricia's fingers.

"Patricia," Duana said. "You need to wash your

hands again and finish your soup. Then you can play with the doggy."

After a little more coaxing, Patricia sat down. She looked over at Blake, who smiled at her. "The dog is called Charlie," he said.

"Charlie," Patricia repeated and plunged a crust of bread into her soup.

Blake looked over at Freya Finley. "Have you been here long, Freya?"

"A few years," she said. "How do you know my name?"

"I'm a police officer. I worked it out." He looked at the big man. "You must be Grant Rothwell."

"I am," Grant said. "Are you going to find out who…" he gave Patricia a sidelong glance, "who did it?"

"I hope so," he said. "Where were you just before Jonah's body was discovered?"

Rothwell gave a nervous grin. "Where was I? I was with Freya in her room. We heard screaming and came running out. Then we saw… well, you know…"

"No," Blake said. "Who did you see, apart from Jonah?"

"Well, there was Rosie, all covered in blood, Duana and Megan. Norris was up in his room, like he always is."

"Right," Blake said, nodding. He drank his soup, relishing the warmth as it spread through him. It even seemed to dull the pain a little. Or maybe he was getting used to it. "How did Jonah end up living here in the first place?"

Grant and Freya glanced at Duana, who put her spoon down. "Jonah's father was a founder member of the Community but he was an old man and not in the best of health. He came here to give Jonah a second chance at life. The boy's mother was a drug addict and died when he was five. But I think Jonah's early experiences marked him. He was a troubled little boy, fractious and full of mischief. As you rightly guessed, he drove a number of residents away from the Community with his behaviour."

"Jonah naughty," Patricia said, with her mouth full of bread. "Norris window."

"Eat your soup, love," Megan whispered, pointing to the steaming bowl.

"We tried to hang on to him when his father died but he was sixteen and a free agent. He came and went, returning when the outside world got too much for him, or if he was in trouble but he never really settled or fitted in."

"You said he got into trouble. Was he involved in any criminal activity when he was away from the Community?"

Duana shrugged, but Blake noticed Freya and

Grant share a look. "He did a spell or two in prison for burglary, I believe. Jonah had a bit of a drug problem. Sad really."

"Do you think his dealers came after him?" Grant said.

Blake inclined his head. "Unlikely. Unless he was deeply involved in supply and sales or owed a ridiculous amount of money, I can't imagine anyone coming all the way out here for him. They'd have to know he was here for a start. But it can't be ruled out."

Patricia finished her soup and jumped back down to play with Charlie. "I think you've got a new friend, there," Megan said.

"Well, it's good to have at least one," Blake muttered, scanning the table.

CHAPTER 17

Detective Sergeant Luckie didn't sound particularly pleased to hear Blake's voice. Blake was certain he heard a short intake of breath. "Oh thank the Lord, sir, you made it. I'm so glad to hear that our own celebrity scouse copper is on the case."

"What have you got on Jonah Huxley?" Blake said, ignoring the jibe. The snow had stopped, and he'd taken himself outside to make the call. Now he looked at the jagged, snow-laden treetops that stretched above him up the valley side.

"D'you honestly think that I'd share any sensitive information with you? D'you think I want my boss to hand me my arse and my job on a silver platter?"

"Look, are you going to come down and start asking questions yourself? Because I'm stuck here for God knows how long and by the time you dig us out, I think the trail will have gone cold. Freezing cold!"

"Unless we've got the killer here?"

"You charged her yet?"

Luckie cleared his throat. "Well, no... we haven't had the forensic report back... and what with this snow, things are going to be delayed, aren't they?"

"So you're going to have to let her go or charge her soon enough, aren't you? Just help me here, Luckie. This place is messed up. I can think of a few words to describe it but 'paradise' isn't one of them."

"I'm aware of that, sir," Luckie said, making it sound like 'no shit Sherlock'. "I could have told you that. Then again, come to think of it, I couldn't. You aren't an investigating officer."

"Give me a break, Luckie. I'm stuck out here with this lot and one of them could be the murderer. You want the truth, surely."

"I tell you what you can do, sir. Keep an eye on that Crime Scene tent. I don't want anyone running off with it, okay? They cost a fortune." Luckie hung up.

Blake sighed and pocketed his phone. He looked up at the treeline, wondering if it was worth struggling up there. It looked steep and he wondered if he'd even make it. Under normal circumstances, he'd happily walk up there but right now his body was trying to heal and complaining about any kind of movement. The idea of doing something that got him breathing heavily filled him with dread. But it was where Jonah had fled from, so there might be clues.

"You need a stick," Duana said from the door. She held a rather elaborate shepherd's crook.

"Here."

"Thanks," he said, taking the stick from her. "I'm not trying to destroy your Community, you know. It must have something going for it if Rosie has called it home for so long. I just want to clear her name."

"Right," Duana said and went back inside.

The climb up the hill was every bit as painful as Blake had expected it to be. Every now and then, he would trip or stumble, making him cry out in pain and frustration. He would have to pause and catch his breath. The ground underfoot was boggy and the snow only added to that. Blake's boots slithered as he tried to get some kind of purchase on the slope. Eventually, he had to negotiate a path from the base of each tree, bridging any gaps by stepping on dead trunks or fallen branches. Up in the distance, he could see the white of a second crime scene tent that must have been set up where Jonah was first attacked. It was slow going but eventually he reached a clearing and another tent. In the quiet half-light under the canopy, it looked strangely ominous. Blake pulled back the flap.

Although the tent had protected the ground from the snowfall that penetrated the trees, something seemed wrong. The stepping plates had slid to the far side of the tent as though the earth beneath them had moved. This would have been a clearing in the forest, Blake surmised, possibly a viewing point down into the valley. An ornamental stone bench sat at one side of the tent as though placed there for the convenience of the investigators. The layers of moss told Blake otherwise; the bench had stood there for many years. Did people come up here to look out on the valley and meditate? Or did the space up in the woods have some other significance? It was an obvious place to arrange a meeting.

Blake peered harder at the muddy ground but it revealed nothing. Not even a bloodstain. It felt like the ground had shifted. Even the stone bench wobbled a little as though it no longer sat on solid earth.

A twig snapped higher up in the woods. Someone was moving around out there. Slowly, he stooped and slipped out of the tent and glanced around. Trees stood silently on guard all around him, their straight trunks vanishing into shadow up the hill. There was no sign of anyone which made Blake's hair prickle. Was he being watched? High above, a pair of crows began arguing with each other, sending small streams of snow tumbling down from their perch. Blake saw a movement up the hill and heard a distant creak. A series of thuds and crashes echoed through the wood and something flashed past the side of Blake's head and continued its journey down the hill.

Staring in horror, Blake realised it was a large rock. A few more inches to the left and that would have taken his head off. Smaller stones bounced down after it and something else groaned up there. It was a wooden sound, like huge branches rubbing together. Diving behind the trunk, he glanced up the hill again and wished he hadn't. A load of logs were bouncing and rolling down towards him as though a giant had tossed them at him. Blake's heart thumped as he threw himself behind a broader tree. The logs clunked against each other, some cartwheeling down the hill end over end, others wedging between trees. A rumbling sound told Blake that something heavier was on its way. Glancing up again, Blake saw a huge shadow, battering its way towards him. It was as big as a car and taking out anything in its path. A tree splintered and tumbled down too as the huge boulder bounced and spun.

Using the stick Duana had given him almost like a pole vault, he slithered down the hill, weaving between the tree trunks as much as he could. Branches crashed and smaller, lighter, stones rattled down on him. He continued his barely controlled fall, ignoring the agonised complaints from his ribcage. Another tree fell to the right of him and Blake tried to stumble his way sideways as well as down. His phone started buzzing. "Jeez, you couldn't make it up," Blake muttered, just managing to stop himself from headbutting a gnarly old pine as he hurtled down the hill. The ground under his feet was slithering away now and Blake feared he would be swallowed up.

At last, the big house came into view and Blake realised he'd probably just experienced Jonah's final journey. He broke out of the bushes and sprinted to the shelter of the hall, not stopping until he'd reached the door. He looked behind him. Much of the hillside had followed him down and now covered what had been the parking area, flattening the crime scene tent completely. The massive boulder stood on top of it all, glowering at Blake.

Opening the front door, he staggered into the lounge and fell onto the sofa by the fire, cursing.

Patricia sat on the floor, playing with Charlie in the warmth. She looked up at Blake and smiled. "Charlie," she said.

"Yeah, Patricia, Charlie. He likes you," Blake panted, catching his breath. Charlie scampered over and gave Blake's hand a cursory lick before hurrying back to his new friend.

"Window," Patricia said, looking, levelly, at him.

"Right," Blake said, glancing outside. "Window."

Patricia fell back to tickling Charlie's tummy. Blake heaved himself up and went to look out of the window. The courtyard looked like a disaster zone. A clear track of earth ran up through the woods to the trees on the skyline that stretched up into the darkening sky. "Where is everyone," he muttered.

The door creaked open and Duana stood there, looking flushed and wearing her outdoor coat. "Are you all right. What happened?"

Blake shook his head. "A landslip and I don't think it was an accident. Someone just tried to kill me."

They walked outside and Duana stared at the mound of earth that now occupied the space in front of the big house.

"It could have crushed us all," Duana said, her face paling. "How could anyone do all this on purpose?"

"The hillside was loose anyway. The land under the crime scene tent up there had shifted. I'm not sure whoever started rolling boulders at me intended to bring the hillside down but that's what happened. Do you mind telling me where you've been this last couple of hours?"

Duana's face darkened and her voice became icy. "After I handed you the walking stick, I went for a walk to have a look at the lane and see if it's passable."

"Right," Blake muttered. Unless there was a quicker path up to the top of the valley, it would have been difficult for Duana to get to higher ground than Blake. She was in the house as he set off. "And is the lane still blocked?"

"Irving has managed to drag your car to the side of his house with his tractor but we'll need the plough to clear the snow."

"You saw Irving then?"

"Yes," Duana said, pulling a face. "He seemed very pleased that you were 'stirring things up' as he put it."

"When did you see him?"

"Half an hour ago, maybe forty-five minutes."

"Unlikely to be him, then," murmured to himself.

"The valley sides are riddled with little pathways, Blake. Irving knows this place inside out. If he wanted to get up into the woods quickly, I'm sure he could."

"The same could be said of you," Blake replied. "It could be anyone here and it's more than likely that the killer hasn't left the valley."

Megan Yule appeared from round the back of the house followed by Freya Finley and Grant Rothwell. "What happened? I heard a rumbling sound... oh my God..." Megan said, her eyes wide.

"A land slip," Grant said. "Do you think we're safe here, Duana?"

"Maybe that's the worst of it," Duana said. "There's nowhere to go anyway. If you took the risk of climbing the hill to the top, there's just miles of moorland buried in three foot of snow. Our best bet is sitting tight and waiting for the plough to dig us out."

Blake looked at each of them. Megan wore little more than a dressing gown and shivered. "I was getting a shower when I heard the noise. I thought the house was coming down," she said, noticing Blake's puzzled look.

"And you two?" Blake said, looking at Freya and Grant.

Duana gave a patronising smile. "Mr Blake thinks someone did this on purpose to try and kill him."

"Really?" Freya said. "How would anyone even start a landslip."

"Somebody was just up there rolling boulders down the hill at me. It was enough to bring the hillside down," Blake replied. "So? Where were you just now?" he looked down at Grant's muddy boots.

"Screw you Blake," Grant snapped. "We don't have to tell you anything." He stormed off towards the back of the house.

Freya closed her eyes and shook her head. "I'm sorry, Mr Blake," she said. "I was in the workshop. Grant was just outside chopping wood."

"All the time?"

"Unless he had a recording of someone hitting logs with an axe, yes," Freya said.

"I heard him too just before I got in the shower," Megan said.

Duana glanced up at the window where Norris Evans stared down on all of them. "He's been there all this time," Duana said. "So who on earth could have been pitching rocks at you?" There was a mocking undertone that Blake didn't like.

"I don't know," he muttered, "but I'm going to find out." He looked up at the window. "I think I should have a proper conversation with Norris. He must have seen something."

CHAPTER 18

Jeff sat in his front room, luxuriating in the heat from the gas fire. It was a little early for a glass of red, but he'd succumbed anyway. He wasn't planning to go anywhere else today. When he'd returned from visiting Josh Gambles, he'd fully intended to write up the notes from his interview but the comments about Eric Lambert had intrigued him.

Now Jeff sat with an old Encyclopaedia of Rock on his lap. He had heard a couple of Lambert's albums in the past but they'd seemed very operatic and toothless compared to some of the Punk offerings he was listening to at the time. Abaddon's Confessor was the name of the band. It was a title meant to shock the middle-aged mainstream of the time as Abaddon was the name of a demon, apparently. Not that Jeff imagined that your average sixties, churchgoing Anglican would recognise that. He read the entry for Eric Lambert.

"Born, Dagenham, 1943, died Moffat, Scotland,1997. Lambert was the lead singer for the notorious Acid Rock band Abaddon's Confessor. Noted for his wailing falsetto voice and flamboyant dress sense, Lambert shocked audiences by performing Satanic rituals on stage and even sacrificing live animals. He is credited with making Abaddon's Confessor a cult band and single-handedly raising their public profile with his antics and lifestyle. Other members of the band were less enthusiastic about the rumours and allegations that dogged Lambert and finally led to the collapse of the band."

Jeff wondered what the allegations were. He knew that Lambert had a reputation for dabbling in the occult. Gambles had mentioned Lambert's daughter, Duana, who ran the Community.

What was Gambles hinting at? He did have a habit of trying to insert himself into the Blake family's story as he had done when he stole their mother's body. Jeff didn't imagine for a second that Rosie was mixed up in some kind of Satanic cult but, given that she was in trouble, it might be worth letting Will know what he'd discovered at this stage and that Gambles might be involved.

*****

By the time Blake reached Evans' room, his heart was thumping. It struck him that nobody, apart from Megan, seemed to care what happened to Rosie or that somebody's life had been taken. They all just went on with their lives as normal. He tried to think of one instance where anyone had asked after Rosie and failed. They were all so wrapped up in themselves. And Evans was probably the worst example of that. A man who sat and watched everything unfold in front of him but did nothing. A man who couldn't even be bothered to come and get his own food. Blake hammered on the door. "Evans! I want a word with you."

Eventually, the door swung open and the hairy man stared at Blake with a hooded gaze. "I'm busy." Evans began to close the door, but Blake jammed his foot in the way and eased his shoulder forward. He was a head taller than Evans and clearly stronger even in his weakened state.

"Well, you're going to have to interrupt your crazy schedule to answer a few questions. A young man died just under your window the other night. Someone tried to kill me this afternoon and my sister's sitting in a cell. You know what that's like, don't you?"

Evans blinked and stepped back. "I dunno what you mean."

"Oh, come on. The way you looked at me when we first met. You asked me if I was a copper. Always a giveaway. So, what did you do time for?"

Evans shrugged. "This and that. Burglary, petty stuff, really. Back home. Moved up here and left it all behind."

Blake had recognised the obvious scouse twang in Evans' voice but there were many kinds of Scouse, all with different intonations. A Bootle Scouse was more guttural than an accent from Aigburth for instance. And a Wirral accent was different again. “You sound like you’re from my neck of the woods. Birkenhead maybe?”

“Full marks, Captain,” Evans said, nodding and flashing his yellowed teeth in a rare smile. There wasn’t a lot of mirth in it. “I haven’t been back since I landed here, though.” He looked like he’d been on a desert island for the last twenty years.

“You must have seen everything when Jonah ran out of the woods. What happened?”

“I sit here a lot, but I don’t always see this world, I go elsewhere,” Evans muttered. “I don’t expect you to understand. Jonah was running out of the woods. He fell. Rosie came out of the front door and knelt down by him. She had a knife in her hand.”

“She didn’t stab him, though…”

“Like I say, I didn’t see the fine detail. She never raised her hand if that’s what you mean.”

“What about this afternoon. Did you see me running out of the woods? Did you see the hill-side coming down?”

Evans shook his head. “Wow! That was real? Half the time, I see things and I’m not sure. Yeah, I saw you, but I never saw anyone else, though. I just sit here and dream, Blake.”

Blake looked over Evans' shoulder into his room. It looked spartan. Blake imagined that once it had been quite a grand chamber with a four-poster bed and thick curtains. Everything had been cleared out of it, even the floorboards were bare. He glimpsed a metal single bed, a rough table and a couple of chairs. A large wardrobe stood against one wall but that was the only sign of the opulence that had once occupied this room.

"How could you just sit there when you saw my sister was in distress?"

Evans' face remained blank. "I knew Duana was down there. I knew she'd be at Rosie's side before I could get down the stairs. No point in us all crowding round a dead body, is there? I live a simple life, Mr Blake. I don't need it complicating."

"Very selfless of you," Blake muttered.

"I never said I was a saint. I sit up here for my own peace of mind. I don't bother the world and it doesn't bother me. If people want to carve each other up, that's their lookout. Anyway, if you're looking for a malcontent, you'd do a lot worse than to have a word with Thomas Irving. He's constantly causing trouble for us."

"Really? In what way?"

"Arguing about access to different parts of the woods, blocking the gateway deliberately, complaining to the police about all kinds of nonsense. He makes Duana's life a misery."

"And you think he'd be capable of killing a young man like Jonah?"

"I dunno, do I? He shoots things, crows, rabbits, his own sheep sometimes, when he has to. There was no love lost between him and Jonah, though, I can tell you that much."

Blake thought back to Irving's own comment about using a shotgun on the boy rather than a knife. He was joking, though, surely.

"And nobody in the actual Community would want to kill Jonah?" Blake said.

"Nah, we're a peaceful bunch, we are."

"So I believe," Blake murmured. "Well, I won't trouble you any longer."

The door closed almost before Blake had finished his last words. He stood in the corridor, frowning. At the end of the passage, the door to Patricia's room stood open. It was almost dark outside now and he could just see the shapes of the figures against the weak twilight coming through the window.

He stepped into Patricia's room and switched the light on. The cut-outs nodded at him in the cold draught and stared with their blank eyes. Blake shivered, edging past the celebrities. He had to admit, they were good, if a little bit creepy. There were some faces he didn't recognise at all and he wondered if they were ex-residents. He saw Rosie's figurine again and felt the weight of responsibility. What was she doing now? Had they charged her yet? Then he stopped dead. Standing by the window and looking out over the courtyard was a cut-out of a young man. At least he thought it was a young man; the body was slighter than the others and he wore a leather jacket and tight jeans. But the face had been scribbled out in red crayon, deep score marks lined the face and the word 'Jonah' had been scrawled across the forehead.

Pulling out his phone, he texted Norris Evans' name to Kath. If he'd had a chequered past on the Wirral, then he should show up on their database. Then he hurried downstairs and found Duana sitting in the small office by the front door. She was sifting through some papers and looked up nervously when Blake appeared at the door.

"I'm going to need a room here for tonight," he said.

Duana pursed her lips and took her reading glasses off. "Do you think that's wise? I mean, you've hardly ingratiated yourself with the residents, have you? Won't you just upset them further?"

"I think it will be easier to investigate if I'm

based here," Blake said. "I can't help it if that upsets people."

"I hope you know what you're doing, Blake. If you think the killer is still in the glen, then it might be dangerous to stay here."

"If the killer is still in the glen, then it's as dangerous at Irving's lodge as here. I may as well be nearer to the action."

Duana leaned forward on her desk. "Let's just hope you don't come to regret that decision, then, shall we?"

CHAPTER 19

It was difficult to imagine Thomas Irving being a threat to the Community as he sat in his armchair by the fire. Blake had come back to Irving's house to pick up his things, only to be welcomed by the smell of stew and dumplings. There was even a small plate for Charlie.

"There's no rush, Will," he'd said. "I'll not be happy if I have to waste it. And don't think you have to stay at the big house. You're welcome to stay here."

The food was delicious, giving Blake the warming he needed after spending so long in the cold house and outside.

Now the old man cradled a glass of whisky in his bony hands and shook his head as Blake related what had happened that day. He looked worried when Blake had mentioned the landslide.

"I thought I heard something," he said, "but I was stuck in the tractor cab up the lane trying to clear the snow. No disrespect, Will but we need the local polis back here. That lot up at the big house are a funny bunch."

"Tell me about it," Blake said. "Norris Evans told me that you'd made a number of complaints to the police about them."

"Aye, I have," Irving said. "Over the years, they've attracted some real deadbeats. I'm sure there's been drug misuse and all kinds of abuse up at the big house over the years. Some of the kids that came and went were like wild animals."

"And you did it out of compassion, or because you're such a good citizen?" Blake said, raising one eyebrow.

Irving grinned and raised his glass to Blake. "I'll admit it; I usually did it to stir up any kind of trouble I could for them. They're not the best neighbours. Never have been. They don't manage the woods well, what they do grow is full of pests and they're forever knocking down my fences. That landslide would never have happened if they'd been terracing and shoring up the valleyside. Everything round here is reinforced, and I've dug channels to guide the meltwater. It's backbreaking work but needs doing."

"So, if one of their number died and The Community got the blame for it, you wouldn't be heartbroken."

"I've told you. If Jonah Huxley had come sneaking around here, I'd have shot him but that's only because I knew he was dangerous, bigger and younger than me. The idea of me pulling a knife on him and then him running away is for the birds."

"If you knew what you were doing, could you have caused that landslide?"

Irving pulled an appalled face. "It's a bit of a hit and miss way to kill someone, though, isn't it? If you *knew* what you were doing, you wouldn't start rolling rocks around."

Silence fell over the room. Blake longed to share his thoughts with Irving and bounce ideas off him as he would his team. Irving seemed like a no-nonsense sort of man who would chew over Blake's theories and spit out all the objections. The trouble was, as much as he thought it unlikely, Irving was a suspect in the Huxley murder investigation. He was as likely a candidate as any other and he had a grudge. Blake looked down at Charlie asleep in front of the fire. "He seems to have made friends wherever he's been."

"That's pups for you. They open doors wherever they go."

"Hmm. He didn't make much impression on Duana Lambert. I struggle to see why she was so reluctant to phone the police. Poor Rosie had to do it herself."

Irving shrugged. "It's no surprise to me. She's her father's daughter. When Eric Lambert moved into the big house, there was all kinds going on. He managed to fend off most complaints and police enquiries. God knows what he got away with. Even now, people come and go. That Lambert woman doesn't vet anyone. I bet you if your sister hadn't called the polis herself, Lambert would have hidden Jonah's body or moved it or something."

"What makes you say that?"

"Just a gut feeling, Will," Irving said. "A couple of times that I made a complaint to the polis, she claimed I was lying. She even denied that one kid I'd seen wandering around stark naked in the woods alone lived at the big house at all. She's quite capable of a big cover-up that one." He paused and looked closely at Blake. "I'm telling you, if the polis hadn't got involved, Jonah Huxley would be in a shallow grave up in the woods by now."

"You might have a point," Blake muttered. He toyed with his phone and then called Luckie.

"Hello, Detective Chief Inspector Blake, sir," Luckie said. He sounded weary. "What can I do for you?"

"Do you want the bad news or the bad news?" Blake said, taking the call into another room.

"Oh, no, go on."

"The hillside collapsed..."

"The hillside?" Luckie spluttered. "What the are you going on about?"

"The whole hillside opposite the big house it came down, bringing your crime scene in the woods into close contact with your crime scene in the driveway. I wasn't able to save either tent. I'm sorry about that."

"Oh no," Luckie groaned. "The Superintendent is gonna love this! You're enjoying this, aren't you, sir?"

"Not really, I nearly ended up buried in it. Somebody was rolling huge boulders down the hill at me. I think that's what set the landslide off."

"Who'd do a thing like that, I wonder?" Luckie said, his voice dripping with sarcasm.

"Funny. Listen, I think someone didn't want me snooping round the crime scenes..."

"Yes, sir that was me and all of Police Scotland. I said not to interfere with the investigation, remember? Now look what you've done. Brought the whole hillside down."

"It wasn't me..."

"No, it's was those nasty boys up the road. Save it, Blake, I've heard it all before. I knew you'd complicate things."

"I didn't kill Huxley, Luckie. The landslide was going to happen sooner or later. Would you rather it did when some of your team were on it?"

"Of course not. Mind you, there's Harris..."

"Look. Right now, there's a killer on the loose in this valley and the only trained professional you have on the scene is me. I'm not going to sit back and twiddle my thumbs but you need a team here right away."

"With the best will in the world, sir, we can't get to you for at least twenty-four hours, maybe more. The roads are blocked and the snow's melting fast now, but there are floods everywhere and that's going to get worse."

"Then give me something to go on. Some information I can work with. Come on, Luckie, if you were stuck down here, I'd do the same for you."

Luckie paused for a moment, obviously wrestling with the desire to tell Blake where to go. "All we have so far is that Huxley hadn't been at the Community long before he died. He'd been bragging about knowing something that was going to make him a few bob."

"You think he was going to blackmail someone here?" Blake said. "Any ideas what? Duana Lambert's old man had a bit of a reputation according to Thomas Irving. Could it be something to do with him?"

"I dunno, sir. It's possible I suppose? Maybe you could ask Ms. Lambert."

Luckie ended the call and Blake scrolled through his contacts until he found his brother Jeffrey. He didn't like asking Jeff for help. But

Blake needed a good researcher and that was one of Jeff's strengths. His little brother was also well-versed in the Arts, especially music. If anyone could find background information on Eric Lambert, it was Jeff.

To Blake's surprise, Jeff picked up straight away. "It's Eric Lambert, isn't it?"

"What? How did you know, Jeff?"

"Gambles put me onto him. Can you believe that creep had been researching Rosie and the Community? He even stayed there."

"Jeez. That creep was sitting at the same table as our Rosie," Blake said, suppressing the urge to shout down the phone. How could Jeff pander to Gambles. Couldn't he see what a monster he was? He took a breath. "What else did Gambles have to say for himself?"

"He just said he'd spent some time here but that it didn't appeal to him. Then he said that there was something fishy about the place. He said hardly anyone did any work or had any real practical skills but somehow they managed to keep the commune going."

Blake pulled a face. "The place is hardly a luxury spa but, yeah, none of them look like they're starving. Did he have any theories?"

"No. He told me to look into Duana Lambert's background."

"Can you do that for me? For Rosie?"

"Will, you might be angry with me for working with Gambles on his biography, but I bear you no ill will. If it helps you and Rosie, I'll look into it. One thing I have found out is that Danny Melrose, the bass player from Abaddon's Confessor only lives over in North Wales. From what I've read, Lambert and the band's split was quite acrimonious. D'you want me to have a chat with him?"

"As soon as you can, Jeff. I'm snowed in this valley and I'm limited in what I can actually do. A bit of background information might give me some kind of way into what's actually going on here."

"Okay. You be careful, Will. Keep your wits about you."

"I intend to."

*****

It hadn't been the greatest of days for Kath Cryer. She'd moved from reporting the Kinder Egg in the anus incident to the human ears that were found in a public toilet minus their owner. By the time she got to the details of the man with his todger stuck in the exhaust of his BMW, Kath was beginning to wonder if she somehow attracted these weird cases. She sat back and looked at the clock which said, 'time to go home, Kath.'

"Good," she muttered and typed 'Norris Evans' into the database. Sitting back, she put her hands behind her head and stretched out.

"Done for the day, Kath?" Superintendent Martin said, startling her.

"Jeez, sir," Kath said. "D'you have to sneak up on people like that?"

Martin laughed. "Sorry, Kath, didn't mean to startle you." He looked down. "Maybe the carpets are too plush. I could have saved a fortune on cheaper ones."

Kath glanced at the screen as the egg timer symbol turned over and over. "No, these carpets are just fine. Was there anything in particular, sir? Only I'm heading off in a minute..."

"You haven't shut down your computer," Martin said, helpfully.

"No, just checking a name," she said. "This guy stuck a Kinder Egg full of drugs up his backside, can you believe it?" It was one of Kath's sleights of conversation, juxtaposing two separate pieces of information so that they sounded related. It was a great way of lying without actually telling a lie.

"Hope he licked all the chocolate off first," Martin said. Kath winced and looked suitably disgusted. He grinned and continued. "No, I was just wondering if you'd heard from Will at all?"

Kath shook her head. "Haven't heard from him at all, sir." This was technically true as Blake had only texted a name and a couple of other details. He hadn't *actually* spoken to her, and technically, she hadn't *heard* anything from him.

"That's funny," Martin said, and Kath's stomach flipped. He craned his neck and squinted at the screen. "Name not found."

A rush of relief forced a squeak of a laugh out of Kath and she threw her hands up. "I must have put the wrong name in," she said, closing the window and shutting down the computer. "Sure sign I need to call it a day."

Martin nodded. "Fair enough. You will let me know if he gets in touch, won't you? I don't want him going 'off piste' and messing up another force's investigation."

"You'll be the first to know, sir," Kath said, feeling herself reddening. She jumped up and pulled her coat on. "G'night."

"Night, Kath," Martin said. She hurried across the office, feeling his suspicious gaze following her. She'd have to be more careful.

CHAPTER 20

The moment he saw the mildewy, cold bedroom, Blake regretted insisting on staying at the big house. It was high up in the house, probably a servant's room once and so it was tiny. Blake tried not to think about how many times he'd bang his head on the beams that held up the low ceiling. The walls were bare plaster and a small single bed was huddled in the corner next to a small table. A chair and a writing desk completed the furniture collection and managed to make the room cramped and awkward to negotiate.

"It's compact," Blake had said, when Duana pushed the door open and switched the light on.

"There are bigger rooms downstairs, but I can't vouch for the soundness of the floorboards in any of them." They both stood in the doorway, Blake stooping slightly, so he could smell her perfume and feel her breath on his cheek. She leaned in towards him. "Or you could sleep in mine if you wanted to..."

"And where would you sleep?"

Duana raised a perfectly plucked eyebrow. "You're an attractive man, Will, you must realise that."

"This'll do fine," he said, breaking the tension that stretched between them.

"Suit yourself," she said, straightening up. "We tend to fend for ourselves in the morning and meet up for lunch."

"Right," Blake said, already mourning for the fry-up that he could have been enjoying at Thomas Irving's house had he decided to stay there. "It must be hard living in this place. I mean your father's legacy is quite a dark one. There must be memories for you in these walls."

Duana's eyes hardened for a second. Then she gave a short laugh. "You certainly know how to get under a person's skin, Will Blake, do you know that? My father was a complex man and yes, there was darkness in his life, but he never let that touch me."

"Really? From what I understand, Eric Lambert had all kinds of wild parties going on here..."

"Says Thomas Irving," she said with a wry smile. "My father's take on Satanism was a rejection of authority, of the power of the church over ordinary people's lives. I never experienced shame or reprimand. My father taught me how to stand on my own two feet rather than crawl in the dust; to look the world in the eye. Now, he may have got up to all kinds of shenanigans at his 'wild parties' but I was safely tucked in bed by then. My mother made sure of that."

"Your mother?"

"Yes. Surprisingly, I did have a mother," Duana said. "Everybody talks about the infamous Eric Lambert, but they never ask about my mother. Alice Lambert was the real power behind the throne. My father was a great showman, but it was my mother who kept him from burning through his fortune. Sadly, she passed away before him and... well, look around you. It took my father about two years to squander the money and follow her into the afterlife."

"I'm sorry. I didn't mean to rake up bad memories..."

"Yes you did," Duana said, mildly. "It's what you policemen are trained to do, isn't it? You find your suspect's weak point and manipulate it until you get the right answer. Anyway, in answer to your question, I have many fond childhood memories of this place and the fact that we all live here peacefully more than makes up for the few bad ones. The sooner you and the police go away and let us get on with our lives the better."

Blake nodded. He'd noted that she made no mention of finding Huxley's killer. "Could anyone from your father's past be responsible for Jonah's murder?"

Duana shook her head. "I'd imagine most of them are long dead. They didn't lead what you'd call healthy lifestyles besides, I'm probably the oldest member of the Community and I was a child when my father was at the height of his powers. The rest of them were toddlers when he passed away."

"Norris Evans is about your age."

"True but, although he is a founder member of my particular Community, he had no connection with my father."

"Where did he come from?"

"Isn't he from your neck of the woods, Will? Liverpool or somewhere?"

"The Wirral, yes but I meant how did he come to be here?"

Duana shrugged. "He just turned up one day. I'd only just started the Community then. It was a struggle; as I said, my father had left me no money, only this house and the land. Irving was snapping at my heels to buy it. Norris helped us all."

"How? I might be doing him an injustice, but he doesn't look like a man with a wide range of skills sets."

Duana pursed her lips. Clearly, she didn't like being cross-examined like this and she was losing her patience. "I don't know. Sometimes, the right person comes along at the right time. He had that famous scouse sense of humour that seems to have evaded you. He saw off a few deadbeats who weren't pulling their weight… oh, I know what you're thinking, Blake, Norris doesn't do much now but if it weren't for him, The Community would have died at birth." Duana Lambert's eyes narrowed. "Irving would probably have bought the estate for next to nothing. Do you know what he wanted to do with the valley and the woods? Farm wild boar. Can you imagine that? He'd have turned the whole place into a pigsty, literally."

"I see," Blake said. "And what would you have done then?"

"Oh, I get it. You think I couldn't do anything else, so I had to hang onto this place to maintain a certain lifestyle. But I chose this life, Blake. There were many things I could have done."

Blake raised his hands. "I'm not judging you. I just wondered whether your attachment is to this valley or to The Community, that's all. You could set up The Community anywhere, in theory and probably make a better living."

"We do all right, Blake," Duana said. "Anyway. I'm tired now. I'm going to bed. I suggest you get extra blankets from the laundry. There's a large cupboard full of them. Goodnight."

"Goodnight, Duana," Blake said, watching the woman saunter downstairs and wondering just how they made any kind of living in this place.

*****

Stanley the pug was farting rather too much for Kath Cryer's liking. They sounded weird, too, like someone blowing bubbles in a glass of lemonade with a straw. It was putting her off her online search for Norris Evans. "Theo!" she shouted, sitting up on the sofa. There was a definite hint of curry in them. "Theo, can I have a word?"

Kath heard a muffled oath from upstairs and Theo, her boyfriend came thumping down the stairs. He poked his tatty head through the door. Kath hoped he was going to get his thick black hair sorted but he kept teasing her about growing dreadlocks. "What?" he said. "I'm in the middle of a game."

"Did you share a curry with Stanley at lunchtime?"

"No," Theo said, widening his eyes.

"Don't lie to me, Theo. I can tell when you're lying, you make those big eyes at me."

"I didn't share it with him, I just put my plate down for a minute and he was there lapping it up. Honest. It's like he can teleport to any place where food gets put down. I took it off him as soon as I realised."

"He's farting and it really stinks."

"Hey! He scoffed half my dinner. I wasn't happy

about it, you know," Theo said, sitting on the sofa putting an arm around her. The laptop slid between them. He felt solid and reliable next to her. Sometimes, Kath wondered what he saw in her. She never thought of herself as pretty and she fought a constant battle with her weight, while he was a bit of a cliché, tall, dark, and square-jawed. He knew he was good-looking. Mind you, he was a pain in the arse, too. Not many women would put up with him for long the way she did. "What're you looking at?"

"I'm looking for any reference to a man called Norris Evans," she said, scrolling through the search engine results. "He's meant to be from Birkenhead and have done a bit of jail time, but I couldn't find anything for him on the National Database."

"Do you know if he even exists?"

Kath shrugged. "Blakey just texted me and asked me to look him up. He's up in Scotland..."

"Blakey is?"

"Yeah, this fella too, I suppose."

"It could just be a made-up name. Who's called Norris these days? Sounds like an old-fashioned kind of name to me."

"Hmm, yeah," Kath said, absentmindedly clicking a name on ukphonedirectory.com. "Ooh, what's this?" The page displayed: Mr

Norris Evans, 13 Fountains Street, Birkenhead, CH413GX.

"So you've got his address, now what? You can't pay him a visit, he's in Scotland."

"True but I can talk to neighbours, get an idea of what he's like. Pick up any gossip, you know." She clicked off the site. Theo's hand crept down her shoulder and he wiggled his eyebrows at her.

"Really? Is that the best you can do? Whatever happened to the flowers, wining and dining?"

"Well, I never know when you're going to be in. Have to take my chances when I can..." Another bubbling fart erupted from Stanley and Kath looked from Theo to the dog and back. "God, I never knew I was in for such a life of romance..."

CHAPTER 21

The next morning was bright and clear as Jeff drove down the A483 towards Wrexham. Danny Melrose had sounded guarded when Jeff rang him and asked for an interview. Jeff had deliberately avoided mentioning Will or The Community. Having read late into the night about Abaddon's Confessor, he quickly realised that the split had been quite traumatic for some members of the band. Shortly after, the drummer, Quentin Chapple, had jumped to his death from the top of a block of flats. Bob Orton, the lead guitarist, had made several failed suicide attempts.

It had been a long time since Jeff had driven into North Wales. Melrose lived near Llangollen, a small town, nestled in the hills and popular with tourists. There was a ruined abbey and a river that was popular with kayakers. Jeff seemed to recall that there was a steam railway, too. Rosie had wanted the three of them to go on the train once when they were all home for some reason, but he and Will had pulled a face at the idea. He wished they hadn't now.

He turned off the busy dual carriageway and headed into the hills. The roads became lanes as he climbed higher and then the Satnav sent him up a track that was basically two strips of tarmac with grass growing up the middle. Fortunately, a faded sign with 'Melrose' written on it peeped out of the high hedges that flanked the track, which reassured Jeff.

The hedge grew higher and formed a thick tunnel that, even without the summer foliage, blocked the bright winter daylight. Then, without warning, Jeff found himself in an open farmyard flanked by a quaint cottage and outbuildings. He parked next to a muddy Land Rover and watched as two black and white sheepdogs came bounding over, leaping up at the door and yapping excitedly at him.

Jeff looked down at the animals' muddy paws and wondered if he was going to get to the house unscathed, but a gruff voice shouted something from the cottage, and they ran back to their master.

Danny Melrose was a short, burly-looking man with a silver mullet hairstyle, short at the sides and long at the back. His white beard was neatly trimmed, and his thick eyebrows made him look as though he was constantly frowning. He was dressed in a long wax jacket and jeans but what concerned Jeff the most was the shotgun he held in his meaty hands.

Jeff wound his window down. "Mr Melrose? Jeff Blake, the writer. We spoke on the phone last night."

Melrose nodded and lowered the gun. “Come on in. Don’t worry about the dogs.”

Jeff climbed out of the car, wincing as his brown suede shoes sank into the mud. He tiptoed over to the front door and shook Melrose’s hand. “Thanks for seeing me at such short notice, Mr Melrose.”

“I have to admit,” Melrose said, “I was a bit surprised that you were so eager to come over. There hasn’t been much interest in the band lately, thank God.” Danny Melrose made the sign of the cross and looked heavenward, briefly. “Come in, I’ll make you a coffee.”

The cottage had a low ceiling with thick dark oak beams. Dried flowers hung from hooks. A large antique clock ticked away the seconds from the wall, and a large green Aga glowed in the corner. Pots and pans hung in size order above it. The whole kitchen looked as though it had been set up for a magazine shot. The smell of freshly baked bread hung in the air too.

“Have a seat.” He pointed to a refurbished armchair that sat by the Aga.

“Thanks,” Jeff said, settling down and smiling. “It’s lovely. Not sure I’ll want to move out into the cold again, now.” He pulled out his phone. “Do you mind if I record our conversation? It’s just that I’m hopeless at taking notes and I’m sure to forget something if I don’t make a record."

Melrose glanced down at the phone and licked his lips. "Sure. Why not?"

"I hope it doesn't make you nervous. I know some people go to pieces when they realise that they're being recorded."

Melrose settled into another armchair opposite Jeff and sipped his coffee. "Really, it's fine. It's just that you weren't too specific about who you were writing for."

"Well, I write lots of these kinds of articles. I'm hoping to sell this one to one of the rock journals, Kerrang maybe. I don't know yet. I guess, we'll see what I come out with."

"I see," Melrose said and sipped his coffee again.

"So, let's start at the beginning. You started out as the Bluetone Three."

"Yeah, in the early sixties" Melrose said, with another of those fleeting smiles. "We were a blues outfit then, playing all the standards. We had a small following but by the mid-sixties, we hadn't really moved with the times. Bands like the Yardbirds were experimenting with psychodelia and we were still banging out the twelve bar numbers."

"But by 68 you were Abaddon's Confessor and nobody could accuse you of not experimenting. What happened?"

Melrose stared into his coffee. “Eric Lambert happened. He came along and changed everything.”

“He was quite a character, I believe.”

“Larger than life,” Melrose said but no smile joined his words. “You know that story about Robert Johnson?”

“Yes, he sold his soul to the Devil to become the greatest blues guitarist. Something like that, wasn’t it?”

“It was,” Melrose said, darkly. “Well Eric had visited a crossroads somewhere along the line and made a pact with… certain forces. That’s what he told us anyway and we believed him. He opened our minds to so much.” Melrose crossed himself again.

Jeff realised that they were straying into the territory he wanted but he had to temper the interview with questions about musical influences so that Melrose didn’t become suspicious. “It hadn’t really been named as a musical genre, but you were early acid rock, then. Were there drugs involved?”

Melrose rolled his eyes. “Were there ever? It seemed like Eric had a never-ending supply and he was happy to share.” He touched his chest and Jeff saw a chain glinting at his neck.

“I get the impression that he introduced you

and your friends to a lifestyle that you were unfamiliar with."

"You could say that," Melrose said, with a snort. "I mean, don't get me wrong, we had our fair share of groupies and we liked a joint or two, but Eric had a taste for anything dissolute. And the occult side of things."

"But your blues style didn't go out of the window straight away, did it? I mean that last Bluetone Three album had some great rockers on it, Voodoo Potion for instance."

"Eric was with us by then. He played harmonica on that and wrote the lyrics, too. I don't think they'd appeal to today's generation..."

"In what way?"

Melrose's bushy eyebrows shot up. "Have you listened closely to the words? It's not exactly about consensual sex." Melrose shook his head. "It was right up Eric Lambert's street."

"Are you saying he was a sexual predator?"

"Eric didn't really stop to ask anyone permission to do *anything*," Melrose said. He'd put his mug down now and was rubbing his brow as though he had a headache. "That was his strength and his weakness. He didn't ask permission to change the band's sound. It just happened. He didn't worry about the more sinister lyrics even though some of the record label execs were worried about them."

"He just ignored them?"

"Too right. Eric had no belief in authority unless he granted it. These guys didn't know how to cope with him. All these guys were older and posher than us. They all went to private schools and Oxbridge. Eric didn't give a stuff. Plus, he had Alice behind him."

"Alice?"

"His wife. Well, she wasn't his wife at first. She had some kind of double-barrelled name, I can't even remember it now. Anyway, she was a real tough cookie. She and Eric were a force to be reckoned with. Between them, they screwed a fortune out of the record company. They couldn't say 'no' to Eric."

"And what about you and the rest of the band?"

Melrose looked pale. "By the time we changed our name to Abaddon's Confessor, we were all under his spell. Like I said to us it was just part of the 'lifestyle' you know, the rituals and all the Satanic stuff. It was just an act to us, just an excuse for orgies and partying. To Eric it was his religion."

"And Alice?"

"She was more level-headed. I think she worshipped money more than anything. She went along with a lot of things. I don't know that she shared Eric's devotion. She steered him away from the more destructive aspects of his beliefs."

"So, what finished the band in the end?"

"Lambert's wild behaviour was certainly part of it. Quentin, the drummer was under his influence more and more. He went to black masses with Eric and I'm sure he hurt people. Bob dabbled. He went to one of Eric's rituals but saw something that night that tipped him over the edge. He was never the same again..."

"In what way?"

"Haunted," Melrose said. By now, he had pulled the cross that hung around his neck from under his shirt and was rubbing it with thumb and forefinger. "Whatever Bob saw it marked him forever. He's tried to end it all on a number of occasions, unsuccessfully, thank the Lord. Quentin succeeded as you probably know; chased off a rooftop by devils of his own conjuring."

Despite the cosy kitchen, Jeff shivered. "Can I ask? Did Alice and Eric have any children?"

Melrose grimaced. "One daughter, Duana. It's a Gaelic name, apparently. She was a nasty piece of work."

"Really?"

"Yeah, she had her father's self-belief and her mother's sense of entitlement. I knew her when she was a little girl, sometimes she'd be hanging around backstage with her mum. But, wow, she'd grown when I next saw her. She was beautiful and charismatic, like her parents. But she came after me for the rights to certain songs and albums. It was a nightmare."

"When was this?"

"The end of the Nineties, just into the new century. She had a load of lawyers claiming that Eric was the sole creator of anything recorded by Abaddon's Confessor. I thought I was going to lose this place. I mean the claims were kicked out of court in the end, but she must have been desperate for money to do that. Quentin had killed himself by this time and his family were all for rolling over, Bob Orton wasn't in any fit state to fight in court, so she thought I'd be easy meat on my own. Proved her wrong, didn't I?"

"And do you know where she is now?"

"Yeah, she's runs some kind of commune up in Scotland. Probably keeping the Lambert's wicked legacy going, I don't know."

"I see."

Melrose looked up at Jeff. "You're not thinking of going looking for that bitch are you?"

"There might be a story..."

"I'm telling you, steer clear. That woman is bad news. You'd get a story all right. It mightn't be the story you're looking for. She's a chip off the old block, is Duana Lambert. Just think about it, she grew up surrounded by black masses, Satanic rituals, and torture." Melrose lowered his voice. "I wouldn't mess with Duana Lambert if you know what's good for you."

CHAPTER 22

As he expected, Blake had slept badly. The room was cold and even with several extra blankets and Charlie snuggled up close, it took him ages to warm up. On top of that, his sides ached, and his head thumped. He wondered how Rosie was and fretted about whether staying in the house was the right idea. On one level, it made sense to be in amongst a bunch of suspects, but it might also turn out to be a dangerous move, especially if somebody was out to kill him. As a police officer, he was often in harm's way, but those times were more spur of the moment things; confronting angry criminals or challenging suspects in their own home. He'd only ever been targeted by one person and that was Josh Gambles. Even then, the serial killer didn't wish to harm him.

It was early morning but still dark. Blake staggered bleary-eyed downstairs into the kitchen, followed closely by Charlie, eager for food. Megan Yule stood in the kitchen staring out through the window at the few vague white lumps of snow that glowed white in the blackness. A mug of coffee steamed in her hand and she pointed at the kettle. "It's just boiled."

"Thanks," Blake said. "You're up early."

"Couldn't sleep, what with Jonah and then the landslide."

"That's understandable." Blake glanced around the kitchen and started opening cupboards. Megan watched him struggle. "Aha." He pulled out a bag of porridge oats. "Now, I need a pan. Do you know why Jonah had come back to The Community?"

Megan folded her arms and shrugged. "Dunno. I didn't have that much to do with him. He came and went. Duana said he usually rocked up when he was in trouble and needed to lie low for a bit."

"Did he say anything about being in trouble, this time?"

"Not that I know of. He was arguing with Duana about some antique furniture he reckoned a friend could sell for her to make some money, but I don't know anything else."

Blake put some water on the oats and put it on the stove. "I bet you have salt on your porridge, you being all Scottish and that."

Megan tried to suppress a smile. "Who the hell has salt on their porridge?" she said. "Anyways, I canna stand porridge. Give me a good fry up any day."

Blake laughed. "I thought you lot were strict vegies. You seem so ill-suited to this place Megan."

"I told you, it was better than the last place. Free board and lodging for a bit of cooking and cleaning. Simple. Or it was until all this..."

Blake stared out of the kitchen window. It was growing light fast and he could see the huge outline of a building. He frowned. "We're at the back of the house, right?"

"Yeah," Megan said, puzzled.

"So, Rosie would have been standing here by the sink when Jonah died."

"I guess so, why?"

"How the hell could she have heard a groan and seen Jonah from here when he collapsed at the front of the building? It's not possible. Even with the front door wide open."

"I guess so. I was in the front room and I didn't hear anything until Freya freaked out screaming her head off. D'you think Rosie is lying?"

"I'm not saying she's an angel, but I've always known Rosie to be honest to the point of embarrassment. If she was lying, there would have been a very good reason."

"The only reason I can think of to lie about that would be to cover up the fact you weren't outside already, with a knife in your hand," Megan said.

Blake nodded. "That's logical but Rosie's no killer."

"Maybe she killed Jonah by accident. He could be quite pushy sometimes, so I believe. Maybe he went too far and she flipped."

"She'd admit it, I'm sure." It was light now and Blake could see the yard at the back of the house. Several wheelie bins lined up against an old shed which didn't look like it had been opened in years. Next to that was a stack of logs that would have put a lumberjack to shame. A few abandoned growbags and boxes gave testament to some attempt to grow something recently. The back yard was hemmed in by a low wall which made one side of a quadrangle covered in snow. Directly opposite stood a brick-built barn with a large door. On either side was a line of what would have been stables but they had been converted into rooms. "What's that?" Blake said, nodding at the big building.

"That's the workshop. It's where all the Arty stuff goes on."

"You've never been in there?"

Megan shook her head. "No. I just do the cooking and cleaning. It's mainly Freya who works in there. Patricia has her own little workshop upstairs."

Blake poured out his porridge into a bowl and found one for Charlie. He was sure he'd read somewhere that porridge was good for dogs, but he added a little creamy milk to Charlie's. Leaning on the sink, he looked out. "Why has someone put a second log pile there?" The huge heap of chopped wood sat awkwardly on the edge of the gravel right by the side of the road. It looked as though it had been dumped and anyone driving up there would have to swerve off the road to avoid it.

"Search me," Megan said.

"I think I'll check that out when I've finished this porridge. Got any salt?"

*****

Grant Rothwell was a bear of a man. Broad-chested and with a full bushy beard, he pushed a huge barrow laden with logs from the pile by the road. Blake could see the veins in his neck bulging with the effort. Although the snow had stopped and it was still freezing cold, Rothwell was in his shirt sleeves, sporting a lumberjack chic. When he saw Blake and Charlie coming out of the back door, he redoubled his efforts with the barrow and tried not to make eye-contact.

"Mr Rothwell, can I have a word?"

Rothwell dropped the handles of the barrow, so it crashed to the ground, spilling a couple of logs. "If it doesn't take too long. I've spoken to the proper police already..."

Blake stooped down and picked up one of the logs, placing it back on the pile. "I am proper police, Grant," he said, "and my sister, your friend, is under suspicion of murder. So I'm sure you want to do everything you can to help her, right?"

"Sure," Rothwell said, reluctantly.

"So, you were in Freya Finley's room on the night Jonah Huxley died, is that right?"

"Yeah, I told you that."

"What were you doing?"

Rothwell raised an eyebrow. "Well, you know... We were in bed ..."

"Is she a regular partner of yours?"

Rothwell shook his head. "She's my only partner. We're not all at it like rabbits just because we try to live a bit more freely, Blake."

"Right. And you heard the screams from all the way round the front of the house? I mean that's a long way."

"Not that far and it's quiet at night, here. Sound carries."

"Did you hear any other noises before that? Up in the woods maybe?"

"No. It was silent before then."

"I see. What did Freya mean when she said that she had blood on her hands?"

Rothwell blinked and despite his face being

covered with a thick red beard, Blake noticed he went pale. "I-I don't know what you mean..."

"Come on, you were having a row yesterday. I distinctly heard her say that you were okay because you didn't have blood on your hands..."

"You'll have to ask her about that. I can't remember her saying that at all."

"What were you arguing about?"

Rothwell shrugged. "Living here can be difficult at the best of times. I like mucking in with everyone else, but Freya isn't so keen. She keeps talking about moving on soon. I'm not so keen."

"But the current unpleasant business has focused her mind. Is that it?"

Rothwell nodded. "Yeah."

"But I thought Freya was all for keeping the place going. Making it grow. I thought she was making costume jewellery to sell."

"She blows hot and cold about it, doesn't she?" Rothwell said, looking down at the pile of logs. "Like the rest of us, she wants this place to succeed but gets disheartened when there are setbacks."

"How did she get on with Jonah Huxley?"

Rothwell's face regained its colour. "I dunno. Same as the rest of us, I suppose, she thought he was a pain in the arse."

"You didn't like him either then. Any particular reason for that?"

"He was a troublemaker, wasn't he? Always stirring things up between people and causing havoc." Rothwell's eyes hardened even more. "If you ask me, he got what he deserved."

"Does Freya share that opinion?"

"You'd have to ask her about that," Rothwell said, picking up the remaining logs that lay in the snow. "Now I'd better get these inside and get on with the rest of the work that nobody else seems to take responsibility for." He picked up the trolley again and barged past Blake who watched him disappear into the house.

"What did you see in this place, Rosie?" he muttered. The forest surrounded the house, spreading up the steep valley walls behind it. The trees whispered in the breeze, sending sprays of snow hissing through the branches. Maybe the snow was thawing. He hated to admit it, but Blake would welcome Luckie and his team, right now. They could take over and really start grilling this lot. Somebody here knew more, of that he was certain. Blake looked up to see the usual silhouette of Norris Evans in his bedroom window and felt a pang of sympathy for Rothwell. With the likes of Evans doing nothing but stare out of the window all day, it was a wonder anything got done.

Blake wandered over to the workshop, hoping to find it open. As he went, he mulled over his conversation with Jeff the night before. It troubled him that Gambles knew about the Community. The serial killer had intruded in Blake's life already, even from behind bars. He just prayed Gambles' involvement in any of this had begun and ended with him tipping Jeff off. He wondered how much use Jeff's information would prove to be, but at least he felt like he was helping, and Will knew how important that was sometimes. On the other hand, maybe Jeff would uncover what Duana was hiding. Blake paused at the second log pile. It looked hastily assembled, the wood more dumped than stacked. The ground under it was muddy and Charlie sniffed intently at the base of the heap. Pulling the little dog back, Blake crouched down and took out his phone. Some of the bottom logs had mud and something rust brown on it. He took a picture. If it was dried blood, that might explain why Rosie said she saw Huxley from the kitchen. Perhaps he'd died there and they'd covered the spot with logs. But why go to all the effort of dragging him round the front? And why hide the original death site? Blake's stomach lurched as he also realised that would take more than one person to cover it up. Or one very strong person. Like Grant Rothwell.

CHAPTER 23

Andrew Kinnear hated breaking rules. One of the things DCI Blake had taught him was not to assume anything and to go through the proper channels and procedures. So when Kath Cryer had asked him to call in at 13 Fountains Street, Birkenhead and ask a few questions for Blake, he was torn. Kinnear had a great deal of respect for Blake but he'd also heard what Superintendent Martin had said about not getting dragged into another force's case. But then there was Kath Cryer to take into consideration and, on balance, Kinnear decided he was more afraid of her than Superintendent Martin. Besides, he was on another call anyway and could just swing by. If Norris Evans was up in Scotland, he didn't really know what would be gained by calling at his empty house. It may be that it had been rented out to complete strangers But Kinnear was curious.

Fountains Street was a typical old Birkenhead row of terraced houses, now with double glazing and satellite dishes poking out under their gutters. Many of the houses had low walls containing the tiniest strip of soil in front of the house. Some had lost the walls and the little fronts had been paved to hold wheelie bins. Cars lined the street and finding a parking space was difficult.

Number thirteen looked neatly painted, a little trellis ran along the low wall and a bush of some description spilled over the trellis. It looked very much inhabited. Kinnear knocked on the shiny black front door and waited. He looked up and down the street as a young woman pushed a pram past him. Kinnear sighed; it looked like the house was empty as he expected. "Bit of a waste of time, Kath, but hey ho," he muttered and turned to leave. A door chain rattled inside, and the door opened a fraction, bumping as the chain tightened. A pair of watery blue eyes peered out and Kinnear could see an old man in a dressing gown. "Yeah? Can I help you?"

Kinnear smiled, pulled out his warrant card and decided to play ignorant. "Sorry to trouble you but I was looking for the, homeowner, a Mr Norris Evans?"

"Right," the old man said, staring at him.

"Is he in?"

"Yeah," the old man said. "I am."

"I'm sorry. I must have made some kind of mistake. Forgive me, sir, I was expecting someone a little younger..."

Norris Evans' knitted his brow; Kinnear could see his bald head and the silver stubble on his chin. "What's this all about?"

"Something and nothing, really, sir. Is there anyone else in the area called Norris Evans?"

"There was," Evans said and took a deep gargling breath. "A while back now. You'd better come in."

*****

The rear courtyard lay empty, the windows of the barn conversions that flanked it were dark and still. But the barn door at the other end of the yard stood slightly ajar. Glancing round, Blake hurried over and poked his head into the gap.

It was dark inside at first. The smells of Linseed oil and paraffin tickled his nose. Slowly, Blake's eyes adjusted to the half-light and he saw that he was in a huge workshop. A pile of furniture lay stacked on one side of the room and a workbench held a table in place. The other side of the room resembled an artist's studio with an easel and a number of empty gilded frames leaning against each other. Blake couldn't make out the picture and slipped inside to get a closer look. He pulled the door closed so that the noise of anyone coming in would alert him.

The picture on the easel was of an Eighteenth-Century gentleman on a horse but it looked freshly painted. Blake shook his head. If this was just a place where the residents indulged in their hobbies, why lock it? Possibly because the equipment was valuable but, looking round, there didn't seem to be much of value in the room. Possibly some of the power tools over by the furniture would have a limited second-hand value.

A set of stairs led to what would have been the loft in the original barn. This level had been walled off into some kind of upper room. Blake crept up them and tried the door at the top of the stairs. It was locked but he could see through the small window in the door that it was a small office, with a desk and a computer.

The front door rattled and Blake hurried down from the stairs and just managed to hide himself behind an old bookshelf that had been pushed to the back of the workshop. "Hello?" Grant Rothwell called in. "Freya? Are you in here?"

Blake heard footsteps as Rothwell came further into the workshop. "Duana?" Rothwell went up the stairs and tried the office door, giving a grunt of satisfaction when he found it locked.

Another footfall made Blake press himself deeper into the shadows. "Grant?" Freya Finley called. "What're you doing?"

"I saw the door was open and came to check. Can't be too careful with that Blake character snooping around. Why did you leave it open?"

"I thought it was locked. It must have been on

the latch," Freya said.

"You've got to be more careful, Freya..."

"I know, I know," she snapped, impatiently. "I just popped out to check something with Duana. I didn't do it on purpose."

"Well he was giving me a good grilling before," Rothwell said.

"Who?"

"Blake," Rothwell snapped. "The policeman. D'you think he suspects anything?"

"Stop fussing. He doesn't know a thing. Neither do those numpties up in Moffat. Where is he now?"

"I dunno," Rothwell said. "He didn't follow me into the house, so he must have stayed outside. Do you think he came in here?"

There was a moment's silence and then Freya's voice rang out loud and clear. "Okay, Mr Blake, you can come out now."

Blake stepped out into the light. "So what am I meant to suspect?"

Freya gave half a smile. "It's rude to eavesdrop, Mr Blake," she said. "And don't you need a warrant to go snooping around private property?"

Blake shrugged. "I saw the door was open and looked in to have a word with whoever happened to be inside. Turns out it was empty. Anyway, you haven't answered my question."

"Why don't you leave us alone, Blake?" Rothwell said, striding forward. "We might have disliked Huxley but we didn't kill him."

"Calm down Grant. He's only trying to clear his sister's name." Freya grabbed at Rothwell's arm.

"So, what's going on, here?" Blake said, looking round.

"Nothing. We're an artistic as well as a spiritual community, Mr Blake," Freya said. "You'd expect to find a workshop. We do a bit of restoration work for local stately homes, too."

Blake frowned. "What did you mean when you told Grant that you had blood on your hands?"

"That does it," Rothwell roared and charged at Blake.

"Grant, no!" Freya yelled but Rothwell ignored her.

Years of experience kicked in but as Blake jumped aside, a searing pain tore through his chest and he stumbled back, crashing into the stacked furniture. The big man turned on his heel and swung a punch. Blake dodged the blow, but it may as well have landed because the fire in his side made him double up and fall to his knees.

"Grant, stop!" Freya said again, running in front of him and shielding Blake. "Can't you see he's in pain?"

Rothwell stood, panting, and glaring at Blake. "I don't care. You get out of here, Mr Policeman or so help me, I'll kill you."

Freya put a hand on Rothwell's chest but he slapped it away and stalked out of the workshop, slamming the door behind him. "Are you all right?" She said, offering a hand to Blake as he staggered to his feet, clutching his side.

"Thanks. I've been better. Tobogganing down the hillside in my car the other day didn't help," Blake said. He looked towards the door. "Will he be okay?"

"Yeah, he'll calm down soon enough. He's just a little overprotective, that's all." There was a moment's awkward silence. "Look, I suppose I owe you some kind of an explanation..."

Blake raised his eyebrows. "Go on then."

"When I said I had blood on my hands. There was a reason for that."

CHAPTER 24

Detective Chief Inspector Vernon balanced on the edge of Luckie's desk, his hands gripping his knee. It was an irritating pose. Luckie kept expecting him to lose balance when he leaned back. If any of the other officers in the briefing room had done that, he'd have told them to sit up and pay attention. Also, DCI Vernon was younger than Luckie, a fast tracker with a university degree. Luckie wasn't one of those who believed that you had to work your way up from the very bottom, to be a good senior officer. He'd seen a few in his time who were just watching the clock, waiting for retirement and he didn't blame them. But he did value a little experience in the field. Vernon didn't display any evidence of that at all as far as Luckie could see. The snow was receding gradually and many of the main roads had been cleared. This meant the office was full again. But outside, flooding was still a problem and some of the narrower lanes were still blocked. Even the roads that had been cleared and gritted were still slippery which made travel difficult.

"So, as you know, sir, they have the pleasure of DCI Will Blake in Devil's Glen at the moment and he has reported that both crime scenes have been destroyed in a landslip. Deep joy. He claims, too, that the landslide was caused deliberately to try and kill him."

A murmur rippled through the officers, but Vernon remained stony-faced. "Any news on the pathologists report? Any forensics back?"

"Still a bit early even under normal circumstances, sir," Luckie said, "but apparently, the pathologist is still snowed in, so we're not going to get anything back there for a while."

"So we've ground to a halt," Vernon said.

"We're pretty sure that Huxley went back to The Community in order to blackmail someone. He was bragging that he knew something and it was going to make him a fortune, so it seems plausible that someone down there knows something. And if DCI Blake isn't being melodramatic, then the killer is still active."

"What about his sister?" Vernon said. "Rosie."

"I don't think she did it, sir. No criminal record. She doesn't seem capable, to be honest but she's following her brief's advice and making no comment at the moment. The other residents just talked twaddle when we interviewed them. Saying they all killed Huxley. It's a mess, to be frank and if what Blake says is true, then things are set to get worse. "

"This Blake," Vernon snorted. "Is he reliable?"

"Well, he's a scouser but he's also a DCI, sir..." Luckie said, glancing meaningfully around the group. "Of course, he must be totally reliable."

Vernon pulled a face to indicate that he knew he was having his leg pulled and that he was okay with it. Luckie nearly pulled the same face back to indicate he didn't give a shit but thought better of it. "We need to get back on site. I'll have a word with the Super, see if we can't put some pressure on the Highways Authority to clear the lane down to the glen as a priority..."

"Great, sir," Luckie said, genuinely impressed for once. "I think the sooner we can get down there, the better."

*****

Freya Finley sat on the workbench and looked down at the floor for some time, composing herself and clearly wondering where to start. "I grew up in quite a well-to-do family, Mr Blake. My father was an Art dealer in Edinburgh and I dearly wanted to follow in his footsteps. But money can't buy you everything..." She paused for a moment and looked around at the gloomy workshop. "My sister had mental health issues. Eating disorders, depression and anxiety, you name it."

"That must have been tough for all of you."

Freya nodded. "Growing up while your family tiptoe around your little sister like she's a time-bomb just waiting to go off is difficult. I was only a teenager. It affected me badly..."

"You resented her," Blake said.

"Yes. It's a terrible thing to say but I hated her. Or rather, as a kid, I hated her illness. Every night I'd pray that she'd get better and everyday things seemed to just get worse. Outbursts and anxiety attacks. She'd pick a fight with me over seemingly tiny things, the colour of my top or the fact that I'd been to have my hair done. One Christmas, I got some really expensive make-up. I'd have been around sixteen. I used all my tips money from my weekend job to buy it. She threw it all down the drain. And if I fought back, I'd end up being the villain..."

Blake wondered where this story was going. "If this is difficult, you don't need to..."

"No. I have to tell you so you can make sense of what you heard me say." Freya's eyes glittered and she swallowed a sob. "Shortly after that incident, we had a big blow-up at the dinner table. It was something and nothing. My sister was sniffing, she'd picked up yet another cold because she had no energy. She was like a living skeleton. I just lost it with her. Told her to eat something. I can't remember what was said but I do remember telling her to kill herself and give us all a break...." Freya's head went down, and she shook.

Blake watched her silently, uncertain what to do. "Which, I assume she did," he said at last in a quiet voice.

"There was so much blood, Mr Blake. Her last act. I was meant to be looking after her while my parents saw the social worker. She took a razor blade into the bath with her. I found her..."

"I'm sorry."

"So, when I saw Jonah and... all that blood... it all came back to me. That's why I said I had blood on my hands."

"I see. You must realise, though, that you weren't to blame for your sister..."

"Wasn't I? I could have been kinder. Yes, I was just a kid, but she was in my shadow. Are you an eldest child, Mr Blake?"

"I am."

"Then you must realise what a position of responsibility that is. How resentment can build up, how you can overshadow your younger siblings."

Blake thought of Jeff. "In my experience, it can happen either way. Rosie probably had the worst deal in our family as I competed with my brother." He stopped, feeling himself reddening at the confessional turn the conversation had taken.

"I've spent the rest of my life paying for those

cruel words. My parents never said it, but they blamed me for my sister's death. I tried to join my father in his business but there was always a barrier. I've drifted ever since."

"I'm sorry," Blake said again, not sure what else he could add. "You said something else to Grant about me not suspecting anything. What was that, then?"

Freya took a deep breath. "It's nothing. Grant made some mistakes when he was a youngster, too. Drug-related, petty, and certainly nothing with any bearing on Jonah's death. He chose to hide them from the police and thinks it'll look bad if it comes out now."

"Well, he has a point. It's better to be honest with the police, especially in circumstances like this. One thing does puzzle me, though. When I spoke to Rosie, she told me that she'd seen Huxley out of the kitchen window which would suggest that he came off the hill behind the house. Yet the crime scene tent was at the front. Can you explain that?"

Freya gave a nervous laugh. "Well, I imagine Rosie was deeply traumatised by what she saw. Maybe she misremembered..."

"Misremembered," Blake repeated. "So she was actually standing outside the front door waiting for Huxley with a knife..."

"I didn't say that."

"No but I can't see what she would be doing at the front of the house. Her story makes more sense if Huxley staggered out of the woods into the back yard area."

"It would but that's not what happened. Huxley was lying dead in the front."

"Grant is very protective of you, isn't he?"

Freya rolled her eyes. "Overly protective. I've had words with him about it. Wait... what are you suggesting?"

"Just that he's on a short fuse and jealous with it. He described you as his *only* partner. Is that true?"

"What do you mean?"

Blake shrugged. "I can imagine he'd get nasty if he discovered that you'd slept with Huxley. He said to me that Jonah got what he deserved. He's a big man, could've easily taken Jonah down."

"That's ridiculous. Grant is not a killer," Freya snapped. "Now, Inspector, I have things to do, if you'll excuse me."

"Fair enough," Blake said and walked out of the workshop but he could feel Freya glaring at him as he left. He'd hit a raw nerve there and Rothwell would need watching.

*****

There was definitely an atmosphere in the kitchen the next day. Laura poured herself a coffee while Gilmore sat in his armchair scowling at his mug. “You shouldn’t have gone after them, Stacy,” he said. For a second, Laura wondered who he was talking to but then realised and felt a stab of guilt that she’d given him a false name.

Laura had followed the men the previous night, but she hadn’t got very far before she walked straight into a barbwire fence, slipped on what seemed like every cowpat in the field and finally taken a wrong turn and fallen into a ditch. By the time she’d become accustomed to the dark, the men had slipped away in the darkness. “You could have come with me,” she said.

“I didn’t know you’d go on your own. God knows what might have happened to you.”

“I can look after myself,” Laura said, sipping the coffee. “Anyway, they left me far behind. It seems there’s an artform to moving around the countryside at night.”

“It’s called knowing where the ditches are,” Gilmore said, with a snort. “Next time you hear them, just stay in bed. That’s what I do.”

Laura frowned. “Wait, you said that they hadn’t been on your land.”

“They might have once or twice. What am I meant to do? Stay up all night in case they find the badgers?”

"You've got badgers on your land? And those bastards are going to get them? We've got to check they're okay!"

Gilmore stared at her. "Says who? Aren't you meant to be living in the caravan? Bloody hell, you've only been here a couple of days and you're telling me what I have to do!"

"Well," Laura said, indignantly "I mean we're talking badgers here, aren't we? And they want to kill them. It's cruel and their dogs get horribly mauled, too. You want that on your land?"

Gilmore pursed his lips. "All right. I'll call the police then..."

"No," Laura said. "We don't need to do that. Can't we just scare them off ourselves?"

"My dad was the scary one. He'd go raging over the fields, flat cap pulled down, shotgun in hand. They wouldn't have messed with him..."

"But he's not here, Steve," Laura said, softly. "You have to face up to things like this. You can't hide away from them or it just gets worse."

Gilmore looked at her. "Says the girl hiding in a mouldy caravan."

Laura folded her arms. "I'm not hiding from anyone."

"Really? You come here for a holiday, then?"

"I'll take Archie out for a walk," Laura said, ignoring his sarcasm.

"No, he's my dog," Gilmore said, jumping up. "I'll take him up the fields and check on the cattle. He can have a run around up there. You must have lots to be getting on with."

Laura shrugged. "Suit yourself."

For the rest of the morning, Gilmore avoided her, keeping busy, with jobs around the yard in his tractor. He pointedly put Archie back on his chain and Archie settled down to sleep in his kennel.

Laura lay on the bed, trying to read the book but her thoughts tumbled over in her mind. If they called the police, they might want to know who she was and ask her to make a statement and that might get back to Blake somehow. If she gave them a false name, she knew how quickly that would unravel. The only way to save the badgers was to deal with this herself. She was so deep in thought that she didn't hear the van draw up into the yard. The first thing she heard was Archie's barking and Gilmore's voice. "You're out late, Billy. Hardly any daylight left for work."

Laura looked out and saw the red van that had stopped in the lane the day before. Gilmore stood flanked by three men, two of them, Laura recognised. "We were just wondering if you wanted us to keep an eye on your fields for you.

You know for pests and such."

The men were close to Gilmore, trying to intimidate him. He towered over them but he looked cowed. "No, it's fine, thanks, Billy. I've got it under control."

"Are you sure? Cos we can lend a hand. Terrible business all this TB that's being spread around by the little bastards. It can put a man out of business."

"No TB on my land," Gilmore said. "Now, if you don't mind, I have work to do…"

Billy held Gilmore's arm. "Oh, go on, Stevie, be a sport."

Laura came out of the caravan. "You okay Steve?" she said.

"Oh, look boys, it's the Judy," Billy said. He winked and gave Gilmore a nudge. "You dark horse, Stevie, I wondered where she'd come from. Got yourself a bit of rough, eh? Good for you."

"I think you were asked to leave the yard, lads," Laura said. "Better jog on, eh?"

"They're hard them Liverpool Judies," Billy said, smirking. "We'd better move along before we get our butts kicked. Nice dog, Stevie. If you ever want to sell him, let me know. He looks like a fighter!"

The three men sauntered back to the van and

drove off.

Laura started to say something, but Gilmore raised a hand and stalked off into the farmhouse. Archie whined and watched him go.

CHAPTER 25

Budgerigars were something Kinnear had never got used to. He wasn't great with feathered creatures at the best of times but when they were couped up in a small cage and jumping back and forth, they freaked him out. He'd been sworn at, punched, kicked even shot at in his time as a police officer but the dry rustle of feather on feather just clawed at his nerves. Sometimes, he wondered if he had some kind of allergy to birds. Sitting here, in this cosy living room, he could feel the dust from the creature in the cage coating the back of his throat. It was a harmless enough thing, bright blue and chirping cheerfully but it was kryptonite to Kinnear.

Mr Evans sat in the armchair opposite him, lost in a huge dressing gown with a big family album full of faded photographs. "This is my son, Norris Evans Junior," he said, holding the album up.

Kinnear squinted at a picture of a skinny, smiling boy standing by a sandcastle, the wind blowing his blond hair. "That looks like a happy time," Kinnear said.

"Yeah," Evans Senior said, smiling. "He'd have been about eight then. We lost him when he was ten."

"I'm sorry," Kinnear said. Wondering how he was going to extricate himself from this. Clearly, neither Evans Senior or Evans Junior were pertinent to Blake's case, given that one was dead and the other about to join him by the looks of it. A mountain of paperwork awaited Kinnear back at the office and if he was too long, he'd have to account for his time and Superintendent Martin might get suspicious. But Kinnear felt sorry for the old man; he seemed to live alone, and he'd had a tough life by the sound of it. "How did you lose him, if you don't mind me asking?"

"No, not at all. It was back in the Eighties. Young Norris was a bit of a knockabout, you know, full of life. He was always exploring things and getting into trouble. He wasn't a bad lad, just inquisitive, you know. If Elsie, his mum, told him not to go somewhere, then he'd do as he was told but, sometimes, we didn't find out what he'd been up to until afterwards. He'd climb anything, buildings, fences, he spent half his life on the garage roofs at the end of the street."

"He sounds like a handful," Kinnear agreed.

"But he was a good lad," Evans Senior said, leaning forward. "Until he met Vincent Tanner. Then it all went wrong."

"Vincent Tanner," Kinnear repeated. The name rang a bell. A loud, alarm bell. "Anything to do with the Tanners from Beavan Street?"

Evans Senior looked as though the milk in his tea had gone sour. "The same family. Yeah. Bad news. I'm not surprised that you've heard of them. A right bunch of crooks the lot of them. Vincent was the middle boy. A feral kid, which might be fine coming from me, but our Norris always came home in time for his tea before he met that little shite."

"So, what happened?"

"He was out with Vincent and the little toe-rag suggested playing chicken on the railways," Evans Senior said, his face hardening. "They were seen climbing on a bridge over the lines near Birkenhead Central. Vincent Tanner said that Norris had fallen but there were quite a few witnesses who said that Vincent pushed him."

Kinnear shook his head. "On to the rails?"

"He died instantly. Of course, once the police picked up Vincent, the Tanner family got to work on the witnesses. Tried to stop them from standing up in court and telling the truth. A few brave ones held out and Vincent went off to some home for naughty kids for a bit. He was back before you knew it, though. It broke our Elsie's heart to see that little monster running free."

"That's awful. I'm so sorry, Mr Evans," Kinnear said. He was genuinely shocked by the story and felt the weight of guilt under the pressure of time. “Is Vincent still around, then?”

“Nah, thank God for that. He buggered off in the early Nineties, up to Scotland or something. He was a big gangster or something. Last I heard, he’d disappeared. I hope he’s propping up a motorway flyover somewhere or feeding the fish at the bottom of a lake.”

“You said he went up to Scotland,” Kinnear said. “Where did you hear that?”

“His brother was bragging about it in the pub one night. I heard that much and left. I steer clear of the Tanners. But a few years later, I hung about a bit the night his brother came in saying he’d vanished. I had myself a little whisky that night.” Evans Senior gave a secretive smile.

Kinnear nodded and pulled a card from his pocket. “I don’t blame you, Mr Evans. Listen, I have to go, but if you think of anything else, please don’t hesitate to get in touch.” He stood up and Evans did too.

“What was all this about? You didn’t say,” Evans said. “Why were you looking for someone with my name?”

“I don’t know yet, Mr Evans. It could be nothing. I can’t really tell you, I’m sorry. I hope you understand.”

His marbled skin went a shade whiter and he put a hand on Kinnear’s sleeve. “You haven’t found him have you? Vincent Tanner? You won't tell his family I spoke to you, will you?"

Kinnear patted the old man's hand. "No, Mr Evans, it's nothing like that, I'm sure and you can rest easy. I won't be telling anyone I've been here. Not even my boss."

"Just be careful. Those Tanners are a law unto themselves." He showed Kinnear to the door and glanced up and down the street as the young Detective Constable left. The door had slammed shut behind him before Kinnear reached his car.

*****

To say that Blake was surprised to see Norris Evans in the hallway of the big house would be an understatement. Blake had convinced himself that the man was incapable of leaving the upstairs room where he meditated. Evans was holding a piece of paper and looking at something on the floor.

"You all right, Norris?" Blake said.

The man looked startled. He was wearing a stained LFC tracksuit that looked like it had been pulled out of a bin in the Nineties. His hair hung in greasy ringlets around his shoulders. "What? Yeah. Just got this pushed under my door and there was this on the floor." He squatted and picked up what looked like a stubby wooden arrow, a steel point at one end and black plastic flights at the other. "It's a crossbow bolt."

"What does the note say?"

Evans looked down at it. "Just says, 'meet me in the hall if you want to know the truth about Jonah.'"

"Evans!" Blake yelled and launched himself forward, pushing Evans off his feet. Once more, Blake's whole body exploded with pain and on top of that, Evans swore loudly, hammering his fist down on Blake's shoulder.

As Blake landed on top of Evans, a deafening metallic clang filled the hall, cracking into the ground and sending splinters of tile pinging everywhere like little bullets. Somewhere, Charlie gave a yelp of surprise. A bronze bust lay partially embedded in the floor.

"Jeez," Blake said, staring at the bust of Ramsay Reid, the original owner of the big house. Charlie scurried across the cracked tiles whimpering and burying himself in Blake's coat. "That was straight out of the Wily Coyote play book. If I hadn't pushed you out of the way, you'd be dead."

"Shit," Evans said, sitting up. "Think you bruised my backside. That's police brutality that is."

"You're welcome," Blake muttered. A thump upstairs brought him, wincing, to his feet. "Whoever did that is still up there. Come on Norris. Let's go and say 'hello.'"

“Seriously?” Evans said. “Have you listened to yourself? You’re wheezing like a set of punctured bagpipes.”

“I just saved your life,” Blake said.

Norris held up the crossbow bolt. “And what are the chances he’s got the thing that fires these?” He dragged a decorative shield off the wall. “This is metal. It’ll take some of the force. Get the other one.” Evans nodded at a round buckler about the size of a dinner plate.

“You can go in front, then,” Blake said. Putting Charlie in front of the fire in the living room and hoping the lure of the heat would be enough to keep him there.

Evans led the way, his shield held high. Every creaking step made Blake almost groan out loud. The landing was silent. Evans nodded at the empty plinth by the banisters. Blake wondered how heavy the bust was and who would have been capable of lifting it.

Room by room, they made their way around the first floor but found nothing. When they came to Evans’ door, he stopped. “I’ll check in here.”

“Is that wise? I mean, they were after you, weren’t they? What if they’re waiting inside and I don’t hear your cry for help?”

“I’ll keep the door open.” Evans pushed the

door wide and Blake watched him check under the bed and even inside the big wardrobe. His room was so spartan that it took all of thirty seconds.

Blake remembered the bedroom next to Evans' as the one that had been invaded by the crow. He stepped inside and shivered at the cold breeze. "The window's open. I think our attacker has gone, Norris." He went over and poked his head out of the window. The yard below lay empty. Blake could see the pile of logs that covered the real site of Huxley's death. He looked down the wall at the bruised leaves of the ivy that clung to the wall and wrapped around the drainpipe at the side of the window. It was as good as a ladder.

"I think you're right," Evans said.

"Let me see that bolt."

Evans pulled the bolt from his pocket. Blake turned the thing over in his hands. "Does it mean anything to you?"

"No," Evans said but Blake thought he sounded haunted. "Who has a crossbow these days? I mean I thought that was all knights in armour and all that shit."

"They're becoming the criminal's weapon of choice in some areas. Especially as the technology improves and makes them more powerful. You sure you don't recognise this?"

"No, Haven't a clue about it. Get off my case, will you?"

"Someone's after you, Norris. What about the letter?"

Evans pulled it from his pocket and flung it at Blake. "You can have it. I can look after myself, Blake. Don't you worry. Now all this chasing around has messed up my balance. I need to get my head straight." He punched the wall and stalked out of the room.

CHAPTER 26

Andy Kean wasn't best pleased to see Luckie on his doorstep and made it clear that he felt it to be some kind of betrayal. "I helped you, Luckie," he whined. "You said you wouldn't come round here." He was a tall, skinny young man with sunken eyes and a deathly pallor. He wore baggy jeans and a fleece top. His mousey brown hair was lank and long. At some point in his life he'd decided that a badly executed tattoo of a butterfly just above his right eyebrow would make him an individual.

"It's all right, Andy," Luckie said, looking up and down the street. "Nobody's seen me." As far as Luckie knew there were no 'mean streets' in Moffat. A lot of its problems travelled in from more challenged areas. But Kean had set up in a small, terraced cottage in a back alley off the High Street. Most of the properties were what you'd call quaint, painted in pinks and turquoises and freshly double glazed. Kean's house was in need of attention. It clung to the back of a row of shops, looking more like a workshop than a house. "Not really sure why you set up business here of all places," Luckie said. "It's hardly a thriving hub of drug marketing..."

Kean's eyes hooded over. "I don't know what

you're talking about, Luckie. I'm a legitimate businessman. I don't sell drugs anymore. I'm more into buying and selling antiques."

Luckie rolled his eyes. "Can I come in for a moment?"

Kean glanced over his shoulder. "Aye but you can't search for anything, right? You need a warrant for that."

Luckie pushed past him. "Why would I want to search for anything, Andy? You're a 'legitimate businessman,' remember?"

"Come on in, then," Kean said, sarcastically. Andrew Kean had clearly made some money for himself one way or another, judging by the inside of his house. It was small, a front room with stairs up and a kitchen in the back but everything looked modern and brand new. A huge television filled one wall of the room.

"I don't see many antiques here, Andy," Luckie said, sitting down on the sofa.

"I buy and sell them, I don't keep them. That'd be like being an alcoholic who runs a pub..."

"Or a drug dealer who can't help sampling the goods," Luckie said.

"All right," Kean said, sitting in an armchair opposite Luckie. "I confess, I do dabble still now and then but I don't deal anymore, scout's honour. I'm telling you, I'm going straight. In fact, funnily enough, Jonah was going to come in with me."

"Really? I can't see that working very well. Huxley wasn't the most diplomatic of people, so I'm led to believe."

"Yeah, he could be a dick but he's a great salesman and the stuff in that big house down in the glen, some of it's two hundred years old and in mint condition."

"The Community wanted to sell you antique furniture?"

"And old paintings. Jonah was going to set it all up, man. The Americans love this shit. They see it on holiday and want to take a slice of history home with them. Kerching!"

"So, Jonah talked about this the night he came here?"

"Yeah him and his girl."

"His girl?"

"Aye, what was her name?" Kean clicked his fingers. "Megan, yeah, that was it. Megan."

Luckie sat forward. "What did she look like?"

"Small, dark haired," Kean said. "Hang on." He rummaged in his pocket and pulled out his phone. "I've got a picture of her somewhere. You can have it if it helps." He scrolled through a few pictures then held up the phone.

"Megan Yule," Luckie said.

*****

Once more, Blake found himself sitting in Irving's living room, stroking Charlie and warming himself in front of Irving's fire. The big house seemed so hostile and after nearly being brained by a falling statue, he just needed to unload. It seemed a remote possibility that Irving was involved in all of this and, anyway Blake needed to talk it through. So he'd walked down to the lodge house, looking for a friendly face and possibly something meaty and hot to eat.

"You were lucky again, Will," Irving said. "That bust of Ramsey Reid would have crushed your skull or that hairy fella's if it had hit either of you."

Blake grunted and sipped coffee laced with whisky Irving had given him. The old man had been horrified when Blake had suggested it but grudgingly acceded to his request. "Evans knows something, Thomas. When he saw the crossbow bolt, he looked..."

"Spooked?"

"No. Angry. There was a fury in him that I haven't seen before. And then there's the landslide. I don't know if that hill is stable. We need more people here."

"I called the Polis. Devil's Glen is tricky to get

to. They can trek across the tops but then they'd have to find a way down into the valley which is dangerous right now."

"Don't they have a helicopter?"

"Nowhere to land, the valley is too narrow and deep. That's its appeal. It's not just remote, it's inaccessible."

"That Grant Rothwell is hiding something, too. Jeez, they all are. If Jonah Huxley came to blackmail someone, he upset something or someone and it cost him his life. I'm worried someone else is going to die, Thomas."

Irving's eyes glittered in the firelight and he sipped his whisky. "That's Devil's Glen for you. It's the curse, I'm telling you..."

"Strangely, I'd rather stick to facts and leave superstition out of this, Thomas. Is that okay? So Evans sits up in his room all the time, trying to keep 'in balance' whatever that means. But someone is trying to draw him out and kill him. Why?"

"Well, it's not random," Thomas said. "He's been picked out. Whoever tried to drop that bust on him planned it carefully and even had an escape route planned."

"True. We're pretty certain that Huxley was blackmailing someone. They agreed to meet him but whoever he met turned on him and stabbed him. He ran away and almost reached the house but died at the back of the house."

"So does Evans know who killed Huxley? What if he's picking up where Huxley left off and blackmailing the killer?"

"It's a theory. I hate theories. I want the truth. Why did they move Huxley's body when he fell at the back of the house?"

Irving grinned. He was enjoying this. He was removed from it and this was just a puzzle to him. "To keep inquisitive noses away from something at the back of the house, perhaps?"

Blake nodded. "That makes sense but then why not just hide Jonah Huxley's body up in the woods?"

"Perhaps whoever did it didn't have time. What if Rosie saw Jonah lying there before the killer could do anything about him?"

"But they moved him after Rosie had seen him. Presumably when she fainted. I need a proper timeline of events. Who turned up and when? Rosie said Duana was there first, but she was hazy about that. And none of them thought to phone the police."

"Huxley's body was moved before the police were called. Which suggests that they are all in on it."

"Someone like Grant could have dragged the

body on his own and then carried Rosie to the front of the house before running off to get cleaned up."

"Could have, might have," Irving said. "None of these are certainties are they, Will?"

"No. I'd better get back. One thing is certain, if Evans knows who is after him, then he might decide to take the fight to them." Blake stood up, wincing at the pain.

"You wanna get that strapped up," Irving said.

"I thought they didn't do that these days."

"Pffft! Get your shirt off and let me wrap a bandage around your ribs. It'll help. Have you been taking the painkillers I gave you?"

"Jeez, Thomas, when did you turn into my dad?" Blake muttered but he pulled his shirt off to let Irving wrap his ribs.

"That's some fancy bruising," he muttered, "but they don't seem broken, as far as I can tell."

"You're a medical expert, too?" Blake said, wincing as Irving pulled the bandage tight.

"I've tended to enough sick livestock in my time to know a broken bone when I feel one and I'd say it's just bruised."

"Thanks, dad," Blake said, with a grin.

"Aye, you can laugh but if that gets infected, you'll be sorry. Now can you ride a quadbike?"

*****

The reception area of the Dumfries Custody Suite was surprisingly quiet. A couple of ragged looking down and outs sat muttering to each other on the chairs put out in the public waiting area but otherwise, the place looked empty. Rosie Blake stood by the front door, wrapped in a blanket. She felt a bit silly but the woman on reception had insisted, clucking on about Will and Searchlight. Rosie supposed she was glad of his minor celebrity status then.

Detective Sergeant Luckie was stammering his way through an apology, his face as red as his hair. Behind her she could sense Simon Carver, her solicitor, staring frostily over her shoulder "I'm sorry you ended up being detained longer than I intended, Ms Blake," Luckie said. "It was purely down to the weather. I hope you understand."

"By rights, we ought to make a formal complaint, Luckie," Carver growled.

Rosie Blake smiled, tightly. She felt sorry for Luckie. She knew from Will how difficult it could be sometimes being a police officer. "It wasn't your fault Detective Sergeant. Your team could hardly throw me out in the snow and they did stress that I was free to leave. Under other circumstances, it would have been quite an adventure and the staff here made me as comfortable as possible…"

"You're very gracious, Ms Blake," Luckie said. "I hate to say it but, although we haven't charged you, we do need to know where you'll be staying while our investigations continue."

"I've left the hotel address with the receptionist," Carver said, before Rosie could answer, which annoyed her a little. "Ms Blake will be staying there until such time as she can return to The Community."

"Have you heard from Will? I haven't had my phone and it's run out of charge now I have it back."

"I have. There have been some… developments down in the glen. Nothing I can discuss directly but your brother is fine. Can I ask you a question? Just off the record?"

Rosie glanced at Simon Carver, who nodded suspiciously. "Okay," she said.

"Is there *anyone* there, even remotely connected with the glen or The Community who might be capable of murder?"

Rosie shook her head. "No. Not really, I mean…" she stopped and shook her head. "No, it's silly."

"I can decide if it's silly, just try me."

"Well, Thomas Irving once threatened Grant with his shotgun. I mean raised it at Grant and made him get on the floor. We'd been walking in the woods and strayed onto what he liked to think of as his land. He stopped us and asked us what we were doing. Grant is a bit of a hot head and gave him a mouthful."

"And Irving lost it with him?"

"No, that was it. He was really calm and his voice was dead steady. He just stepped forward and pressed the barrel against Grant's forehead and told him to get down."

"That must have been frightening," Luckie said.

Rosie nodded. "It was. I mean, he let us go in the end, but the coldness in his voice was horrible. I've kept away from him ever since. If anyone in the glen was capable of murder. I'd say it was Thomas Irving."

CHAPTER 27

Sometimes, it's best to just do something rather than think too hard about the possible consequences. That's what Jeff thought anyway. It had got him into no end of trouble and quite a lot of debt from time to time, but it had made life interesting and opened doors for him too. So, he picked up the phone and dialled the number that Danny Melrose had given him.

He'd only intended to spend an hour at the most with Melrose but time seemed to fly past. Once their chat had drifted away from the unsavoury side of Abaddon's Confessor, and into more general antics and anecdotes about life in a rock band, it had been well into the afternoon before Jeff and Danny realised that they'd been talking for hours. They'd even hatched a plan for Jeff to write an official biography of Danny and the band.

Danny had scribbled down lead guitarist, Bob Orton's number and handed it to Jeff, not letting go of the paper as Jeff reached to take it. "You need to be careful with Bob. He's fragile but I think getting all this off his chest would be a kind of therapy for him." Jeff had nodded and taken the number.

As he drove home, Jeff mused over the turn his life had taken. He'd started out writing literary fiction, hoping to be the next big prize-winning name. Now, here he was thinking that dark and twisted biographies might be a more lucrative venture. More interesting, too, if he was honest with himself. Maybe there was something in the Blake DNA that made them inquisitive. Will certainly couldn't keep his nose out of things and had made a profession out of it. Even Rosie's spiritual quest suggested a curiosity that couldn't be satisfied. And Jeff had to admit, digging up the bones of the past and uncovering truths made him feel more alive than he had in years.

Now he was back home, Jeff wondered at the wisdom of contacting Bob Orton and raking up a painful past. He knew that Duana had been in the thick of Eric Lambert's depraved lifestyle and that she'd come after Melrose for the rights to all Abaddon's music. She must have been desperate for cash. Danny had given him a pretty good pen portrait of Eric Lambert, nothing he didn't know already or couldn't imagine. But he knew that Bob Orton had seen Eric's true nature close up and that might be worth something.

The phone rang for a while and Jeff was just about to end the call when it was answered by a young female voice.

"I'm sorry," Jeff said. "I'm looking for Bob Orton. I wonder if you can help me? Danny Melrose gave me this number."

"Ah, right. Yes. He did ring to tell me to expect a call. I'm Yvette, his daughter. Look, I'm afraid my father isn't in a great place, right now. I don't think he'd be up to talking about the past."

"I totally understand. The last thing I want to do is to cause him any distress. Anyway, I don't know how much Danny told you but I'm interested in the history of the band, Eric Lambert and his daughter..."

"Duana," Yvette said, scornfully.

"Yes," Jeff said. "You've met her?"

"She gave my family a terrible time when she tried to steal the rights to the music from the band. But..." Yvette stopped as though there was more that she wanted to share but was wary.

"Yes?" Jeff said. "There's more?"

Yvette hesitated. "Well, not long after all that unpleasantness, she approached me privately. I had just won the Feldmann Galleries Award. You won't have heard of it..."

"I have, it's for work in oils, isn't it?"

"I'm impressed, Mr Blake. Not many people outside my sphere of Art know of the Feldmann. But you're right. The gallery holds and preserves a rich collection of works focusing on oil paintings. What you might call the works of grand masters."

"So you're an artist?"

"In a very narrow and what some might consider conservative discipline. I focus on landscapes. I'm also a restorer of old paintings, too."

"I see, and what was Duana Lambert's interest in all of this?"

"She was very cagey about what she wanted and wouldn't come out and say it. So, you must understand that what I'm telling you now is my own opinion. The last thing I want is for her to come after me with accusations of slander."

"I understand," Jeff said. "Anything you tell me will be in the strictest confidence."

"She wanted to know if I ever perfected my technique by copying old works. I told her that I had done that in the past and she seemed very interested. She wondered how easy it was to tell the difference between my painting and the original and if I'd ever thought of trying to sell a copy."

"You think she was sounding you out to start an Art forgery business?"

"I never said that Mr Blake. You did. She just asked me if I'd be interested in restoring and maybe reproducing some of the works in her house up in Scotland. I got the impression that it was more than that though. She did mention John Myatt, the famous Art forger. I turned her down of course. I can't abide the woman after what she did to my father. The idea of living in her house would unbearable."

"I see."

"Believe me, Mr Blake, Duana Lambert is an opportunist criminal. She tried to steal the rights and royalties away from my father, the only thing that put food on our table and a meagre feast it was too. Then this business with the Art. And you wonder if she was any different from her father? His evil blood runs through her veins, still."

*****

The dark woods flashed by, caught briefly in the headlights as Blake's quad bike bounced him along the rough track that led up to the big house. As there wasn't a spare seat or any kind of basket on the bike, he'd left Charlie curled up in front of the old man's fire. He'd been rather surprised that Thomas had let him borrow the quadbike. Not that Irving had just thrown him the keys, he'd clucked over Blake and given him a lecture about not letting it tip over and keeping his speed down.

Now he hurtled along the path, he had time to think. At least two of the residents had criminal pasts: Norris Evans and Grant Rothwell. Freya Finley was traumatised by a past tragedy and seemed a very unlikely killer. There were so many options, it was bewildering. Everyone seemed to be hiding something. Was there anyone in The Community who wasn't lying? And what did that say about Rosie? Was she telling the truth? He refused to believe that she could be anything but an innocent bystander. Once again, he cursed the fact that he didn't have his team to back him up.

The living room window threw a yellow light across the melting snow. Blake could see the gravel beneath as he steered around the earth that had slithered across the drive in the landslide. Evans' silhouette filled his bedroom window, as usual. Blake raised a hand, but Evans ignored him. Bringing the bike to a halt, Blake stared through the living room window. Grant Rothwell was waving his arms around and shouting something. An argument was in full flow and they hadn't noticed Blake's arrival.

Sliding off the quadbike, Blake walked softly into the hall and stood by the living room door.

"I'm telling you, we can't wait any longer. You know it Duana. She needs to go. They both do..."

"No," Duana said. "It's only a matter of time before they clear the lane and the police come back. We've got enough explaining to do without complicating matters."

"I'm telling you, Duana..."

"No, Grant. You don't get to tell me anything.

I tell you," Duana snapped. "Understand? You do as you're told or you can just leave The Community. Now keep that childish temper of yours under control and we'll be fine. Okay?"

Blake heard Grant Rothwell's heavy tread nearing the door and hurried into the next room, keeping the lights off and pressing himself against the wall. Rothwell stamped past towards the kitchen, not noticing Blake in the shadows. With a sigh of relief, he slipped back into the hall and crept upstairs.

As soon as he got into his bedroom, Blake's phone buzzed and he thanked his lucky stars the call hadn't come a few minutes earlier. Jeff sounded excited as he related his day to Will.

"Duana Lambert is a nasty piece of work by the sounds of it, Will," Jeff said. "She tried to screw the remaining members of Lambert's band out of royalties and rights when they were on their knees. They said she seemed desperate for money..."

Blake lowered himself onto his bed, trying not to let the pain sound in his voice. "When was this, Jeff?"

"About twenty years ago?"

"Not exactly breaking news then, is it?"

"I'm doing my best," Jeff said, sounding hurt. "The next bit of history will probably be so underwhelming that I may as well not bother you with it then."

Blake closed his eyes and shook his head. "Sorry, Jeff, it's been a bit of a long day. Go on, try me."

"So not too long after that, Duana approached the daughter of one of the band to make some copies of old masters..."

Blake sat up on the bed and peered out of the tiny window to the back courtyard of the house and the workshop. A light shone from there, someone was working late. "Really? You mean she wanted to make forgeries?"

"The woman was a bit careful with her words, frightened of Duana coming back to bite her in court but she said that Duana mentioned John Myatt."

"Who?"

"Oh come on Will, you're meant to be a police officer. He was a famous forger back in the Eighties. Made a fortune selling fake oil paintings. He did his time and is actually a reformed character now, advises the police on forgery cases."

"Now that is useful information, Jeff. Thanks. That's one piece of the jigsaw sorted, I think."

He hung up and peered over at the workshop and thought about what he'd seen in there. It might be worth another look, after all. A creak of floorboards made him freeze. Someone was outside his room. The stairs didn't lead anywhere else. Easing himself off the bed, he crept to the door and flung it open.

Megan Yule gave a stifled scream. And fell back. "What d'you think you're doing?" Blake snapped. Then felt awful. Megan looked terrified. She hugged herself tightly. Her eyes and nose were red with crying.

"I'm sorry. I-I didn't know who else to go to," she stammered and her face crumpled again. "You're the only person I can trust."

Blake stepped back from the door and held it open. "Come in."

Megan glanced over her shoulder once down the stairs and then swept past Blake and sat hunched on the chair by the desk. Her shoulders shook. "I'm sorry. I'm sorry."

"Megan, what is it?"

She looked up at Blake, her tear-streaked face pale. "Someone just tried to kill me."

CHAPTER 28

There were moments when Kath Cryer stood in Superintendent Martin's office and she felt like a naughty school kid. This was one of those moments. Kath's insides squirmed under Martin's stern look of disappointment. She'd been doing well, recently, leading a press conference and getting some approving nods as though Martin had just woken up to her existence. Now he'd remember her forever as the Inspector who'd disobeyed a direct order and gone behind his back.

It was Kinnear who had insisted that they had to go to Superintendent Martin with what they had found. "If we were just ruling someone out of our enquiries, and ringing Blakey to say, 'yep he's the fella, a couple of burglaries, a bit of jail time' then I'd agree with you and leave Martin out of it but this could be part of something big. It's bound to come out. Then where would we be?"

"God, I hate it when you're right, Andy, it just does my head in!" Kath Cryer said. "Come on, let's go and get our arses kicked."

Now they stood in front of his desk. It was late in the day, very late by the look on Martin's haggard face. Kath had to think fast. "It's my fault, sir. DCI Blake texted the name through and

I asked Kinnear to check it out without telling him to keep you informed..."

Superintendent Martin looked as though he was sucking a wasp. "So, Andrew logged onto the National Database as you, then? Do you think I'm a mug? Have I got a handle sticking out the side of my head?"

"No, sir," Kath said, thinking she'd hate to be a real criminal being grilled by Martin.

"I may spend most of my time in this office or at meetings, but I'm still a policeman, Kath. I can tell when someone is lying."

"Sorry sir. But Andrew was just doing what I asked him to. He didn't know that you had an interest in DCI Blake's activities."

Martin cast a sour eye over Kinnear. "Well, he should have guessed. It's not like we aren't spread thinly enough without going off on wild goose chases for friends."

"Thing is, sir, we think we might have uncovered something quite important. When I went looking for Norris Evans, it turns out his son died at the hands of a lad called Vincent Tanner. A few years later, Tanner takes himself off up to Scotland and gets mixed up with the Dumbarton Three..."

"More than mixed up," Kath butted in. "He's the ringleader."

"The Dumbarton Three," Martin said, holding his hands up. "Forgive me, but it sounds like half a football score. Who the hell are they?"

Kinnear opened the file he'd prepared and passed it to Martin. "Between 1995 and 1999, they committed a string of violent armed robberies in Edinburgh and Glasgow. Each incident was characterised by unnecessary, brutal violence. Security guards were not just intimidated, they were badly injured, even mutilated. Several died."

Martin leafed through Kinnear's file. "It says here that two of them died..."

"They were found dead soon after the robbery of a jewellery shop. It was a big haul. Millions of pounds worth of stones and pieces. The van was dumped somewhere in the Lake District with two members of the gang dead in the back. They'd been shot. Vince Tanner wasn't among the dead. Officers assumed that Tanner had killed the two men and made off with the loot."

"But he'd have needed an accomplice, surely," Martin said, unable to resist the mystery. "Otherwise, where did he go? He would need another vehicle to get away, surely."

"That makes sense. The murder weapon was never recovered, and Tanner was never seen again," Kath said, hoping the revelations would save their bacon. "But there's a guy at the crime scene up in Scotland who claims to be Norris Evans, a small-time crook from Wirral. The only Norris Evans on the Wirral is the old man Andrew interviewed. Prior to that the last Norris Evans was his great grandfather in 1922."

"So there's a possibility that the Norris Evans that Blake is worried about is in reality a ruthless killer called Vincent Tanner," Martin said. He looked up. "Well, what are you waiting for? You'd better call him. I'll have a conversation with the team up at Dumfries and smooth things over."

"Thanks, sir," Kath said, winking at Kinnear and heading for the door.

"And Kath," Martin called just as her hand touched the handle.

"Sir?"

"Pull a stunt like that again and it'll be disciplinary, understand?"

"Yes, sir, sorry, sir," she said. She saved her smile for when she was safely out of sight of Martin.

*****

Megan sat on the chair and shuddered silently. The cramped conditions and the fact that there was only one chair made it impossible for Blake to comfort her, so he stood awkwardly. His phone buzzed but he ignored it. This wasn't the time to take a call.

"Did you see who attacked you?" he said at last.

Megan shook her head. "It was dark. I was going back to my room when I heard someone behind me."

"You didn't recognise the way that they moved or their voice?"

"No, they didn't speak. Just wrapped an arm around my neck and tried to choke me," Megan lifted her head up to reveal a growing bruise on her neck. "I thought I was going to die."

"How did you break free?"

"I elbowed them in the stomach and threw all my weight to one side. It threw them off balance and they fell over. I jumped up and ran here." Tears began streaming down Megan's face once more.

"Okay. You're safe now, Megan. Trust me. Can you give me an idea of their size? Were they big or small? Strong?"

"Not big, not like Grant. But I think it was a man..."

"Why?"

"I don't know. Just the way he grabbed me. He smelt funny too."

"What like?"

"I've smelt it before when I worked in a charity shop for a while. It's meant to keep bugs and stuff out of your clothes…"

"Mothballs?"

"Yeah. That's it. D'you think it was Irving?"

Blake stared at Megan in disbelief. "Why would it be him?"

"He's a creep. I've seen him sneaking around the plunge pool…"

"Sorry, you've lost me. What plunge pool?"

"At the head of the valley, there's a waterfall and a pool. That's where the burn comes from that formed the glen. We go skinny dipping in there. I've seen him in the bushes with his binoculars…"

"Do you think it was Irving?"

"I don't know. It wasn't Grant and Norris is up in his room. I saw him as I ran in."

"Really? Well if other men are ruled out, he's the only other in the valley although I didn't hear his car and I've got his quad bike. Unless he ran up from his house, it's unlikely to be him."

"Could it have been someone from outside? What if the snow up on the moors has thawed enough for someone to get in?"

"Let's save any speculation for the morning, if we can, eh? The main thing is that you're safe and sound here."

"Can I stay here tonight? I can't go back to my

room."

Blake could see she was frightened. "Sure. You can stay here. I can get some more blankets from downstairs and sleep on the floor." His body groaned at the idea let alone actually trying it. Listen. You sit on the bed. There's a bolt on the back of this door. You can lock yourself in. I'm going to have a little look around and get some blankets. I won't be long. I promise."

Blake stood outside the door and listened to the bolt sliding across on the other side. Leaving Megan safely locked away, Blake crept downstairs. He didn't share Megan's theory about Irving. Spending all this time alone and living so close to a lake where people swam naked, he might be a Peeping Tom but Blake didn't think he would attack anyone. Not that he knew him that well, but Blake liked to think he was a good judge of people. Irving might be low on patience and might even resort to threats, but he didn't strike Blake as predatory.

Even though the snow was melting now, there was enough of it to reflect the starlight and give the night a twilight feeling. That made the shadows in the corners deeper and Blake tried to keep to them as he made his way around the back of the house.

Megan's room was situated in the stable blocks that flanked the courtyard. Blake hadn't really expected anyone to still be hanging around but her bedroom door was open. Peering inside, it was clear that it had been turned over in a frantic search for something. The bed lay on its side, chairs scattered around and the contents of drawers lay strewn all over the floor. Even the cushions had been ripped open. A couple of large spots of blood dotted the floor, too. He glanced around the confusing mess. He couldn't hope to make any sense of this without Megan here.

A light still glowed in the workshop windows and Blake could detect the low bass thud of music being played inside. The windows were high up and the only way for him to get a look through was to drag one of the wheelie bins over from the back of the house. The bin rumbled across the ground horribly but the music still thumped inside the workshop, hopefully masking the noise. He pushed the bin against the side wall of the workshop, and climbed up. The bin wobbled slightly and every correction he made, sent electric shocks through his ribs. Finally, he steadied himself and peered into the workshop.

Freya was mixing paints and working at the easel that Blake had seen last time he was in there. But Grant was tacking another painted canvas to what looked like an old frame. It was hard to make out but Blake could see the bleached wood. As he tacked each one, he took a pinch of dirt from a bowl and sprinkled it under the canvas. Blake didn't know much about Art forgery but he was pretty certain that was what he was looking at.

Something moved behind him and, instinctively, Blake turned to see a fox dart across the courtyard. But the damage had been done. As he twisted, Blake had set off a chain reaction. Pain seared in his side and he hunched up, sending his weight to one leg which overbalanced the bin. With a rumbling boom, the wheelie bin crashed to the ground and Blake on top of it.

CHAPTER 29

The clatter of the bins echoed across the courtyard. The loud music inside the workshop stopped abruptly. Glancing around, Blake could see nowhere to hide and prepared to brazen it out with whoever appeared around the corner. All he really wanted to do was curl up in a ball and hug his aching body.

He heard the door open at the front of the building and two heavy footsteps scrunch on the gravel. Freya's voice drifted out. "What was it?"

"Fox or something, I think. Just saw the wee bastard scurry across the square."

"Well come back in, and shut the door, you daft oaf. You're letting all the cold in."

"All right, all right," Rothwell grumbled and shut the door. Blake let out a long breath and leaned against the brick wall. Making his way back, a thought occurred to him and he slipped around the front of the house. Norris Evans still sat, a black outline against the light.

"Nobody could meditate for that long, surely," Blake muttered to himself and went into the house.

Evans' door was shut but Patricia's was open. Blake could hear her humming tunelessly to herself. He leaned in, looking around the sea of figurines. "Patricia? Are you there?" The humming stopped and Patricia appeared from between a cut out of Duana and one of Cliff Richard. Patricia looked at him. "Charlie," she said.

"Sorry, Charlie's asleep," Blake said and pointed at the figures. "Patricia, where's Norris?"

She pointed over Blake's shoulder. "Norris window."

"I see," Blake said. "You've been telling me all along, haven't you?"

Patricia's face creased with concentration as though she was trying to process what Blake had just said. She nodded. "Norris window."

"Patricia. Should we get Norris back?"

Patricia's round face split into a smile. "Norris back."

Blake tried Evans' bedroom door. To his surprise, it opened. What he saw inside didn't surprise him, though.

Norris Evans stood facing out of the window or rather, the effigy of him that Patricia had painted did. The real Norris Evans was nowhere to be seen. A bright spotlight had been placed on the floor to make sure that the figure was always seen in silhouette.

"Norris," Blake said, handing the cardboard cut out to Patricia. She gave a short laugh, clapped her hands, and grabbed it. "Thank you, Charlie's dad," she said and scurried back into her studio, leaving Blake alone in Evans' bedroom.

Wherever Norris was, he could return at any moment. So Blake had to be quick. He glanced down the corridor then hurried over to the wardrobe. He pulled open the door, noting the smell of mothballs, straight away.

A few items of casual clothing hung there along with a dark suit. It was double-breasted, with padded shoulders, the style dated it. Blake imagined it had been used for funerals or court appearances and was only kept in reserve now for some extremely formal circumstance. The pockets revealed a pen, and an order of service from a funeral for a Mavis Tanner at a Landican crematorium in 1987. It looked as old as the suit. Landican was the main crematorium for Wirral. He put the items back, then realised he hadn't checked the breast pocket. Crumpled at the bottom, almost unnoticeable was a pink slip of paper that read: McCoist Dry Cleaners, 2 Glenburn Street, Oxton. Beneath that was scribbled in faded blue ink: Mr V. Tanner, Beavan Street, Bhead.

"So, who is V. Tanner?" Blake muttered. Was he a previous owner of the suit? That was very possible, the slip was well crushed at the bottom of the pocket and hard to detect. On the other hand, something told Blake that this suit had only seen one owner. The order of service matched the vintage of the suit and why would Evans keep a memento of Mavis Tanner's funeral if it meant nothing to him?

Smoothing it out on the small pine table, Blake took out his phone and photographed it several times. Then he returned the slip to the pocket. Evans would realise that Patricia had rumbled him and taken her figurine back, but he might not suspect anything else if Blake left things as they were.

Megan was waiting anxiously in the bedroom and let Blake in. "I heard a noise down in the courtyard. What happened? I didn't think you were coming back. Why did you take so long?"

Blake sat on the chair, catching his breath. Eventually, he looked up at her. "I had to get some more bedding but I did a bit of snooping round, first. Can you think why anyone would want to search your room, Megan?"

"What? No, why?"

"Whoever attacked you broke into your rooms and turned them over. There was blood on the floor, too."

"Blood? Oh god."

"Don't worry. We'll be able to work it all out

tomorrow." He remembered the phonecall he'd ignored before. There were a couple of missed calls and a voicemail from Luckie.

"I hope you haven't managed to destroy any more of Devil's Glen, sir. Ask Megan why she didn't tell us she knew Huxley before she came to The Community." He'd texted a picture of her with Jonah.

Blake held up the picture. "Would you care to explain this, Megan?"

*****

Even to Rosie, who put little store in material possessions or the idea of luxury, the Old Smithy Hotel was stunningly appointed. Simon drove his Range Rover through the huge iron gates and Rosie almost gasped. The snow had been cleared off the gravel drive, but it had been piled onto the extensive lawns and reflected the moonlight. "My God, Simon. How did this place ever get called the Old Smithy? I can't imagine any blacksmiths getting near this place unless it was at the back door."

The hotel had once been the country seat of some seriously moneyed family, that was clear. "I think there was a blacksmith's house somewhere back along the road once," Simon said, laughing a little. "You could hardly describe it as quaint, could you? Duana wanted you to have a little pampering after all you've been through."

Rosie frowned. "Did she? Doesn't sound like Duana, to me."

"Believe me, there are lots of things you don't know about Duana. And anyway, she said that the poet, Blake wouldn't see anything wrong with enjoying the more earthly pleasures once in a while. He was hardly a monk, was he?"

Rosie smiled as they pulled up. "It's just that I feel a bit guilty living it up like this while they're in the valley worrying."

"Relax. We'll have you back with your friends as soon as possible. For now, just relax."

Rosie followed Simon in through the huge wooden doors and into a plush lobby with deep carpets and a huge grandfather clock ticking in the corner. The place smelt of polish and freshly cut flowers, and suddenly, Rosie felt grubby and unkempt. The receptionist behind the mahogany counter retained a professional, fixed smile as Simon checked Rosie in.

"Your room is on this floor," the receptionist said, leaning over the counter and pointing down the corridor. "Straight down to the bottom and second on the left."

"I took the liberty of buying some fresh clothes," Simon said. "They're in your room. I know it's late but you must be famished. Do you want to freshen up and grab a snack? I completely understand if you don't."

Rosie didn't know what to say. She was tired and worries flitted round her head like caged birds but she felt like she owed Simon. Besides, sitting in a prison cell, she had time to think about what had happened and that had left her with a hundred questions even before she found herself in this luxury hotel. "Yes. Thank you, that would be lovely," Rosie said.

Simon raised his eyebrows. "Right, well, my room is this way. I'll book us a table. Shall we say half an hour?"

"Suits me fine," Rosie said and watched him disappear down the corridor.

Although Rosie had made a point of leading quite an austere life since leaving home, she could still appreciate a bit of luxury. It had been a long time since she had stayed in a hotel and her room in this one was something else. Everything looked brand new. Rosie reckoned she could live here for a few days without leaving, there was a coffee machine, chocolate, crisps, other small snacks, and wine.

She was also pleasantly surprised at the clothes that had been bought for her. When Simon had mentioned this, she'd worried that there would be some kind of Bond girl low-cut silk gown spread across the bed. In her experience, men were rarely practical in matters of clothing for women. But what she saw was a pair of serviceable trousers, a t-shirt, a fleece top, and cotton underwear all in her size. As she showered it occurred to her that most of the shops in the nearby towns would probably stock more practical, country clothing unless you were going for a wedding dress but even so, Simon had done well. She was impressed.

The hotel corridors were hushed, the few residents having turned in for the night and Rosie relished the thick carpet under her silent tread. There were lots of things to fret about, of course; Will was trapped in the valley and, thinking back to the night Jonah died, she had plenty of worries. But Will was tough enough to look after himself. She'd realised that when he'd talked to her in the custody suite. She never really reckoned with what he actually did in his line of work, what he encountered day-in, day-out. But she'd worry about all that later. Right now, she would enjoy the moment, however brief.

Simon rose from his chair in the dining room as she entered and pulled a seat out for her. "I'm glad everything fits. I hope it's not too... practical for you. I didn't imagine you'd want to be wearing anything too fancy..."

"It's perfect, Simon, thank you. It's so thoughtful of you." Rosie settled herself at the table.

"I've had enough experience to know that people come out of the custody suite wanting to hose themselves down and get a complete change of clothes," Simon said, "especially if it's the first time." He looked apologetically at Rosie. "Because it's late, the only thing they could offer us is some vegetable soup. I assumed you would want meat free but I don't know if it's vegan or not I can..."

Rosie laughed and raised a hand. "It'll be fine. Honestly. That sounds great to me."

He picked up a bottle. "Fortunately, the wine cellar was still open so I got a nice bottle of red. Would you like some?"

"Yes, please," she laughed. She leaned forward and rested her chin on her hand. "Don't take this the wrong way, Simon, I mean, I'm very grateful, but how on earth can Duana Lambert afford all this?"

CHAPTER 30

Megan Yule cowered on the bed, pressing herself into the corner of the room. "Where did you get that photograph?" She sounded more angry than afraid.

"I'm a police officer, Megan," Blake said. "My colleagues in Police Scotland aren't just sitting up in Dumfries twiddling their thumbs. They're investigating a murder. This lad's murder." Blake pointed at Jonah. "Now why don't you tell me when you first met him and why you lied about not knowing him?"

Megan glanced around the room and at the tiny window as if she was considering jumping out. Then her shoulders slumped. "Jonah and I were together in the summer before we came here. I was doing a crappy job waiting on tables in a tourist café and getting ripped off by the owner. We met at a party and he was full of ideas and ambition. It put me to shame."

Blake looked at the picture. It was the first image he'd seen of Huxley. He grinned out of the phone at them, his face framed by a mop of dark corkscrew locks. His eyes looked sharp and full of humour. Blake could imagine him getting up to all kinds of mischief. "He's a handsome lad."

Megan nodded. "He said he was going to start up in the antiques business and make a fortune selling paintings. He said he knew where he could get them..."

"So all that stuff about leaving a women's shelter and coming here was made up," Blake said. "More lies."

"Jonah didn't want Duana to know we were together. I don't know why. He said I could be his eyes and ears..."

"Did Jonah say anything about forged paintings?"

Megan shook her head. "He didn't tell me anything. Nothing at all. He sent me here just before Christmas and I worked like a skivvy. It was worse than the café I'd left. Then he swans up about a month ago. I was furious with him..."

"Angry enough to kill him?"

Megan looked shocked. "No! I- I wouldn't know how. I think he was trying to get Duana to let him take some of the paintings from the workshop. I heard them arguing about it once. Jonah said something about having the gift of the gab, that kind of thing and being able to sell to the tourists, but Duana just laughed at him. I just wanted to go then but Jonah had a bee in his bonnet about it all. We hung around, him antagonising everyone, picking fights with Grant. I tell you, I almost left two weeks ago. I wish I had."

"So what kept you here?"

"Dunno," Megan said. "Nowhere else to go. Besides, it's this place, isn't it? It gets to you. It pins you down. I was all set to leave the night Jonah was killed."

"What about Norris Evans?"

"What about him?" Megan said, taking a deep breath to calm herself.

"I think he was the one who attacked you…"

"But he was in his room. I saw him in the window."

Blake shook his head. "No. You saw one of Patricia's figurines. I checked in his room and I also looked in his wardrobe. It stinks of mothballs. Is there any reason that Norris Evans would want to attack you?"

Megan jumped up and peered out of the window at the courtyard below. "So he's out there, now? Lurking about."

"Megan is there something you're not telling me?"

"No. No. I just don't like the idea of him roaming free. You should go and arrest him or something."

"I don't have enough evidence. Outside this valley, we'd swab you, get any DNA or forensic evidence that might have been transferred onto you in the struggle. When they get through to us, the police can test the blood on your floor and see who that belongs to but for now, there's not much I can do."

"No. There never is," Megan muttered.

"What d'you mean by that?"

"Nothing. I've been let down by your lot before that's all."

"Really? When?"

"It doesn't matter," Megan said, sulkily.

"Look, even if I did arrest him. What would I do then? Lock him in his bedroom? It doesn't work like that. We have to wait for the cavalry to arrive, Megan."

The young woman just went back to the bed and pulled a blanket over her. Blake tried to make as comfortable a nest as possible on the floor with the extra blankets he'd taken and switched the light off. He suspected it was going to be a long and painful night.

*****

Detective Sergeant Luckie leaned against the bar of the Black Bull Inn and contemplated the bottom of his glass through the last dregs of beer. He liked the pub, it had a pleasant atmosphere and the locals were friendly enough to chat to but wise enough to know when to leave you be. He liked the low ceiling beams and the warmth of the wood burner. Luckie was well-known enough in the pub to have a pint set up on the bar waiting for him whenever he came in. This might have been a bad sign, Luckie wasn't sure.

The talk in the pub was all about the weather this evening and Luckie had had enough of it. The snow had derailed his investigation and enabled Blake to spend far too much time down in the glen. He just hoped whatever Blake had uncovered, there was enough admissible evidence left to make any kind of prosecution otherwise a murderer would walk free and that didn't sit right with Luckie at all. He set his pint down on the counter and turned to bid the Landlord goodnight.

Old Angus, a local farmer who lived not too far from Devil's Glen sat at the table just by the bar. He was a ruddy-faced, bear of a man, with a thick white beard and a flat cap that he never removed. Some locals speculated that he even bathed in it but others who had known Angus longer disputed this on the grounds that he'd never taken a bath. "Have you got into the glen yet, Luckie?" he said, in a loud voice, just as the DS turned to leave.

Luckie looked down at the farmer. "No, the snow is still too thick in the lane. The plough is wary of going down a hill like that. Never know where it might land."

"Aye, it's a dangerous hill, that's true. Has Tom Irving started at the other end?"

"I think he has."

The old man's bushy white eyebrows shot up and he gave a mischievous grin. "I'm surprised he's helping you at all."

"Really?" Luckie said, pulling up a chair. "Why's that then?"

"I'd have thought he'd want them trapped down there so he could have them all to himself for as long as possible," Angus said, chuckling into his pint. "He's no love for the hippies and layabouts in the big house."

"You're joking of course," Luckie said.

"There's many a true word spoken in jest, though, eh?" Angus said. "If I had a bunch like that on my land, I'd run them off any way I could."

"It's not his land though, is it?"

"In Thomas's mind it is..."

Luckie dismissed the idea with a wave of his hand. "Get away with you. I was given the old 'Rightful Heir of Devil's Glen' lecture when I interviewed him. It's all ghost stories and nonsense..."

"Not that load of bollocks, Luckie," the old man said, leaning forward. "Irving goes on about how the Lamberts drove his parents to an early death, but the truth is, they were thick as thieves with the old rock star. You wouldn't go down into the glen on your own back when Eric Lambert was alive."

"Really?"

"Aye. I'm telling you, things went on in that place that shouldn't have. And the Irvings were the gatekeepers to the valley. It was up to them who came and went."

"So, why does Thomas Irving hold such a grudge now?"

Angus shrugged. "It's all rumour and hearsay but it's said that Eric Lambert promised Thomas Irving that he'd leave the land and the house to him. He was like a son to Lambert, and Irving kept the valley running."

"I assume that in this story, Lambert doesn't provide for him in the will..."

"Apparently, he just didn't leave a will at all. So everything went to that stuck-up cow, Duana. I saw Irving at market the week he found out and he was fuming. He even suspected that there was a will, but she destroyed it. It's a wonder he didn't take a shotgun up the valley and settle it then."

"I'm glad he didn't."

"Aye well, maybe if he had, you wouldn't be

investigating a murder down there now. Irving has been festering away in that valley for years. It was only a matter of time before something went wrong."

CHAPTER 31

It took a couple of glasses of wine, and no small amount of flirting, to loosen Simon Carver's tongue enough for Rosie to learn anything. By the time the soup bowls were scraped clean and only a few crumbs of the bread were left, Carver sat back in his chair sipping his wine and watching Rosie carefully. When she'd asked him straight out about Duana's money, he'd been cagey and slipped into another topic of conversation almost without her noticing. But she kept topping his glass up and little by little, he became less cautious.

"So you've never actually been to the big house?" Rosie said. "That surprises me."

Simon Carver looked at her quizzically. "Why is that so surprising?"

"Well, you said that you'd conducted a lot of legal business for Duana over the years. I'd have thought at some point, you'd have ended up at the family home."

"I imagine it's a grand place," Carver said, "Judging by Duana's lifestyle..."

"It's a virtual ruin," Rosie said. "About fifteen or twenty years ago, she converted the barns and stables at the back into rooms and a workshop, but the main house has been left to crumble."

"Strange," Simon said, sipping at his wine. "Mind you, it doesn't pay to think too hard about some of my client's personal foibles."

"You must be used to this kind of rich living if you meet Duana here all the time," Rosie said, not entirely certain what type of business Simon would have to do with Duana on a regular basis.

"This is probably the most upmarket place we come to. When she meets with customers, she often lowers the tone a little..."

Rosie laughed, the mention of customers confused her but she tried not to show it. "Lowers the tone?"

"Well, you know, puts on a show of poverty to keep the price high. It's always better if a customer thinks you need the money. It makes them feel like they have the upper hand but it tempers their instinct to drive too hard a bargain."

"Clever," Rosie said, beaming and pouring the last of the wine for Simon. He didn't even notice. "I mean these people buying must be seasoned..." she struggled with the last word and prayed it wouldn't give the game away. She hadn't a clue what kind of business Duana conducted but needed to tease it out of Simon without him realising. "Tradesmen..."

"No," Simon said, as though the thought had only just struck him. "Often, they're fairly new to the game. They haven't invested in Art before in their lives. I mean, they might have bought stuff direct from a gallery, but they've never bought privately. Duana meets them online apparently."

Rosie tried not to look surprised. "They must have money to burn," she said, conspiratorially.

"I know," Simon said and for the first time, he looked troubled. "You know, I'm surprised that her father had such a big collection of old masters. I mean, he was some kind of Ozzy Osbourne character, wasn't he? I can't imagine he had an eye for fine artwork." He narrowed his eyes. "Especially if you say the big house is a virtual ruin. I mean, these pieces can't be kept in an old damp cellar or something." He laughed to himself. "You know, if I didn't know better, I'd say she's got a whole workshop of elves down there churning out forgeries of old masters."

"What makes you say that?"

"Just the regularity with which she meets her customers. She always has something that someone wants. It's almost like shopping to order." Simon blinked and rubbed his head. "Golly, I must have had most of that bottle. Were you trying to get me drunk, Rosie Blake?"

Rosie leaned her chin on her hands. "What's

your role in all this Simon?"

"Duana's a very private woman. I'm not surprised, given the notoriety of her father in the past. As well as the bills of sale, she asked me to draw up non-disclosure agreements that she insisted customers sign."

"Doesn't it all sound a little dodgy to you?" Rosie said.

Simon laughed. "Yes. Yes, it does."

"What are you laughing at?"

"Well, at the beginning of the evening, I was going to get you drunk and see if I could find out what was going on in Devil's Glen... looks like you did it to me."

Rosie smiled back but inside she felt like she was falling down a well. Duana had been good to her and had created The Community. She'd been so happy there but now, to realise it was all founded on lies and deceit was too much. "I think we need to talk to Detective Sergeant Luckie with our concerns, don't you?" Rosie said.

*****

The evening dragged on and Laura looked across the yard at the kitchen window. She wanted to go over and make peace with Gilmore but all she did was stick up for him when he wasn't sticking up for himself. He could have sent them packing there and then, making it clear that he'd call the police if he found them on his land again. Instead, he let them take the mickey out of him. She knew that they'd be coming back again tonight. She could just tell.

She didn't feel hungry or sleepy and so sat at the window of her caravan with the light off and Archie on her lap, watching the dark fields and waiting. But at some point, her eyelids grew heavy and her head bumped against the cold glass, waking her with a start. Torchlight flashed in the distance.

Pulling her jacket on, Laura hurried out of her caravan. With a brief glance at the house, she set off towards the flickering lights. Archie padded after her. The ground was rough and she stumbled a few times but remembered the previous night's disaster and waited until she got her night eyes. It was still hard going, at one point, she had to squeeze through a gap in a thorn hedge that tore at her skin and almost ripped her coat. Her toe caught on a strand of barb-wire, sending her face first into the grass. Eventually, she could hear the yapping of dogs and see the bright torchlight pointed downward.

Dark figures moved around in a shallow pit they had been digging. Archie growled and then exploded into a fury of barking. "We told you to go," Laura yelled. "The police are on their way."

"What the..?" someone shouted. A bright light shone in her face, blinding her. Laura became aware of someone moving towards her and grabbing her arm.

"I can't see anyone else."

"She's on her own!"

This announcement was followed by a scream of pain as Laura grabbed the hand that held her and broke its thumb. The howl gave her an idea where to punch, so she did, feeling the painful but satisfying crunch of her knuckles on the man's rough chin. He fell to the ground.

"If you want your arse kicked, Billy, then I'm your girl, where are you, you nasty little shit?" Laura bellowed, running towards the light. Archie was busy barking and worrying the fallen man's leg.

"Watch out Billy," the man holding the light called and stopped holding it as Laura barrelled into him, sinking her head into his gut and sending him sprawling. No longer dazzled, Laura could make out the dark shape of Billy wielding a shovel. He swung it down and all she could do was hold up her arm to defend herself. A jolt of hot pain shot up her arm and she screamed, kicking out and catching him between the legs. Billy staggered backwards, cursing. And then the world exploded.

A beam of light illuminated them all and a tall

figure in a wax jacket, his flat cap pulled down low on his brow stood over them. He held a shotgun in one hand and the light in the other.

"Bloody hell it's old man Gilmore..."

"Don't be stupid, he's dead!"

Steve loomed over them. "I'm going to give you thirty seconds to grab your stuff lads and if you're still here, I'm gonna blow you away."

Laura grinned. She felt sick with pain and cradled her arm as she staggered towards him.

The men grabbed what they could, Billy staggered to his feet and began to limp after them. "And Billy," Gilmore said. "If I see you on my land again I'll bury you in it, You got me?"

"Yeah, Stevie..."

"You what?"

"Yes, Mr Gilmore..."

Gilmore gave a grunt of satisfaction. "Good. Now piss off."

Laura grinned. "That's more like it," she said weakly and blacked out.

CHAPTER 32

The bare, wooden floor turned out to be every bit as uncomfortable and painful as Blake had expected but he must have slept because he awoke cold and shivering. A feeble twilight leaked through the thin curtains and Blake realised that Megan's bed was empty. Groaning, he dragged himself up onto the bed and lay there while the pain in his ribcage subsided a little. He stretched cautiously and shivered, pulling the blankets on the bed round him. They were cold. Megan had been gone quite a while, then. That worried him.

Dressing quickly, he hurried downstairs to the kitchen. Duana stood in there sipping a cup of coffee. She barely acknowledged Blake. Patricia sat spooning cornflakes into her mouth, the milk slopping back down into the bowl. She stopped and looked at Blake. "Norris naughty. Norris leg."

Blake smiled at her. "Norris leg?" he said and pointed at his thigh.

"Ow," Patricia said and went on eating her breakfast.

"Right," Blake said and strode towards the hall.

"Blake, no," Duana called after him but he'd got

the message and stamped up the stairs. Blake didn't even bother to knock, he just steeled himself against the pain that would inevitably follow, raised his foot and kicked the door by the handle. The door crashed open and Norris Evans sat up in his bed.

"What the hell were you up to last night Evans?"

Evans tried to jump out of bed but gave a squawk of pain instead. The covers fell off as he tumbled back revealing a rather grey pair of boxer shorts and a fresh bandage wrapped around his thigh. It was spotted with blood. "What's going on?" he yelled. "You can't just burst into my room like that..."

"I just have, soft lad, now why did you attack Megan last night and where is she now?"

"Attacked her? I didn't attack her," Evans spat, gripping his thigh. Duana appeared at the door and Norris Evans nodded at her. "Show him, Duana."

Duana held up a clear plastic bag containing a rather bloody crossbow bolt. "It's the same as the one Norris found on the floor in the hall," she said.

"Yeah, just before someone tried to brain me with that bust. Well, we all know who it was now, don't we?"

"Someone fired that at you?" Blake said to Evans.

Evans rolled his eyes. "You bizzies. Thick as pigsh..."

"Just explain what happened Evans," Blake said, "or that leg will be the least of your worries. I'm not in the mood, okay?"

"Fine," Evans said, pulling covers over his bare legs. "I was out there last night. Just round the courtyard at the back. Suddenly I felt this pain in my thigh. I've never felt anything like it. I looked down and there was this bloody bolt sticking out of my leg."

"What did you do?"

Evans gave Blake another look of disgust. "I fell over."

Blake massaged his forehead. "Right. Then what happened?"

"She came at me, didn't she? Bloody Megan Yule. I managed to fight her off, though. Duana took that out of my thigh. She was trying to kill me, Blake. She's a bloomin' psycho."

Blake nodded. "And did you turn over her room before or after she attacked you?"

Duana took a step forward. "We've had our suspicions about Megan for a while. We think she knew Jonah before she came here. I think they were working as a couple and planning to steal things from the house."

"What kind of things? The place looks like it's about to collapse..." Blake said.

"It is in a bad state of repair, Blake, I admit that but we just don't have the funds to renovate it. That doesn't mean that the contents are worthless, though. We have silver, ornaments and furniture from the Reid family who built the house. Most of that is over two hundred years old. I asked Norris to check her room for any stolen goods. He might have been a little overzealous, but he didn't deserve to be injured so badly."

"None of this explains why she tried to drop the bronze bust on your head, Norris," Blake said. "And why did you use Patricia's figurine in the window to make everyone think you're sitting at your window?"

"Well, it gives me the element of surprise, doesn't it?" Evans' said wincing and shifting his weight. "If Duana asked me to investigate anything or check around the estate. Nobody knew I was around then."

"Right," Blake muttered. He didn't like Evans' explanation. Something was missing but he couldn't pin it down. There was only one person who might explain all this. "Where is Megan?" Blake said. "Has anyone seen her this morning?"

*****

Apart from parking being a total pain in the arse, Luckie hated going to Dumfries and Galloway Royal Infirmary because it usually meant that he was either ill or going to watch a post -mortem. Then again, he didn't think anyone turned up at a hospital voluntarily for a laugh. The parking was a given. He didn't know of any hospital that he'd visited that hadn't given him a 'nightmare parking' story. It was a brand new building, virtually, with loads of spaces to park but what was the saying about nature abhorring a vacuum?

Inside was light and airy, with wide corridors and smooth, clean lines everywhere but that was no compensation. He could really do without watching Jonah Huxley being dissected today, especially as meeting old Angus last night meant he'd stayed for an extra pint. That weighed heavily on his frontal lobes and his stomach this morning. Luckie had made the fact that he was such a lightweight with alcohol into a virtue. The prospect of even a mild hangover meant that he usually went easy when he was at the bar.

Now he stood behind a glass screen, watching Iain Armstrong cut a 'Y' shaped incision in the boy's chest. Armstrong had to be the hairiest man Luckie had ever seen. He had long hair and a thick beard which necessitated him wearing a head and face covering. The hairs on the back of Armstrong's hands could be seen through his gloves. Armstrong was a Geordie and Luckie struggled to understand everything he said.

DC Ashleigh Clarke sat next to him, making notes. "Doesn't this bother you?" Luckie said at last.

"Well, it's not my idea of a grand day out, Sarge but no, not really, why? You feeling a bit peaky?" she said, pouting at him.

He gave her a sneering shake of the head. "Yeah, right. I just hate this bit of the whole procedure, to be honest. That poor lad down there, dead and getting minced up by Guy the gorilla…"

"You're just queasy, aren't you, Luckie?" Clarke said. "Go out and get some fresh air if you want. I can handle this."

Luckie shook his head. "And risk you missing some vital detail because you're too busy ogling Mighty Joe Young down there? No chance."

"Eww, cheeky!" Clarke said, whacking him with her note pad. "Anyway, I *will* miss a detail, several details if you keep chunnering on."

Luckie watched as the post-mortem continued. He tried his best to concentrate but his mind drifted back to what it was that had brought Jonah back to the glen. His phone buzzed and he frowned at it, taking it outside into the corridor. Rosie Blake sounded excited on the phone as she repeated everything that she'd learnt last night. Luckie found himself wondering if it was a family thing. "I hate to say it, Sergeant but I suspect that Duana is running some kind of Art forgery business from the glen."

"That's interesting, Ms Blake. Would you be willing to drop by the station at some point to make a statement?"

Rosie agreed and added that Simon Carver would have some input as he had worked with Duana Lambert on a lot of the sales. Luckie turned his phone around in his hand a she thought. If Jonah was trying to blackmail Duana about forgery and maybe wanted in on the business, that might be a motive for her to kill him.

DC Clarke appeared at the door. "Armstrong has found something." They went back into the viewing booth to see the pathologist holding up a gore-smeared length of wood.

"Looks like a crossbow bolt to me," he said over the intercom. "It was lodged in his stomach. Would have been painful but probably wouldn't have killed him."

"What killed him, then?"

"Someone stabbed him in the throat once with a pointed piece of metal..."

"Commonly known as a knife," Luckie said, "but I think you have something to add..."

"Hard to say but the incision looks to be from

something fairly blunt but pointed at the end like a trowel or a palette knife..."

"Like you use for painting?"

"Yeah, and funnily enough, there are flakes of something in the wound. It looks like it could be paint but we can't be sure. Once we've analysed it, we'll let you know."

"Thanks," Luckie said and turned to Clarke. "So Jonah goes to the glen tries to blackmail Duana over the forgery business..."

"What forgery business, Sarge?"

"I'll explain later. They kill him but why the crossbow bolt?"

"Unless they ambushed him or something? They disabled him then delivered the coup-de-grace, so to speak?"

"Come one, Clarke, let's go and see if they've opened up the lane down to Devil's Glen yet. I'm getting tired of guessing."

CHAPTER 33

Everyone stood in front of the big house. Duana, Freya, Grant, Patricia and even Norris Evans. Clearly not having forgiven Evans for stealing the cut-out, Patricia kept giving him sidelong glances and pouting. The snow had melted here, revealing what gravel hadn't been buried by the edges of the landslip.

Grant had just joined them having searched the upper rooms of the house. He shook his head. "There's no sign of her."

"Well she hasn't taken any of her stuff from her room as far as I can see," Freya said. "She must be out in the woods, somewhere."

"She can bloody well stay there too," Evans said, spitting into the gravel. "I hope she freezes to death."

Blake stared into the woods. "We need to find her. She could be in trouble."

"She's in trouble all right, Blake," Duana said. "She tried to kill Norris, twice. I personally can't wait for the police to return and arrest her. In the meantime, we should lock ourselves into the house. She's armed and obviously dangerous. I wouldn't be surprised to find out she killed poor Jonah Huxley, too. It would make sense if they were stealing things and she wanted a bigger share of the spoils..."

"Are we talking about vast wealth here, Duana?" Blake said. "What spoils are there to be had here?"

Duana stopped and for a second, Blake thought she looked trapped by her own words. "Well, not much," she said at last. "Family silverware..."

"I don't think many people would kill over a few silver spoons," Blake said, looking meaningfully at Evans. "It usually has to be higher stakes than that."

"What are you staring at me for? I don't know nothing," Evans snapped.

"Unless she's got a taste for violence now," Duana said. "I've seen it before amongst some of my father's less reputable friends..."

"Shall we save the psychology for the experts? All I know is that she's out there, presumably in little more than her indoor clothes and it's cold. She was very upset last night. I'm concerned she might come to some harm."

"That's her lookout," Duana said, folding her arms.

"Wow," Blake muttered. "What happened to all that 'see a World in a Grain of Sand' compassion, Duana? Or have you stopped believing that someone like Megan could be a victim of her own 'mind-forged manacles?'"

"I don't imagine your namesake would have had much compassion for someone who had murdered a fellow human being, Blake."

"Suit yourself," Blake said, "but I'm going to look for her." He zipped up his jacket and turned to walk towards the woods.

"Wait," Duana called. "Grant. You go with him. There'll be safety in numbers if you do get into any trouble."

"What?" Grant said, staring incredulously at Duana. "Why should I go? If Blake wants to commit suicide, that's fine by me but I'm not..."

"Grant. Just do it," Duana said, giving him an arched look.

"Bloody Hell," Grant snapped and stalked off into the house, like a sulky teenager. Freya ran after him.

"Just give me a moment," Duana said. Blake watched her go after Grant and Freya. He could see Grant through the living room window, waving his arms around. Duana appeared and put a hand on his arm, explaining something to him.

"She doesn't like being told, 'no,'" Evans said, grinning. He patted his leg. "I'd come with you but I reckon I'd only slow you down."

Blake looked at the skinny man. He was dressed in a hoody and jogging bottoms but no shoes. It was a wonder he wasn't shivering. "Yeah, I bet you would. Why do you think Megan targeted you, Norris?"

"I really don't know," Evans said, his face falling. "I hope you find her, Blakey. You better find somewhere to lock her up. I'm telling you she's a headcase." He walked into the house, leaving Blake on his own. For a second Blake watched the man vanish into the house then he got his phone out. There'd been a missed call from Kath Cryer. It was probably just her confirming that Evans was a local Wirral scrote who had been collared for petty theft way back but he should ring her. His phone buzzed before he could do anything though.

"Any developments?" Luckie said. "You haven't managed to pull any more of the Glen down or set fire to the house, yet, have you?"

"Megan Yule's gone missing," Blake said. "She took a pot-shot at Norris Evans with a crossbow..."

"Really?" Luckie said. "That's interesting because Jonah Huxley's PM found a crossbow bolt buried in his gut. It didn't kill him, someone stabbed him in the throat with what the pathologist thinks is a flat bladed knife, like a palette knife..."

"A what?"

"You know, they use them in painting and stuff.

They found fragments of something in the neck wound, too. They're checking exactly what they are but the pathologist thinks they look like paint."

Blake lowered his voice and watched the house. Duana and Grant were still talking but he looked calmer now and was nodding as though taking instructions. "There's something not quite right about this, Luckie. Okay, maybe Megan Yule might be mentally unstable or maybe jealous of Jonah and killed him because he had a fling with someone. Not that there are that many candidates for having a fling with. Why then target Norris Evans?"

"The one who looks like an undernourished Charles Manson?"

"The same. And it looks like Duana is heavily involved in..."

"Art forgery. Yeah your sister told me..."

"Rosie? God she isn't mixed up in it, is she?"

"I don't think so. She's been quizzing that Carver guy, Duana's solicitor, he's full of stories and information. If you ask me, we've got the wrong Blake doing the investigating down in the glen."

"Very funny. There's something we're missing, here, Luckie I can feel it in my bones. How far are they from clearing the lane? Things are getting tense here and I feel a tad outnumbered."

"I'm at the top of the lane now, nagging them as much as I can, but it'll be a good few hours yet. Just try not to cause any more destruction, okay, sir?"

"Thanks Al," Blake said.

Luckie got the reference straight away. "This isn't bloody Die Hard, sir. You're not John McClane and I'm not Al Powell!"

"Yippee-ki-yay, Luckie," Blake said and hung up.

Grant came out of the house with Duana. It crossed Blake's mind that sharing Luckie's information about the crossbow bolt might frighten Grant off which wasn't necessarily a bad thing. He couldn't do that, now, though. If Duana was tangled up in this somehow, then any inside knowledge might help her evade justice. Blake would just have to keep quiet and put up with Grant.

"Come on, let's go," Grant said.

"Great," Blake said, he turned to Duana. "We'll call you if we find her."

*****

Luckie shook his head and grinned as he pocketed his phone and wandered back to the car. DC Ashleigh Clarke looked curiously at him. "Something tickling you, Sarge?"

"Our celeb down in the glen. Called me Al…"

Ashleigh frowned. "Why, doesn't he know your name?"

"No. No. It's from Die Hard, right? The film? Only he called me Al, but it just occurred to me that when I answered I was more like Dwayne T. Robinson..."

Clarke's smooth brow puckered a little in confusion. "Who's...?"

"It doesn't matter," Luckie said. "Let's go back to the office."

"You know part of me wishes Blake wasn't down in the glen, but I don't think we'd have got half as much out of The Community if they'd had all this time to put their heads together, concoct a story and hide the evidence."

"I suppose his presence has shaken them up," Ashleigh conceded.

"The bugger was right, too."

"About what?"

"There's something missing, a piece of the jigsaw we haven't found yet."

"None of them were particularly helpful when we interviewed them, Sarge," Ashleigh said as they pulled off, windscreen wipers fighting the constant rain. Luckie filled Clarke in on what Blake had told him.

"Megan Yule has no previous convictions,"

Luckie said, "but she seems to have been in on Jonah's plot to blackmail Duana about the forgery business. There's something about her, though. Something that seems familiar and I can't pin it down."

"Could she have got jealous of Jonah for some reason?"

Luckie shrugged. "It's possible, I mean it's said that they have a pretty relaxed attitude about the whole... you know..."

Ashleigh smirked. "No, Sarge, what?"

Luckie could feel himself blushing. "You know... sex and all that..."

"All what?"

Luckie pursed his lips. "I don't think Megan would be jealous from what Blake told me. Anyway, unless Megan's a really predatory and sinister individual, then surely she'd have killed Jonah in the heat of passion, not lured him up into the woods, shot him and then chased him down to the house before stabbing him in the throat."

"There could be any number of reasons why Jonah was up in the woods that night, Sarge," Ashleigh said, watching the road as she drove.

"Too many. There's something about this that we've missed. That I've missed. I can feel it. We need to retrace our steps. There'll be plenty of forensic evidence soon enough but we need some kind of motive for each suspect."

Cars swished past them and Luckie stared out at the sodden landscape.

"Duana Lambert's a sure-fire candidate for killer, Sarge, and the revelations about the Art forgery, don't help her cause. Maybe she killed Jonah to shut him up."

"But she isn't particularly linked to the cross-bow, as far as we know, whereas Megan is, as she used it to attack Evans. It's possible that she'd paid Megan to do it, I suppose."

Ashleigh drummed her fingers on the steering wheel and for a moment. "What about Grant Rothwell?"

"He has a record but nothing remarkable, a handful of cautions, fines and a short stretch in prison for possession." Luckie snorted. "They only locked him up because of his persistence in carrying grass around. He strikes me as a bit of a dogsbody but he could easily have done Jonah in. He's big and ugly enough. What about Freya? Isn't he a bit soft on her?"

Ashleigh shrugged. "According to her file, Freya Finley was a student of Fine Art at Edinburgh University. She could easily be involved in the forgery business."

"Aye, we know next to nothing about Finley's

background. I mean, she's educated, obviously, but she's got a clean record."

Ashleigh grinned. "Even serial killers often have clean records until they're caught, Sarge."

"Her parents are Art dealers," Luckie said, fiddling with his phone. "They live not far from here up in the hills." He looked over at Ashleigh "What d'you reckon. DC Clarke? Think we can get over to the Finleys and back before they open that glen up?"

Ashleigh smiled. "It's possible, Sarge. Shall we?"

CHAPTER 34

Valley sides and mountains showed no mercy, Blake thought. Compared to walking on a treadmill that you could adjust, a real hill got you in a sweat in no time. The fact that he was in constant pain and probably not in the peak of physical fitness didn't help, either. The woods were thick here, large deciduous trees dotted the slopes, interspersed with pines and saplings. Here and there, mounds of snow huddled at the base of trees and between the roots but most of it had gone. The melt water from the snow trickled everywhere making the ground boggy underfoot. Solitary crows cawed and flapped from branch to branch as though following them. Grant Rothwell strode ahead, the gap widening between them until the big man seemed miles away. He'd stop and wait for Blake but then set off again the moment he reached him, giving Blake no time to rest.

They were walking up to meet a track that ran along the side of the valley rather than up it. Grant had suggested they get to the head of the valley and work their way back down, keeping their eyes peeled for Megan as they went. Grant stopped for the fourth time and Blake reached him, gasping for breath. "Wait," Blake said, bend-ing double and resting his hands on his knees. "I need to get my breath back."

Rothwell rolled his eyes and leaned against a tree. He was breathing heavily but not fighting to breath like Blake was. "I'm not used to the hills," Blake panted.

"Don't worry, old man, I won't abandon you here," Rothwell said, without a hint of humour in his voice. "Do you think Megan did it? Killed Jonah, I mean."

"Do you?"

"It's possible. She attacked Norris, didn't she?"

"It looks like it," Blake said, "but appearances can be deceptive. I mean you'd think a commune called Paradise Found would be a heavenly place to live but it's not, is it?"

"It's all right," Rothwell said, folding his arms and looking at the ground.

"All right, isn't really the definition of paradise, is it Grant? Let's be honest. You and Megan seem to do all the work. Rosie pitched in too by all accounts. What do Duana and Norris do all day?"

"It's fine," Rothwell muttered. "I don't mind hard physical work and simple tasks. Give me a pile of wood to chop or a floor to sweep and tell me to get on with and I'm happy. I don't like uncertainty and brainwork."

"That sounds fair enough..."

"You just hate The Community. You're jealous because your sister would rather live with us than down in Liverpool."

"Really? You think that?"

"Yeah, Rosie told us how you and your brother slag off her 'hippy shit' ways. Always taking the mickey out of her lifestyle choices..."

"We were just pulling her leg. I never realised she took it so personally."

"People like you never realise. You don't see the good in a place like this. The security it provides for people. If it wasn't for this place I'd be nothing. I'd be..."

"What? Freya told me you'd been in trouble with the law. Minor drugs stuff, that kind of thing."

"We need to move on. It'll be dark before we get round the whole valley." He pushed himself off the tree and strode off up the path. Blake glanced around, searching between the branches for any sign of movement. Whether or not Megan would attack them, he wasn't sure. If she had wanted Blake dead, she'd have done it in the night, when she was in his room surely. And if she'd attacked Evans deliberately, why flee to Blake? For security? Did she know that they wouldn't touch her in his presence?

They walked on deep into the valley. The sides

grew steeper so that the path was the only place to walk. Some trees had failed in their struggle against gravity and had tumbled down, so Blake and Grant had to climb over their trunks. The branches hung low here and pine needles scratched the top of Blake's head. Blake could hear the thunder of water and suddenly, they were looking down on a small lake that frothed at the force of the fall that plunged into it. The head of the valley was a wall of stone and the brook ran straight over the edge of it.

"The snows have swelled the flow," Grant said. "We have to go down here and go around the pool. Be careful, it's slippy."

Blake looked across the opening. He could imagine it being an idyllic place to swim in the summer. Right now the water looked black and freezing cold. A narrow path ran down the valley side against the rock wall. They began inching their way down, hacking the heels of their boots into the soft earth for better purchase. Grant Rothwell was no longer charging ahead but stayed close in front. The wall of stone felt cold to Blake's touch and offered a false sense of security because although it felt solid, there was nothing to grip if he fell. The pool looked far below.

Something rattled against the stone face, not far from their heads and Blake wondered what it was at first. Then he looked down and saw the crossbow bolt at his feet. Rothwell saw it too and his eyes widened. He started to slither and crash down the narrow track, slipping onto his backside in a controlled fall to the bottom. Blake winced and followed him, trying to keep upright. Every twist and jerk sent waves of hot pain through him but the jarring he felt when he lost his footing was worse. Another bolt pinged against the wall, not far from Grant and Blake paused to see where the shots were coming from.

A dark figure, dressed in black with a hooded top and stout boots stood at the poolside, reloading the crossbow. Blake couldn't see the face but it was a slight figure and he guessed it to be Megan. As he staggered down the hill, he saw her raise the crossbow once more and threw himself down, flattening his back against the muddy path. He felt water and dirt seep into the back of his trousers and winced.

Looking down, he saw that Rothwell had copied him and was unhurt. The crossbow was obviously cumbersome to reload and Blake reckoned they had a few seconds grace to get down. But when he got to his feet, Megan had vanished. She had probably worked out that stopping to load one more shot might give them the time they needed to catch up with her.

Grant and Blake stood panting at the bottom of the hill. "You okay?" Blake said.

Rothwell nodded, his hands on his hips. He looked pale and worried. The air was humid with the spray from the waterfall and the pool lapped onto the path around it.

"This is your plunge pool, eh?" Blake said, trying to distract him.

"Aye. Lovely in the summer. The burn runs off down the glen, then twists behind the house. She went up there," he said, pointing at a break in the bushes on the other side of the pool. He glanced at Blake. "What if she's waiting for us?"

"Come on, I'll go in front if you want," Blake said.

They slipped under the canopy of pine needles again. Blake kept himself low and scurried to the first tree trunk, Rothwell close behind him. There was no crossbow fire. "Could be lulling us into a false sense of security," Blake said. "Or she might want to keep a bit of distance from us. The crossbow is slow to load. If she misses first time, she has to run if we're too close."

Rothwell narrowed his eyes and looked further up the path. "Look it forks there. If we take the right-hand path, we can go up to the top of the hill again. If she hasn't gone that way, we might be able to skirt round her and take her by surprise."

Blake shook his head. "I don't know. I wish we knew what she's doing."

"Trying to get out of the valley, I guess."

"She's had plenty of time to do that, hasn't she? Besides did you see what she was wearing?"

"Well, she didn't look like she was dressed in casual wear when she was firing that crossbow at us. She was dressed like a bloody ninja!"

"She must have put a bag of appropriate clothing out at some point, last night. Maybe even earlier. But if that's the case then she planned this. She must have realised that there might be a chance that things could go wrong. This is her plan B and that's never good."

"What d'you mean?" Rothwell said.

"Think about it, plan B is never the preferred option is it? It's the messiest way out of something. I think we might be in trouble, Grant."

CHAPTER 35

It had been a bit of a punt, calling Freya Finley's father and asking for an impromptu interview but it had paid off and Luckie was left wondering if he should buy a lottery ticket. Mr Finley had sounded weary on the phone. "What has she done now?" he said.

"I'm not certain that she's done anything," Luckie had said, "but we just want to flesh out her background and get a few details, that's all. We're nearby, could you see us in, say, thirty minutes?"

"I'll put the kettle on," he'd replied.

Finley lived up a side road off the A708. Here, the valleys were wide, with open fields flanking the road. The snow-capped hills glowered down at them. Although the lane took them closer to the hills, they never started to climb. The snow piled up around them, but someone had managed to grit the road. Eventually, they came to a large farmhouse built of grey stone. A few outhouses lay behind it. It clearly hadn't been a working farm for some time as the yard was clean and there was no sign of animals or machinery. The contrast between this house with the open skies above it and the crumbling manor skulking in the secretive pines couldn't have been more marked.

Freya Finley's father was a lion of a man, with a mane of long, silver hair and a flattened nose. He reminded Luckie of a boxer or a rugby player rather than someone who bought and sold paintings for a living. He smiled but there was a sadness in his wrinkled face as though he'd deliberately tried to adopt an attitude of happiness against a sea of troubles. He wore a green tweed suit and yellow waistcoat, which could have looked affected and silly but somehow, he carried it off.

"Come on in," he said, waving a huge shovel-sized hand in to the exquisitely decorated hall.

Luckie glanced back at Ashleigh, who looked impressed, too. "It's good of you to see us at such short notice, Mr Finley."

"Call me Leo," Finley said, leading them into the living room. Ashleigh mouthed, 'Leo,' at Luckie and raised her eyebrows. She obviously thought that his name suited his appearance, too. "Freya is my cross to bear, I'm afraid. If I can help clear up any mess she has made, then I'm all for it."

A tea tray with teapot, cups and saucers sat on an antique occasional table waiting for them. Leo Finley poured them each a cup and then sat back in a deep armchair and stirred his drink.

"Help yourselves to milk and sugar."

Luckie dropped two sugars into the cup and wished it had been a mug. He and Ashleigh perched on the huge sofa, and Luckie glanced around. "You've a very nice place here, Leo," he said.

"Thankyou. Yes, it's taken years to build up and renovate but I think we're nearly there," he leaned forward and lowered his voice. "The kitchen is still in a terrible state. Hideous Eighties fitted units, all fake country kitsch. That's the last thing. So, what do you need to know about Freya?"

"There's been an incident at The Community..."

"What community?" Leo said, his cup frozen between saucer and lip.

"The commune where she lives. It's in Devil's Glen..."

Leo Finley clinked his cup down on the saucer. "She went there? It makes sense, I suppose. Birds of a feather and all that."

"I'm sorry, Leo, you've lost me. Do you know of The Paradise Found Community?"

Leo gave a bitter laugh. "Is that what they're calling it these days? Yes, Mr Luckie, my interest is Art, so I had some dealings with Duana Lambert and her father briefly, too. Horrible man.

Made my skin crawl."

"Really? Why?"

Leo took another sip of tea. "Maybe it was his reputation, you know, that Godawful rock band of his with its outrageous antics and image. But I think it went deeper. I'd look into his eyes and see no soul there..."

"I see," Luckie said, not noting that down.

"It sounds silly, I know, but you must have worked with criminals and you look in their eyes and they're just dead inside. Lambert was like that."

Luckie nodded. He had met a few psychopaths in his time and shivered at the memory of that cold, reptile stare. "What about Duana Lambert. What do you mean by 'dealings with her?'"

"Literally that. She brought some pieces to my gallery a few years back. I was dubious about them..."

"Dubious?" Luckie said and sipped his cup, only to find he'd drained it already.

Leo paused and then looked Luckie in the eye. "The Art world is a funny place, Luckie. It runs on trust and reputation. Big auction houses rely on being able to verify that works of Art are genuine. When this trust is broken, it's very hard to repair. But people are fooled all the time by clever forgeries. Even the provenance of works can be manufactured if you're clever enough..."

"Provenance?" Luckie said, putting the cup down and refilling it. He knew it would be lukewarm already, so tried to keep the milk to a minimum.

"Where a piece of Art has come from," Leo explained. "If a piece has been owned by the National Gallery for three hundred years, then you know exactly where it's been and who's had it. That's an extreme example but if you have a picture and a bill of sale to your great grandfather from a hundred years ago, then the principle is the same. You can be pretty sure where that picture has been all its life and that it hasn't been tampered with or altered to make it seem older or by another artist."

"Right," Luckie said. "So, people not only have to forge a painting, but they have to manufacture provenances too?"

"There are lots of other physical things forgers do, obviously, using old frames, rusty nails to hold the canvas, even sprinkling vacuum cleaner dirt into all the cracks and scars on the picture."

"And you think Duana Lambert was doing this," Luckie said, sipping his tea and trying not to grimace. He glanced around in a vain search for any biscuits.

Leo smiled. "I have no proof. The works she brought to me were old masters. She said they belonged to Ramsay Reid, the first owner of the big house and had bills of sale, household inventory when the place was sold. It was perfect."

"Too perfect?"

"For me, it was. And knowing what I do about *her* provenance, having met her father, I felt I couldn't in good faith find her a buyer for the pieces. I think she sold them some time later for a considerable amount of money. And Ramsey's collection seems inexhaustible. More tea?" Leo reached for the pot.

"No!" Luckie almost shouted but managed to soften his voice. "Thank you." He glanced at Ashleigh who smiled benignly at him, obviously having realised that a third cup would be one too far.

She took over to cover Luckie's outburst. "You said something about 'birds of a feather' when we told you that Freya was down in Devil's Glen. Why was that Leo?"

Leo Finley stood up and strode over to the French windows that looked over a long, well-tended garden and beyond to the hills behind the house. He sighed. "My daughter had everything, you know. She wanted for nothing. When she was a little girl, she had a pony, toys galore, a beautiful bedroom. But she didn't have the love of her parents. We were too busy amassing the wealth that paid for all those things. Networking, schmoozing, wining and dining people." He gave a derisory snort. "We could have just been comfortably off and given her the time and attention she deserved but we wanted to be rich. Money is like a drug; the more you have, the more you want."

"So, Freya went off the rails?" Ashleigh said, gently.

"Not exactly, no. There wasn't one terrible incident that made us realise something was wrong. A sudden melt down or explosion of rage that made us see what we'd done to our daughter. In fact, I don't think we realised that until much later. But we both noticed a distance in her, a self-absorption that we couldn't deal with. She would spend all her time up in her room, lost in painting..."

"Painting? Was she good?"

"Very good for a young, inexperienced teenager who never left the house. She could copy anything. Paint in any style, given the materials. Ha, it seems so odd now, us being so concerned about how self-obsessed our daughter was. She only had the same flaws we did."

"So what happened?"

"Hoping it would bring her out of her shell, we sent her to a boarding school up in the Highlands. She fell in with the wrong sort there. Oh you can raise your eyebrows but every school has the wrong sort; bullies, thieves, weak-minded individuals who succumb to every narcotic going. The only difference is that in the poorer schools, they don't have mummy and daddy to cover for them."

Luckie nodded. He'd seen this himself first-hand. Privilege didn't necessarily protect you from criminality. "That must have been hard for you."

"It was. Freya was caught smoking cannabis in the dorms. Not a mortal sin in our eyes but the school tried to expel her. It took a lot of charitable donations to keep her there but then there was the accident…"

Luckie glanced over at Ashleigh in alarm. "Accident?" he said.

"They called it an accident but we knew better the moment we looked into Freya's eyes. A youngster in her dorm had only just joined the school and was dreadfully homesick. She was from Singapore, I believe. One night, she jumped out of the dorm window. Two storeys up. She didn't die but she was in a wheelchair afterwards. I'd imagine she hasn't recovered."

"And Freya was somehow involved?"

"Some of the girls claimed that Freya had been calling her names, goading her to jump or to kill herself. As the school investigated, Freya went on a campaign of intimidation and silenced them. In the end, all parties decided that she should find another school."

"And the girl from Singapore?" Luckie asked.

Leo hung his head. "There was no further action taken. I heard second-hand that the school had concocted a story about her sleep walking. The child denied it of course but the parents were so eaten up with guilt, they took her home."

"And Freya?"

"It was like it had never happened. We employed a home tutor and she eventually got into Edinburgh University to study Fine Art. She really was a talented painter. A terrible human being. We heard other rumours of people suffering because of her. Youngsters would even turn up at the house with horror stories of how they had been treated by her. Some of the characters were quite scary, saying she owed them money and I had to pay them off just to get rid of them. My wife and I separated over my constantly bailing her out. And now you tell me she's down in Devil's Glen."

"Do you think she's helping Duana Lambert make forgeries there?" Ashleigh said.

"I have no evidence, of course but it really wouldn't surprise me."

Luckie took a breath. "I hate to ask this, but,

would your daughter be capable of murder, Mr Finley?"

Leo Finley held Luckie's gaze once more. "I'm sorry to say so but yes, without a doubt."

CHAPTER 36

When Blake's phone rang, he nearly leapt behind the nearest tree trunk. He and Grant Rothwell had been inching their way up the path that led up the other side of the valley, trying not to imagine that every sapling or rotten stump was Megan Yule pointing the crossbow at them.

Mainly to shut the phone up, Blake pulled it out and jabbed the screen, inadvertently answering it by mistake. "Boss? It's Kath. Is this a bad time?"

"I'm crouched in the middle of a dense wood, trying not to be shot by a crossbow," Blake said. "So, yeah..."

"We were worried when you didn't call us back last night. After what we found out about Evans..."

"What?"

"Okay. So you didn't listen to the voicemail," Kath paused. "You were joking about the crossbow, right?"

"No but go on. I'm not about to die imminently. This better be good."

"So, Norris Evans is one of two people and you can take your pick. He's either Norris Evans Senior, an old man who lives in Birkenhead and has never moved away from there all his life. Or he's Norris Evans Junior who died under suspicious circumstances at the age of ten at the hands of a scrote called Vincent Tanner..."

"Go on," Blake said, remembering the dry-cleaning ticket in the jacket pocket in Evans' wardrobe.

"So it turns out Vincent Tanner is a member of *that* family..."

"I know them. I arrested Dougie Tanner for handling stolen goods a few years back. The whole family were involved but we could only pin it on him. So what about Vincent, did he move north?"

"Spot on, sir. He was connected with the Dumbarton Three robberies way back. A violent and sadistic fella by all accounts. Then he just vanished after topping the other two in his criminal trio. He's never been seen since."

"Jeez, Kath. That's brilliant work. Why didn't you call me sooner?" Blake looked around. Grant Rothwell had vanished out of sight.

"We did, but you didn't pick up. Is it significant? Do you think your Norris Evans really is Vince Tanner?"

"Could be. Look I've got to go. Have you let DS Luckie in on this?"

"We fed back. Hopefully, he's been made aware."

"Great," Blake said. His stomach lurched. He'd been on speakerphone. Rothwell would have heard it all. A sudden movement behind him made him turn then a stabbing pain exploded in his head and everything went black.

*****

Ashleigh and Luckie sat in silence for a while as they drove back towards Devil's Glen. Each was mulling over what they had learnt from Leo Finley and wondering how it fitted in with the knowledge about the forgery business.

"So, we're pretty much agreed that Jonah Huxley and Megan Yule were trying to blackmail Duana about the forgery business, right?" she said at last.

"That makes sense but why would Megan kill Huxley? Unless she didn't want to share the blackmail money."

"And why finish Huxley off with a palette knife?"

"Maybe it was the only thing to hand," Luckie muttered.

"Out in the front of the house, Sarge? In the middle of the night? Other things might be more handy; a rock, a big stick. If he was badly wounded by the crossbow bolt, you might even be able to strangle or suffocate him."

"When did you become such an expert on how to kill a young man," Luckie said with a grin.

"It's working with Harris, Sarge. You know what he's like..."

"Aye, he'd drive anyone to murder. What if Finley and Yule were in it together?"

Ashleigh glanced over. "What? So, Yule shoots him in the gut, he runs away. Straight into Finley who has just emerged from the studio, paint-covered palette knife in hand."

"It's possible."

"Except Finley is part of the forgery business. Why would she want to blackmail Duana lambert? You aren't going to bite the hand that feeds you, surely?"

"Dunno, depends how hungry you are."

Ashleigh nodded. "So, Duana is creaming off the money for her lavish lifestyle outside The Community, Freya resents it and talks her way into blackmailing Duana with Megan and Jonah but that's splitting it too many ways..."

"Hmm, seems a little thin." Luckie said, staring at the passing landscape. "And I can't help thinking I know the name Megan Yule or at least part of it but I can't think where from."

"Have you tried Googling it?"

Luckie gave an impatient snort. "Really? What good would that do? Does Google have a direct link to my brain?"

"Suit yourself, Sarge, but if it's a name you've read recently or that has been in the news, you might have just absorbed it. A quick check wouldn't do any harm."

The car was silent again as Luckie got his phone out and started scrolling through. "Probably uses up tons of data too," he muttered, giving Ashleigh a sidelong glance. She smirked and Luckie focused on the search.

Cars swished by and Luckie ploughed through page after page of Instagram, Facebook, and Pinterest accounts. "You wouldn't believe how many Megan Yules there are Ashleigh." There was a Sound Cloud account, a number of personal trainers and then a whole load of life coaches. "What does a life coach do, anyway?"

"Make you a better person. Maybe you should hire one, Sarge," Ashleigh said.

"No, I think I'm done, now. I'm getting onto Yule logs and we've only just had Christmas," he said, sitting back.

"Keep going. Put the local paper's name in too or the word, 'news'"

Luckie gave a disgusted sigh and did as he was asked. "Oh great. Now I get to find out about

Meghan Markle's latest thoughts."

"Keep going. There must be something in there about *our* Megan. Try images. You might recognise her face."

"This isn't very scientific. Oh God," Luckie groaned. "There was someone on Love Island called Megan. Now I'll have to explain to HR why I was looking at swimsuit models on a works phone..."

"Really," Ashleigh said. "You're going to use this moment to cover up your sordid internet searches, sarge..."

"No I..." Luckie stopped in mid flow. There staring back at him was Megan Yule. She was younger, almost a teenager, with her hair in bunches but it was her all right. "Here we are." He clicked on the link to a website called 'Unsolved Crimes, Scotland.' "Oh God."

"What is it?" Ashleigh said.

"Stop the car," Luckie snapped. "Stop the car now. Pull over."

*****

Someone was tapdancing on Blake's skull with size twenty hobnail boots. That's what it felt like anyway. Part of him thought that at least it took his mind off his ribs which also felt as though someone had given them a good kicking. He rolled over, groaning, and frowned. The ground felt cold and damp but solid. He lay in semi-darkness. His heavy breath echoed off stone walls. Dragging himself to his feet, Blake banged his head and realised he was in some kind of cave. The entrance had been blocked off with a brick doorway. The door looked solid and reinforced with steel bands. A single grille let light in. Blake clutched his head and looked around the room. Water dripped from the ceiling which was so low that Blake had to stoop. Green slime covered the walls.

A large chair stood against the wall opposite the door. It reminded Blake of a throne, with its high back and elaborately carved arms. Woodworm riddled the legs and back, but he could make out a faded painting of a serpent. Rusty, metal travelling cases were stacked in the corner.

"Rothwell!" Blake yelled, running to the door. And gripping the bars on the small window. "Let me out!"

Grant's pale face appeared in front of him. "Just shut up. I'll come back for you later but for now, I've been told to leave you here." His voice trembled. "This was where Duana's dad made all his sacrifices to the Devil."

"I'm not really interested in ghost stories, Grant. Assaulting a police officer is a serious crime. You're in big trouble now, I'm telling you.

Just unlock the door and we can find Megan."

"Not so Mr Big-High-and-Mighty now are you?" Rothwell sneered but he looked nervous and fidgeted as he spoke. "You're all the same, your kind. Bullies who think a badge gives them the right to push other people around."

"I'm telling you Grant. Obstructing a police officer during his investigations is an offence, too."

"I'm going back to the house. I hope it's bloody cold tonight. I hope the hill collapses on top of you. This is all your fault!"

"I didn't kill Jonah Huxley, Grant. You know that. I came here to help Rosie. How's she going to feel when she finds out you've locked me up in here, eh? Come on, let me out."

"I can't," Grant said, scowling like an over-grown toddler. "Duana said to keep you here. She won't be happy if I let you go."

"No, but DS Luckie's going to lock you up and throw away the key when he realises what you've done, here. It's not just a caution for a bit of weed, this, Grant. This is major crime."

Rothwell pressed his fists to the side of his head. "Shut up. Shut up! I can't. She'd kill me..."

"Is that what she wants to do to me, Grant? Because the moment I'm out of this cave, I'm talking to the police. About this, about the forgeries, about everything."

Rothwell's eyes widened. "How did you know?"

"I'm a police officer. It's my job to figure things out. You moved Jonah from the back of the house to keep the police from becoming interested in the workshop. I saw you working in there the other night, rubbing dirt into that painting to make it look older. Was Jonah going to blackmail you all?"

"That little shite got what was coming to him," Rothwell spat, his eyes wide. "And so will you, when we come back." He vanished from view for a second and there was a metallic click. The big man staggered back into view. He looked at Blake. "Oh no," he said and collapsed.

CHAPTER 37

Detective Constable Ashleigh Clarke had never seen Luckie so incandescent with rage. He had gone straight past punching the dashboard and screaming to a silent white heat. His knuckles were white as he gripped the phone. His jaw was white, he clenched it so hard. Even the tips of his ears had gone from bright red to icy white. Ashleigh wondered where all the blood had gone and if a human being could pass out from fury alone.

"You didn't want to bother me with it, what with everything else that was going on? Is that what you just said to me, Harris?"

"Erm, aye, Sarge. I thought it was just a bit of tittle tattle from the scousers. You know, trying to look good at our expense." Harris' voice crackled over the speakerphone and Ashleigh physically winced as he spoke.

"Right. Just repeat the 'tittle tattle' that you received last night, for me, please, Harris. Just so I can take it in, again."

"What? Okay then," Harris said, there was the sound of rustling paper as he read from his notes. "DI Kath Cryer rang to say that they'd looked into the background of Norris Evans and found that the only living Norris Evans was an old man who was still resident in Birkenhead. But…"

"But?"

"But Evans had a son also called Norris who died when he was ten years old. Apparently, a boy called Vincent Tanner was involved."

"Brilliant."

"Are you okay, Sarge? You sound a bit… terse…"

"You and I are going to have such a conversation when we next meet," Luckie said and killed the call. He looked over at Ashleigh.

"Norris Evans is Vince Tanner," she said.

"Vince Tanner of the Dumbarton Three who hospitalised my partner and put him in the state he's in now. But who also blinded and crippled Gerry Yule, a security guard on their last jewellery heist and father of Megan Yule."

Ashleigh felt her throat tighten. "Oh my Lord, Sarge," she said. "This hasn't been about forgery or anything. It's revenge pure and simple. She's out to kill Tanner."

"Put your foot down, Ash, if anyone is gonna have that pleasure, it'll be me."

*****

The sound of metal grating on metal filled the cave as the bolt on the door was drawn back. "Come out slowly, and keep your hands where I can see them," Megan called in.

"How do I know you won't kill me?" Blake said, angrily, "like you just killed Rothwell."

Megan snorted. "Grant's not dead. I winged him and he fainted. Now come out or I'll just lock the door again and leave you here with him."

Blake inched out of the cave, blinking in the light. Megan stood, dressed in a black Gore-Tex hoody and over trousers. She had the crossbow levelled at him. Rothwell lay moaning on the floor. A crossbow bolt was lodged in the insulated padding of his thick coat. Blake wondered if it had even got through.

"Drag him into the cave," Megan said.

"I'm not sure I can," Blake said, massaging his ribs.

"Just do it, quickly before he recovers and realises he isn't dead."

Blake gritted his teeth and gripped Rothwell under his arms. The sideways stagger required to pull the big man backwards sent splinters of agony across Blake's chest and he wondered if he'd done some permanent damage. He lowered Rothwell's head gently, swallowing down the wave of nausea that swept over him. Megan was still there when he came out. "What now?" he said.

"Close the door and bolt it."

Blake did as he was told. "What's going on, Megan? This is more than a blackmailing scam gone wrong. Why did you kill Jonah?"

"I didn't," Megan said, lowering the crossbow slightly. "Or at least, not on purpose."

"You shot him by accident?" Blake murmured. "You weren't aiming at Jonah, were you? It was Norris Evans, otherwise known as Vincent Tanner. You were after him, weren't you?"

"How did you know?" Megan said.

"Long story. My team back in Liverpool found the real Norris Evans. I found a dry-cleaning stub…"

"There's no time. Turn around and walk. We need to get to the big house. I've wasted enough time already with you chasing me up the valley. The police will be here soon and I've got things to do."

"All right," Blake said. "Do I have to keep my hands up?"

"Just walk and don't dawdle."

Grant Rothwell's face appeared at the bars on the window. "Let me out you bitch!" he snarled.

"You stay there, Grant," Megan said. "The police will find you when all this is over. You'll be safe enough."

"Duana's gonna kill you," Rothwell said.

"We'll see," she replied, hefting the crossbow up and making Rothwell duck away from the window. "Come on, Blake. Let's go."

They trudged up the path that Megan pointed out to him. He could hear her steady tread behind him. "Why are you so intent on heading back to the house? Why traipse around the woods all this time?"

"I told you, I would have waited by the house but you two came out looking for me. I had to run before you caught me."

"And what are you waiting for, a chance to get Tanner alone? Are you going to kill him? Is that it?"

"He left my father blinded and crippled after their last robbery. My dad was a security guard, a funny man, a tough man too but I watched him waste away after that attack. He didn't last more than a couple of years. Our family fell apart. I never really settled to anything. And Tanner disappeared with everything."

"How did you find out he was here?"

"Pure chance. For years, I fantasised about hunting him down and handing him over to the police. I even channelled my energies into learning martial arts and weapons skills. A total pipe dream, though, until I stumbled across Jonah in a club in Glasgow. He was charming and good-looking and I was drifting at the time. And then he told me his secret."

"About the forgery business here?"

"About Tanner. He didn't know anything about Art forgery. Neither did I. No, he'd worked out that Norris Evans was Tanner."

"But how? I mean Tanner's van was dumped down in the Lake District. He could have gone anywhere. How did Jonah work out that Tanner was here?"

"You're slowing down, Blake," Megan said. "Walk faster. I'm not sure how he made the connections. An overheard conversation here, maybe looking at the maths..."

"The maths?"

"Eric Lambert died, leaving virtually no money, just the property. Duana sets up her commune, a strange man appears at the right time and within a couple of years, she has the workshop converted followed by the barns and a bunk house. Building like that costs serious money. Where did it come from?"

"But that wasn't infinite, she needed money from elsewhere. Hence the forgeries."

"I think Jonah heard rumours in prison too. They talked about the Dumbarton Three like they were heroes; the one's that got away with it. Ignoring the fact that one of them killed the other two. There's no honour among thieves really, is there?"

"No," Blake conceded. "I've never seen it. Just fear."

"Part of the story told about the Dumbarton Three was that they had a secret hideaway, like Robin Hood or something," Megan said, the disgust in her voice apparent. "Tanner had been seen out on a couple of occasions with a 'classy lady.' Someone way out of his league, really."

"Duana Lambert."

Megan stopped and Blake halted too. "The silent, invisible member of the Dumbarton Three."

The chimneys of the big house were visible through the trees now. Blake turned to Megan, keeping his hands raised. "Megan, I'm not sure what you're planning but it won't change the past. What's done is done. Let's go up to Irving's house and wait for the police. You haven't actually killed anyone, yet. There are mitigating circumstances. Jeez, after that landslide, I wonder if there's any actual evidence left anyway. If you succeed in your plan, then you'll be a murderer. No better than Tanner. Don't go down that path."

"I won't be a cold-blooded killer. It's payback, Blake, don't you see that? Tanner didn't just destroy my dad's life that day, he destroyed my mother's and mine..."

"But there'll be bloodshed. Do you want Patricia to witness all that? She's down there painting her pictures, innocent of all this. What will that do to her?"

A shotgun barrel slowly slid from the bush next to Megan and pressed against her cheek. "I'd listen to him, lassie. Nobody wants blood on their hands now, do they?"

CHAPTER 38

Even though it was a freezing cold jumble of baler twine, rusty spanners and plastic bags, Irving's Land Rover felt like a sanctuary to Blake. Charlie sat on his knee, tail wagging like a broken metronome, licking his neck and chin. With Blake holding the crossbow and Irving still levelling the shotgun at Megan, they had walked down a steep track that ran straight to the road on the valley floor. Blake looked at Irving's back and mused at his luck, literally landing on his doorstep that first night.

Irving slammed the back door of the Land Rover where Megan lay, her hands and ankles zip tied securely. Blake felt bad about that but he had no cuffs and realised that she needed to be secured until the police arrived. Megan squirmed and yelled obscenities at Irving but he seemed oblivious.

"I thought you'd have called to see how Charlie was," Irving said, reproachfully. "Little fella's been pining for you."

"Sorry," Blake said. "Things got a bit out of hand. What were you doing up on that side of the valley?"

"Checking up on you. When you didn't call, I

wondered if you had your hands full. I drove up the valley and found a couple of crossbow bolts by the pool. You and Grant were making so much noise up there that I knew which path you were taking. So I headed you off at the pass as John Wayne would say."

"And you just lay in wait until we stopped right by you."

"That was a stroke of luck and I heard all I needed to, to know you were in trouble," Irving's leathery face wrinkled into a smile. Then it faded. "I'm afraid young Grant broke free, though. I saw him running down the main track back to the big house. The door on that cave is strong but the masonry in the breeze block wall is perished. A big lad like him could kick it down no problem."

"What was that place?"

Irving pulled a sour face. "Eric Lambert's den. Where he played all his silly games. Sacrificing goats and cavorting around naked with his so-called friends."

"You saw it?"

Irving glanced over at Blake, and he saw a sadness in the old man's eyes. "I was there, Will, Lambert took me under his wing and corrupted me. I'm not proud of it but it's a truth I regret every day. He was a charismatic man, a charming devil. He could get you to do anything. Duana

Lambert is cut from the same cloth. I'm sure your Rosie is innocent enough but the Lamberts attract bad souls. Part of me wants to give this girl my shotgun and unleash her on the lot of them."

Blake put a hand on the old man's arm. "But you won't, Thomas, will you?

"No. I won't. but Grant will have reached the big house by now, so we might have little choice."

"We always have a choice," Blake said, glancing out of the window and stroking Charlie.

They drove in silence for moment as the outline of the house appeared. Just before the house, the river which had flowed on their left, suddenly meandered right under a stone bridge. At the end of the bridge, just where the road entered the rear courtyard, a trailer full of logs had been pushed in the way. The land to the left of it was boggy with melt water, on the right stood the back wall of the workshop.

"Hold on tight," Irving muttered, hitting the accelerator. He swerved left, taking the Land Rover onto the muddy earth and spraying dirt everywhere. The rear end slid out, clipping the trailer, and sending them into a spin. Megan yelled as she was thrown about in the back. Irving muttered curses and dragged at the wheel, trying to get control of the vehicle again. Blake watched the treetops swirl above his head and wondered if the Land Rover was going to turn over when Vince Tanner appeared fleetingly from behind the trailer, holding a bottle full of liquid with a flaming rag stuffed in the neck.

"Thomas, look out he's got a..."

A sheet of flame erupted as the improvised petrol bomb burst across the windscreen. Fumes filled the cab, snatching Blake's breath for a second. "Watch My Landy!" Irving bawled, whirling the steering wheel round and hammering the accelerator. Charlie howled and buried himself in Blake's coat. The car did a little skip and then hurtled back onto the road. The spirit flashed off the bonnet, killing the flames and leaving a foul, acrid smoke. Grant appeared at the side of the road, with a huge rock held above his head. "Ya wee shite!" Irving snarled and, before Blake could say a word, jagged the steering right, clipping Rothwell with the wing of the Land Rover. Rothwell went down, and the rock followed him. Blake looked away, hoping he wasn't dead.

"Oops," Irving said, a wild twinkle in his eye. "I lost control, then, Will, sorry." Was this the Irving of his youth? The one who joined Eric Lambert's madness. Blake could well believe it looking at the excitement on the old man's face. Blake shook his head and stared out of the back. Duana and Freya stood on the road staring after them.

"I don't think they're finished," he said. "We'd better get to your house as quick as we can."

They pulled into the driveway of the lodge where Irving lived and climbed out of the car. As they did, the sound of an engine echoed up the road. Irving looked outraged. "That's my quad-bike." He grabbed his shotgun. "Cut the girl's feet free and get into the house. I'll deal with this."

"Do not shoot anyone, Thomas. I'm telling you. I swear, I'll arrest you myself if I have to," Blake said.

"Get inside," Irving snapped, passing him a knife.

Blake cut Megan's feet free and saw stars as she kicked him full in the face. "Bastard!" she spat. Staggering back, he saw her roll out of the back of the Land Rover. "Megan stop!" Megan crouched, staring up at Blake like a cornered animal, her wrists still bound. "Don't run now. We stand more of a chance if we stick together. You go now and they'll pick us off one by one."

"Cut me free, then," Megan said extending her arms towards him.

The roaring quadbike drew nearer, and Blake saw Rothwell, his head a mess of blood, glaring at them. The sound of the bike filled the air and Rothwell showed no signs of slowing down. "I hate to do this," Irving muttered, and fired. The front tyre exploded, sending Grant Rothwell cartwheeling over the handlebars and bouncing along the rough road surface. The quadbike tumbled nose over rear and crashed through Irving's garden fence. "Five grand that cost me. Five bloody grand!" He strode over to Rothwell, but the big man lay still. "Ah well, he's out cold."

Blake picked Charlie up out of the front of the Land Rover, pushed the door to the lodge open and looked at Megan. "Come inside and I'll cut those ties."

Megan shrugged and pushed past him into the house. Irving hurried after them. "The others won't be far behind," he said. "I'll close the shutters. I don't know what weapons they've got but you can't be too careful." He disappeared into the house.

Putting Charlie down by the fire, Blake turned to Megan with his knife. "Don't run, Megan. It won't be safe out there and I won't let you go if I think you're going to harm anyone."

Megan held out her hands and Blake cut her free. "I'm sorry," she said, and punched Blake hard in the ribs. Gasping for breath, Blake doubled up, sliding down the wall as she jumped over him and slammed the front door behind her.

Irving burst out of the kitchen. "What was that? Oh, she's gone then?"

Unable to talk, Blake nodded and gripped his

side, willing the breath back into his body. Irving dragged him to his feet. "I think you need some painkillers. Strong ones."

"Thanks," Blake gasped, as Irving led him into the kitchen. The old man rummaged in a drawer for a few second and then pulled out a box.

"Here, take two of these," he said, pouring out a tot of whisky.

Blake necked the tablets and swigged down the spirit. "What are they?"

Irving scratched his beard. "Not sure, really. The vet gave them to me when I kept a few head of cattle. You'll be fine. Okay?"

"A bit better," Blake said, blinking and pouring himself another whisky. Irving joined him. "I don't know where the polis are. It's taking them an age to get down here."

Blake patted his pockets. "I lost my phone up in the woods when Rothwell jumped me. We'll just have to sit it out."

"Aye well, we've got this," Irving said, patting his shotgun. "Did you bring the lassie's crossbow from the Landy?"

"Jeez, Thomas, I had Charlie in one hand and Megan to keep an eye on..."

"You did a good job there, Inspector," Irving said, smirking. "She'll have taken that, no doubt but it's worth checking."

"I'll go," Blake said. "You cover me."

"You don't cover someone with a shotgun, Will. Anyone on the wrong side of this gets diced, including you. Just sneak out, keep low. I'll fire over your head if I have to."

"That's what I said. Covering fire," Blake said, he peered at Irving. "Are you enjoying this, Thomas?"

Irving looked like an angry garden gnome. "Enjoying it? Oh, aye. I love having my precious Landy set fire to and having to shoot at my own quadbike. It's great fun. Just get out there and see if you can find the crossbow."

Blake grinned, he felt light headed and suddenly, this all seemed rather comical. He opened the front door to see Duana standing at the gate. The quadbike smouldered behind her and smoke drifted around her legs. She looked like a witch. A very beautiful witch, Blake thought.

"Hello, Will," she said. "I think we need to talk."

CHAPTER 39

It was going dark and there was a smell of smoke on the air at the top of the lane into Devil's Glen. An officer had reported that she heard a gunshot earlier. Luckie kicked the wheel of his car. "Bastard." Ashleigh Clarke came back from the lane and looked warily at Luckie.

"What's the worst then?" he said.

"There's a crane on the way to pull the tractor free. But they're concerned about the gradient of the lane and if it's safe..."

"Well, it's clearly not safe otherwise the tractor wouldn't have tipped over when it turned on the lane," Luckie growled. He raised his hands. "Sorry Ashleigh, it's just so frustrating. I just wanna get down there and find that bastard, Vincent Tanner."

"Why don't we kit up and walk down, Sarge? Get a team together, just to make sure everything is okay down there."

"I'd love to, Ashleigh, but that gun shot before and the crossbow bolts suggest we might need armed back-up."

"They're here, sarge, getting paid for sitting on their thumbs. Why not call the Super and tell him how much his budget is haemorrhaging while armed response sit drinking hot chocky and playing cards?"

"But they aren't drinking hot..." Luckie began to say but Ashleigh raised one eyebrow. "Aye," he said, scratching his chin. "We could try. You're right. Let's go and tell him."

*****

A cold gun barrel brushed against Blake's cheek as Irving pointed it at Duana Lambert. Blake pushed it away. "Jeez, Thomas, that'll perforate my eardrum if it goes off."

"What do you want, Duana?" Irving said, ignoring Will.

"It's the organ grinder I've come to talk to, Thomas, not the monkey," she said, smiling at Blake.

"That's not very polite, is it, Thomas?" Blake said, his head floating like a balloon. "You didn't answer Thomas. What do you want?"

"I want to make a deal," she said. "Give us the girl and we'll let you go."

"Seriously?" Blake said, nudging Irving. "Have you ever heard such cheek, Thomas? I'm an officer of the law. Without fear or favour, never heard that expression? Your local bobbies will be here soon enough. It's over, just give up."

"You're right, Blake. It is over but it can only

end in one of two ways. Either they find your dead bodies, murdered by poor, mad Megan and her crossbow or they find you alive and we all managed to subdue the wild girl of the woods."

"Are you threatening us, Duana? You'd never make it look like Megan killed us."

Duana Lambert shrugged. "The place is a mess. It'll get messier if we have to burn you out of that miserable cottage. Come on, let's catch wee mad Megan. I'd say it's a no-brainer, what would you say?"

"I'd say Thomas has a shotgun pointed at you and you insulted him a second ago. I don't think he likes you anyway, Duana and I'm not his boss. Also, I'd say we haven't got the girl so, sorry, can't help you." He was sure he hadn't meant to say the last bit but somehow it slipped out. He blinked and shook his head. At least now his ribs didn't hurt. Much.

Duana's face clouded. "Very well," she said. "You leave us with no choice." She backed away, slowly and Blake slammed the door shut.

"Well that went well," Blake said.

"You should've let me shoot her."

Blake peered out through the front door window. "Rothwell's back on his feet but he looks like he's had enough."

The big man swayed as Duana spoke to him, but

he just stared at the house and shook his head. In the end, she shouted something and hit him on the shoulder. Rothwell just fell back down and stayed there.

"One down," Irving said. Vincent Tanner limped out of the darkness and hurled a bottle. It crashed on the roof and Blake heard a 'whumpf' as the petrol in the bottle ignited.

"That's my bloody house!" Irving bellowed, smashing the glass in the door panel and letting both barrels loose.

Blake's ears rang and as the smoke cleared, he saw Freya scurrying to the side of the house with another bottle. Irving was reloading. "We can't stay here, Thomas," Blake said. Tanner's petrol bomb had caught something up in the roof space and now smoke was billowing down into the house. Something thudded against the shutters at the side of the house and a fiery light glowed from the bedroom.

"Out the back," Irving said, firing blindly into the night.

"Charlie!" Blake said, running into the living room and snatching up the puzzled dog. Charlie gave a yelp and snuggled into Blake's arms.

They hurried into the kitchen and flung open the back door. Freya stood there, a petrol bomb held over her head, the cloth wick blazing. "Freya, don't!" Blake yelled.

She grinned manically at him but then a crossbow bolt shattered the bottle, showering Freya with petrol. The flaming rag wick ignited the liquid and, screaming, Freya vanished in a ball of flame. The heat singed Blake's face and Charlie leapt out of his arms. Irving dragged him back as he tried to beat the flames with his bare hands. But the fire was all over her petrol-soaked clothes and hair. Running back into the smoke-filled house, Blake found a towel, soaked it under the tap and flung it over the screeching girl who rolled back and forth, writhing in agony.

"They'll kill us, Will," Irving said, grabbing him. "We've got to get away. You can't help her."

Duana loomed at them from the darkness and swung some kind of wooden club. It cracked Irving across the temple and Blake watched him fall. Charlie cowered at his feet, whimpering.

"I told you what would happen," she snarled.

*****

Sergeant Mcbarry was a cautious man, Luckie could appreciate that but time was running out, he was certain of it. They stood by the overturned tractor, the glare of arc lights reflecting painfully on the huge bank of snow that blocked the narrow lane. Meltwater trickled under their feet in small, fierce streams. "You're telling me you want me to send my team down there into total darkness without any real knowledge of the area or what we're up against?"

"I've got a bad feeling about it. Something's going on down there already, I just know it."

"Come on Luckie, I'm gonna look a proper eejit if I say I went down there because of your guts, aren't I? Having said that, you're talkin' such a pile of crap now, I might go down there just to get away from you."

"There's an officer down there already and I think he's in danger."

"An officer down there?" Mcbarry said, concern etched on his face. "Anyone we know?"

"Well, no, he's a scouser, but maybe still worth saving, eh?" Luckie said, trying to open Mcbarry up with a little humour.

The sergeant looked stony-faced. "I'm not sure. What does the Super say?"

Luckie could feel the knot that tied his temper to his patience and common sense slowly slipping loose under the tension. "He agrees with me that instead of sitting around polishing our gun barrels, we should be down that hill by now!"

"Really?"

"Look, time's running..." Luckie stopped as a huge flame blossomed in the darkness below and a shotgun boomed across the valley.

Mcbarry looked at Luckie. "Sod it, let's go," he

said.

*****

Irving lay groaning on the ground, his shotgun out of reach behind Duana. Blake needed time to think and clear his head. The painkillers had really kicked in. Megan was out there somewhere still. Perhaps she could disable Duana.

"Why did you do it, Duana?" Blake said.

"Do what?"

"Why did you kill poor Jonah," Blake said, holding onto the house wall as he went up in some kind of mental elevator.

"It was a mess from the start. Jonah was trying to blackmail Vince. We couldn't let that happen. He'd just keep coming back for more. What was it your namesake said? 'A truth that's told with bad intent, beats all the lies you can invent.' Jonah's truth pulled the whole thing down, didn't it? We didn't realise about Megan until the night Vince lured Jonah up into the woods. She'd followed them up there and was going to kill Vince. She missed and wounded Jonah instead. He came stumbling down the hillside…"

"And you killed him."

"It was Freya actually, she'd been painting in the workshop and when she came out she was first on the scene. She stuck him with the palette knife. I was quite impressed with her decisiveness."

"But then you had to move him. So Grant was called for to move the body but Rosie came out then and things got complicated."

"Yes, fortunately she fainted and we were able to gaslight her enough to think she'd been out at the front of the house. Poor, innocent Rosie. I really didn't want her to get involved, you have to believe me. If you hadn't turned up, then we would have killed Megan and made it look like a remorse suicide. Something like that."

"For someone who professes to believe in the sanctity of life, you seem to talk about taking it quite glibly."

"What can I say? Self-preservation has always been a primary Lambert instinct. Besides, I never go out of my way to hurt anyone. You people just complicated matters."

Tanner appeared, limping behind her and picking up the shotgun. "Duana," he said. "We've got to find the girl yet. We haven't got time. Finish him."

"I'm sorry, Blake. You had your chance," Duana said, raising the club.

CHAPTER 40

Time slowed down. It really did for Blake or maybe it was the drugs Irving had given him. Duana seemed frozen, her face twisted into a grimace of hatred, the club raised high above her head ready to cave Blake's skull in. Instead, Duana's face untwisted and transformed into a mask of pain. She stared down in horror and Blake followed her gaze.

Irving gripped her leg and had sunk his teeth deep into her calf. He looked like a wild animal. Blood trickled down his chin and he waggled his head from side to side, like a wolf worrying at the carcass of a dead cow. Charlie, following the old man's example, sank his needle teeth into the other leg. Duana screamed and, triggered by this, Blake threw his head forward, butting her square in the face. Stars exploded before him and he staggered backwards. Duana fell to reveal Tanner standing behind her, his shotgun levelled at Blake.

Blake hurled himself to one side but the blast never came. Instead, the gun clattered to the ground as another crossbow bolt buried itself in Tanner's shoulder. He fell back against the house, looking in horror at the stump of wood poking out of his arm. Blake glanced out into the darkness behind the house. Tanner had the same thought, Megan would be reloading. The next bolt would be a death shot for Vincent Tanner. The fugitive criminal stared at Blake and spat on the ground once before turning tail and hobbling into the shadows. Blake went to chase after him but Irving had straddled Duana Lambert and was busy choking the life out of her. Charlie barked angrily down her ear.

"Thomas no!" Blake yelled, pulling him away from the prone woman. "She'll go to prison. You don't want to be banged up too."

Irving fought against Blake to get back to the groaning Duana. "Look at my house and that poor lassie over there. This is what the bloody Lamberts do. They twist people and ruin their lives and they wriggle free. Every time. Mark my words. She'll swear black is white, muddy the waters and blame everyone else. You've seen her at work with that 'we all did it routine.' It's all lies with her. She bloody breathes lies."

Duana staggered to her feet, gasping for breath. "You're a barbarian," she spat at Irving, as she bent to hold her bleeding leg. "You'll pay for this. If I go down, so will you Thomas Irving. You did things with my father. Things that should shame you..."

Irving stared at her. In the light of the blazing house and with the blood trickling down his face, he looked like some tired old demon, sick of everything. "I know. And they do shame me, every day but I never killed anyone. If they don't lock you up, I'll hunt you down personally and end your wicked life." Charlie bared his teeth and growled at her.

But Duana's attention had moved beyond Irving and out into the road. Detective Sergeant Luckie strode grimly towards them, flanked by three armed officers.

"Bloody Hell, sir, I thought I told you not to destroy the place. Couldn't you just have asked a few questions and been satisfied?"

"Detective Sergeant Luckie, thank goodness, you're here," Duana said limping forward. "These men were about to kill me..."

"Cuff her," Luckie said, not even looking at Duana. "Arrest her for Art forgery... or something..."

One of the armed officers looked puzzled. "What law is that, Sarge?"

"I don't know, do I? Just do her for obstruction for now, she's in my way," Luckie snapped. "Where's Tanner?"

"He ran off up the valley. Megan Yule is after him. She's armed and intends to kill him," Blake said. "There's a young woman round the back with bad burns."

Luckie glanced down at the shotgun on the floor and turned to the other two officers. "Check the house," he said. "And in the woods behind it. See to the girl." They nodded and hurried off. He looked at the shotgun again. "Is that loaded?"

"Aye, but…" Irving started to say. Luckie stepped past him and snatched up the gun.

"Luckie, what are you doing?" Blake said.

"I'm going after the suspect," Luckie said. "You stay here."

"No chance," Blake said, hurrying after him. He turned back to Irving. "Look after Charlie. I'll be back."

They marched into the darkness and Blake glanced at the woods on either side of them. Megan could be stalking them as they walked along. Not that she was a direct threat to them but if she thought they were going to stop her from killing Tanner, she might take a shot at them.

"What's going on, Luckie? Why have you taken Irving's shotgun?"

"Every week," Luckie muttered. "Every week for the last twenty years I've visited him. Can you imagine that, sir?"

"Visited who?"

"Callum Bane. My old partner. He was a rugby

player. A climber. He loved the outdoors, was rarely inside. Great copper, too."

"What happened to him?"

"Vincent Tanner happened to him. The bastard drove a van into Callum when we were answering a call. Callum eats and drinks through a tube now. Sits in one of them big, padded wheelchairs and never speaks. Dunno if he understands half the shit I talk when I go to see him. His finger twitches every now and then, but doctors say that's just reflex."

"I'm sorry," Blake said. "And all this time you've been wondering where Tanner is. What he's doing."

Luckie nodded. "It's torture, sir. Wondering where the bastard is. Imagining him sunning himself on some poolside in South America. And then to discover that he's been under your nose all this time. Every time I went to visit Callum, Tanner wasn't more than half an hour away, meditating and finding inner fucking peace."

"But you weren't to know," Blake said.

"A slip of a girl figured it out and came here to do the right thing. Well, if she fails, I'll finish the job for her."

"Luckie, no," Blake said. "You can't do that..."

Luckie stopped and raised the gun. "There are two shots in this, Blake. I only need one. Stay away from me or I swear…"

Blake backed away and Luckie strode on, looking lonely and distant in the moonlight that reflected off the banks of snow that remained. Keeping his distance, he followed Luckie along the path. They came to the house and Blake wondered about Patricia and what would become of her if Duana went to prison. There was a light on up in her room and Blake thought he could see movement, but it could have just been one of her many cut-outs.

A wave of weariness swept across him. Irving's medication was wearing off. His nose felt broken from butting Duana but the pain in his face just melded with the general aching pulse that was his whole body. A cold wind rustled the pines around him, and he shivered, wondering where Megan had got to. Part of him feared they would turn a bend in this road and find Tanner on the ground, punctured by so many bolts that he looked like roadkill. He hoped not, but part of him thought that wouldn't be a bad end to all this and it would keep Luckie out of trouble, too.

Luckie had stopped and was looking at the road. Blake did likewise and noticed bloodspots. Tanner had gone this way. When he looked up, Luckie had quickened his pace. Behind them, Blake could hear sirens which told him the lane had been opened up. Hopefully, they'd get a fire engine to save Irving's house and back-up would reach them before Luckie found Tanner. It all felt a little too late, though.

Blake quickened his pace and drew closer to Luckie who had stopped on the bend in the road. When Blake caught up with him he froze.

They had come to the end of the road and Tanner stood at the edge of the plunge pool, perfectly still. Megan was just a few feet away from him, her crossbow levelled at his body. "Oh thank God for that. It's the cavalry," Tanner said, giving Blake and Luckie a pathetic smile. "Come on, lads, take me in. This mad bitch is gonna kill me."

"Don't worry, Vince," Luckie said, raising the gun. "I won't let her harm you."

"Great," Tanner said, relaxing a little.

"No, cos it's me who's gonna be blowing your fucking head off."

Megan and Tanner both stared at Luckie. "What?"

"Constable Callum Bane, Vince. Mean anything to you? No, I didn't think it would. Just one of the many people whose life you destroyed."

"He blinded my father," Megan hissed. "He's mine."

Blake stepped in front of Tanner. "Stop! Luckie, killing Tanner isn't going to heal your friend, is it? It won't bring your father back, Megan, will it?"

"No but it'll stop him from ever hurting anyone else again..."

"Look," Tanner said. "I've changed. I've had a long time to think about what I did and I know it was wrong. If I could go back and change things, I would. I'm not the same fella I used to be."

"Which is why you were ready to kill Blake with a shotgun? Or were you full of remorse when you threw those petrol bombs?" Megan said.

"All this time you were breathing the fresh air and enjoying life while Callum sat, trapped in his own body," Luckie growled.

"Luckie. Think! If you kill Tanner now, you'll be a criminal. You'll go to prison. Your whole career will have been a waste of time. A lie, even. Everyone will look at the headlines and think, 'another hypocrite who told us what to do but broke the law himself when it suited him.'"

"He's got a point," Tanner said.

"Shut up," Blake said, pointing his finger. "You shut up because I'm a fraction of an inch from walking away."

"He'll sit in a prison cell no different from that room he's been in. What difference will it make?"

"He didn't sit there meditating, did you, Tanner? You used Patricia's cut-out figures more than once. I bet you were all over this valley, secretly enjoying your freedom. Besides, there's a difference between choosing to stay in one room and being told you have to. Megan, you haven't actually killed anyone yet..."

Megan gave Blake a sidelong glance. "But Freya," she winced at the memory of the burning girl. "She was on fire..."

"You did that to save us. You have your whole life ahead of you. Why let this lowlife bring you down to his level?"

"You'd be doing the world a favour. Even if they didn't know it," Luckie said, his face hard and cold.

"And when you're in prison, Luckie, who will visit Callum? Anyone? I get the impression that he'll be forgotten. Is that what you want?"

Luckie lowered the shotgun. "No," he said. "That's not what I want. You're right... sir. It's not for me to take his life." He turned to Megan. "Nor you."

Megan looked over at Luckie, taking her eyes off Tanner and that was when he made his move.

CHAPTER 41

It all took place so silently that Blake wondered if it had happened at all. There was nothing either Luckie or Blake could do. Tanner lunged towards Megan but his sudden movement alerted the woman and she squeezed the trigger. Blake heard the 'thwack' of the bowstring and Tanner staggered back, the bolt deep in his chest. A rose of blood blossomed across his dirty shirt. He looked down at the wound and back at Megan. Then he fell backwards into the pool with a splash and floated out, staring blankly into the frozen sky.

Megan dropped the crossbow and put a hand to her mouth. Blake put an arm round her. "Come on, Megan. It's over."

She broke away from Blake and walked over to the pool and stared down at Tanner's body. A single tear trickled down her cheek. "I didn't mean to... He was going to attack me. I had to stop him."

"Yes," Blake said, looking over at Luckie. "None of us meant to harm him." Luckie nodded and gave a tight smile.

The sound of engines echoed up the valley and Irving appeared in the Land Rover with Patricia in the front, beaming at Charlie who squirmed and wriggled on her knee. Behind him came an ambulance and a police car, blue lights flashing. Luckie directed the ambulance to Tanner's body in the pool.

Blake climbed into the back of the Land Rover. Irving looked over his shoulder.

"I brought Patricia along for the ride. Not good her being alone in the big house all on her own. You got him, then?"

Blake nodded and watched Luckie lead Megan to the police car. The stocky sergeant made his way back to the Land Rover and put his head in through the back window. "Thanks, sir," he said. "You saved my bacon, back there. I'll not forget it."

Blake nodded, and grinned. "Yippee-ki-yay. Buy me a beer, Al."

Luckie pursed his lips and gave him a reproachful look and then grinned. "Maybe even two," he said, patting the car and backing away.

"Hi Willum," Patricia said. "Charlie happy."

"That's nice, Patricia. I'm glad," Blake said, his eyes suddenly feeling heavy. "Willum sleepy."

The journey up out of the valley was a blur to Blake. He saw the moonlight through the pines, the outline of the big house, the dying flames on Irving's house, his wrecked car tucked at the side of the road. Then they were driving up hill. When he opened his eyes, Rosie was dragging him out of the Land Rover.

"My god, Will, look at you! What happened?"

Blake remembered muttering something about Duana, Tanner and fire but he wasn't sure it made any sense. Then he fell to the floor and thought it was quite nice down there; cool, soft and a nice place to sleep.

CHAPTER 42

This was the last place Laura wanted to be but the pain in her arm was so intense that she couldn't argue with Gilmore. He had dragged her across the fields back to the farm and almost thrown her into the back of his Land Rover. Archie lay whining his concern at her side and licking her hand.

Laura had tried to sit up and open the door. "Steve, I can't. I can't go there. You don't understand."

"I understand that you've smashed your arm in and you need medical attention."

"But I'm on the run. There are some bad people after me. If they find me, they'll kill me."

Gilmore stopped the car and looked back at her. "And you're the one who told me that I needed to stick up for myself. That if I hid away from things, they'd only get worse."

She'd thrown up twice in the back of the car then and stopped arguing after that. She felt Steve's strong arms picking her up and saw lights blurring into each other. Archie barked somewhere in the distance as she floated into Accident and Emergency. Then she came to rest on a trolley of some kind and heard curtains swish around her.

A nurse leaned over her. “What’s your name, love?”

“It’s Stacy,” Gilmore said, confidently. “Stacy Smith.”

“Stacy? Can you hear me Stacy?”

Laura raised herself and nodded. “I can but my name’s not Stacy,” she croaked. “It’s Laura. Laura Vexley.” She looked at Gilmore and gave him a brief smile. “Sorry. I’d quite like to be a Stacy but I’m not. I’m Laura Vexley.”

“Nice to meet you Laura Vexley,” Gilmore said, returning her smile and holding her good hand. “Welcome back to the world.”

CHAPTER 43

Blake awoke in a soft bed with crisp, clean sheets. He had no memory of arriving in this room. The thick curtains were drawn but he could smell that it was a hotel, tidy and well-swept but with the unmistakable air of a place that is wiped and hoovered every day. He sat up and switched the bedside lamp on. There was a table with a full fruit bowl on it, a huge screen on the wall and a three-piece suite sat in front of some French windows, covered by more long, thick curtains. Everything about this room boasted of its luxury. Blake had no idea of the time. He had slept a long and dreamless sleep. At some point, he'd half awoke and then rolled over and fallen asleep once more. Looking down, he realised that he must have been out for a long time because his clothes lay folded on the suit-case stand, washed and neatly pressed.

He stood up, grimacing at the pain in his legs, arms, chest, neck and head. In fact the only part of his body that wasn't complaining were his toes and, looking down, he saw that one of them was raw and bloody. Naked, he shuffled over to the long mirror that hung on the wall by the bathroom. "Jeez." He looked like he'd been put through a mangle. His eyes were partially closed and puffed up, the lids a yellowy blue, his nose had a black stripe across it which could only be more bruising. His chest was a thundercloud of purples and blues and hundreds of tiny cuts and scratches crisscrossed his arms and legs.

Reaching for the dressing gown, he slid it on slowly and carefully, allowing himself little yips of pain as the heavy fabric scraped his cuts. Just as he got it on, there was a gentle tap on the door. It opened a little slowly. "Will?" Rosie called, softly through the crack. "Are you awake?"

"I am," he said. "Where am I?"

"The Old Smithy Hotel," Rosie said. "How are you?"

"Battered and bruised but okay," Will replied, walking over to the armchair and sinking into it. "Did you bring me here?"

"Yes. I didn't know what else to do. Simon said it would be fine..."

"Simon?"

"Carver. The solicitor. You remember him?"

Will frowned. "Yeah. He's been looking after you then?"

"Will Blake, the protective brother!" Rosie laughed. "Yes, he's been very sweet actually. He's paying for all of this actually..."

"Really? That's decent of him."

"I think he's trying to make amends. He didn't realise quite what Duana was up to but had his suspicions. When we realised she was running a forgery racket from the big house, we notified Luckie straight away."

"Right," Blake said. He frowned and scanned the room. "Where's Patricia and Charlie?"

"They're here too. Would you believe there's a rather luxurious kennels at the back of the hotel? Patrica had a single room of her own. She's quite stressed but seems okay if she can stay with Charlie."

"Good," Blake said. "Poor woman. She's lost her home and family. Everything."

"Well, not exactly," Rosie said, looking sheepish.

"Not exactly? What do you mean?"

"Well, I've decided to look after her. Thomas Irving has offered us a room at his house or what's left of it, but Simon suggested we move in with him until everything is sorted..."

"Move in with him?"

Rosie gave Blake a stern look. "I'm a grown woman, Will, not some dewy-eyed teenager. I know what I'm doing. If Patricia says she wants to stay with me, then I think social services will okay it."

"It's a hell of a commitment."

Rosie looked pinched and tired. "I know but I owe it to her. I've been part of Patricia's life for some time now. Looking back, I can see that the others cared about her but they never did the difficult stuff like getting her to bathe or taking her to the dentist. They'd smile and nod and give her tea but they didn't try to enrich her life. There was only me. So I want to carry that on. She deserves it."

"I see," Blake said. "I was going to ask you to come back to the Wirral with me. I mean, you'd both be welcome but..."

Rosie put a hand on Will's arm. "It's better if we stay up here, where Patricia is settled. Who knows? In the fullness of time, we might even be able to buy the big house."

"How?"

"Simon reckons that sometimes they sell off the proceeds of crime. I don't know if Duana will want to settle back down there after she's spent time in prison."

"Not with Irving on her doorstep," Blake said, remembering what Thomas had said to her about what he'd do if she ever returned.

"Simon says it's a good business proposition. It could be an outdoor pursuits centre or a hostel."

"Simon says," Blake repeated, smiling. Rosie gave him a playful punch in the arm which made him double up.

"Well that'll teach you not to tease me," Rosie said, grinning.

"Seriously, though, you know you can always rely on us, if you need to come back, Rosie, yeah?"

Rosie smiled. "I know I can rely on you, Will. Look what you did here..."

Blake looked sidelong across the room. "Erm, destroyed your Community, put most of them in hospital or prison? Yeah. Nice work, Will."

"No, Will. Sooner or later, something terrible would have happened there. I can see that, now. Duana's nature was destructive and controlling. It's like scales have fallen from my eyes. If you hadn't been there to sort things, I think the poison of that place would have infected me in the end. So thank you."

"Okay, any time you need a house burning down, a landslide and a forgery ring breaking up, I'm the brother to do it."

"Shall we get breakfast?"

Will grinned. "Only if Simon is paying."

*****

Detective Sergeant Luckie stood next to Callum's chair and stared out into the garden again. "Well I got the bastard, Callum. Or rather a girl called Megan did. Shot him right through his black heart with a crossbow bolt. You'd have loved it."

Callum swallowed and his finger twitched. His eyes gazed out with no focus that Luckie could discern. Luckie carried on. "He'd been living down in Devil's Glen all this time. I reckon that Duana Lambert was his accomplice, too. Picked him up after he'd topped the other two in his gang. Maybe we can prove that, eh? That would be the icing on the cake, I'm telling you."

Luckie drew a short breath. "I couldn't do it, Callum. When push came to shove, I couldn't kill Tanner for you." He narrowed his eyes and looked closely at Callum. "I don't think you wanted me to, did you? Blake was right. He's the Chief Inspector I was telling you about. The scouser. Except he insists he's not a scouser. He's okay, though. Good copper, I reckon. He looked like he'd been run over by a tank when we got to him and a lot of people would have walked away when they saw me stomping off with that shotgun in my hands. He stuck by me. Like you would have done."

Silence fell over the room for a while and Luckie sighed in the end. "I nearly blew it, Callum. Just let the monster inside me take over for a few seconds and that was it. I need good counsel, pal. D'you mind if I come here and discuss some cases with you again?"

Callum made a strange gurgling sound but seemed okay as far as Luckie could tell. "I'll take that as a yes then. I might have to move the visiting days around. I'm going to make time to see Megan whenever I can. I reckon she'll need a friendly face once the trial is all over. She's had her life turned over by the same bastard, eh? I'll see you soon, mate."

Luckie patted Callum on the shoulder and left the room.

CHAPTER 44

After a few days of rest, Blake felt a little more human. He'd booked into the Black Bull Inn not far from the High Street. It was a quaint place with low oak beams and a log burner which was welcome. Rosie and Simon tried to get Blake to stay longer in the Old Smithy hotel but Will didn't feel comfortable there, besides, they didn't allow Charlie in the bar. Patricia was sad to see him go but Blake suspected by the look in Rosie's eye that Patricia would have a Charlie of her own pretty soon.

"I think Simon's going to get the shock of his life when you move in with him. You sure he knows what he's letting himself in for?"

"He's not daft," Rosie said. "And anyway, we'll have Mr Irving to impose on once he has his house rebuilt. Spoilt for choice!"

Will nodded. "How do you stay so positive about the future, Rosie? I mean, The Community is gone. Megan is in custody charged with the murder of Tanner. Freya's in hospital, in a serious way. Duana and Rothwell are going to be banged up for quite a while."

"I don't know, Will. How do you stay positive?" Rosie said, raising her chin and staring him in the eye. "You hunt down criminals every day. Half of them go through the justice machine straight back out on the street to offend again. The woman you love is in hiding and you look like you've been run over by a lorry."

Blake laughed and shook his head. "I don't know. You just keep on keeping on, don't you?"

"Well there you go then."

"You better call Jeff and tell him you're alive. He'll fret otherwise. Or get horribly jealous and sulk."

Rosie winced. "Do you think so?"

"I do."

He'd called Jeff himself to tell them that everything was all right and felt guilty that his brother was unaware of the danger they'd faced. That was tempered with a twinge of irritation at his response to the call.

"Will Rosie go to prison, Will? You said you were going to help her."

"She'll be fine. She's got a good brief and it's pretty obvious that she was blissfully unaware of the whole forgery racket that was going on under her nose. Huxley was killed with a palette knife, not the big vegetable knife she was carrying."

Jeff had muttered something about making sure she was okay and apologised for not being any more help.

"You did help, Jeff. I think the whole forgery angle threw Jonah's blackmail plan into clear view."

"Really?" Jeff said, his voice brightening. "It was tough being stuck at home. I was worried sick." There was a pause. "Well done, Will. You did a good job."

Will grinned, confused at why that meant so much to him. "Thanks, Jeff. We need to meet up when I get back, yeah?"

Now he sat in the bar of the Black Bull, with a pint of Guinness in his hand, watching the flames dance in the wood burner. Charlie lay curled at his feet, snoring lightly. Luckie sat opposite him, nursing a pint too. Being a February weekday, it was quiet with only a few punters propping up the bar.

"Daniel Craig," Blake said. "He's from the Wirral."

"Who?" Luckie said staring into his beer.

"Daniel Craig, you know, James Bond."

"Are you just going to list people who are a little bit famous and came from Liverpool all evening? Only I could be at home paring my toenails."

"The Wirral, not Liverpool. Jim Bowen."

Luckie's eyebrows shot up. "Really? The Bullseye guy?"

"Born in Heswall. Moved away when he was a kid, I think..."

"Right. I really didn't want Megan to kill Tanner at the pool you know," Luckie said, lowering his voice. He took a swig of beer.

"I know, Luckie. I've been in that position myself."

"You have?"

"Yeah. A real psycho, mutilated people, held them captive," Blake looked hard at Luckie. "He stole my mother's dead body and I found myself in a position to throw him off a tall building. He almost wanted me to. Sick bastard."

"You didn't then?"

"No. But I get it. The Tanner thing was personal, wasn't it?"

"He was an animal who put my best friend into a nursing home for the rest of his life. I broke the news to Callum, today. I just felt a bit empty."

They were quiet for a moment. "What'll you do now?" Blake said at last.

"What d'you mean?"

"Come on Luckie, I can see it in your eyes. You've had enough, haven't you?"

"Well, I guess I want to get this case put together but, yeah. I'm done. I'm fifty-five and I'll be looking at my pension options soon as I can. It's going to be a long, drawn out business. I hope Rosie's up to it."

Blake nodded. "She's a Blake. Tough as old boots."

"Aye. I'm going to try and link Duana in with the Dumbarton Three. She needs to account for what she did to enable that..."

"That might be a stretch. You'll be relying on rumour and hearsay in the underworld. Maybe some old bank accounts, if they exist."

"I've got a team checking the big house for any evidence that links it with the Dumbarton Three apart from Tanner's existence. There might be something there. She has to explain how he ended up in The Community, too." Luckie paused for a second. "I want to apologise. I was an arsehole when you first arrived. There's no excuse. I'm sorry."

Blake shrugged. "No need, Neil. I'd be as sceptical if someone like me came clodhopping into my patch and it turned out to be quite a case."

"True. And you did cause a landslide... and Irving's house got burnt down... not to mention the minor battle at the end..." Luckie gave Blake a sidelong glance and Blake grinned.

"Disaster is my middle name. Ask my boss. Oh, you have already!"

“So what happens next?”

Blake shrugged. “Back home, I guess. I’ve some unfinished business of my own too that I need to sort out. A woman I need to track down.”

“Well, good luck with that.” Luckie raised his glass.

“Thanks,” Blake said, clinking his pint onto Luckie’s. “I’ll need it.”

CHAPTER 45

The railway station thronged with commuters heading home, their breath pluming in the cold February air. Laura stood with Gilmore and Archie on the platform, her arm in a sling. "Well, this is your train," Gilmore said. "Sure I can't persuade you to stay? Once that arm's better, you'd make a good farm hand. Archie wouldn't mind. Neither would I..."

Laura shook her head and smiled. "No," she said. "I've got to get back and sort things out. I've pretended to be someone I'm not for far too long. Anyway, I'd just cramp your style at the farm, once you've developed your FARMR App, you'll be fighting them off."

Gilmore laughed. "I'll have to do something; I'm too old to join the Young Farmers. I saw a website called Muddy matches that brings like-minded agriculturalists together. Maybe I'll give that a go."

"Sounds great."

"What about you? Will you be okay?"

Laura shrugged. "Who knows? But I'll stick up for myself and I won't be living off Pot Noodles in B&Bs and looking over my shoulder all the time."

"Bring it on, eh?"

Laura picked up her suitcase with her good hand and nodded. "Bring it on." She was going home.

*****

Blake quite liked the hire car he'd been given although he felt guilty for even thinking it. Charlie lay in his safety crate, snoring and oblivious to the speed they were travelling. Blake grinned. Nothing shook or rattled. There were no icy breezes chilling his legs from unseen gaps in the floor. The gears changed smoothly, and the seat didn't feel like it was made of papier-mache. It also went like the clappers and he had to keep watching his speed. He decided that his father's poor, battered Opel Manta could rest in peace up in Scotland. He'd have to scrap it or let Irving have it for scrap. Either way, if he was going to be travelling more in his search for Laura, he should do it in comfort. He wondered where she was and for a moment, longed just to talk to her and tell her what had happened, what he'd seen. If he could, he would explain how all the lies he'd heard in the last few days had convinced him that honesty was the best policy. He didn't care what Laura had done but she once told him that he should face the truth and not live in the past. He needed to find her and remind her of that. And he'd stay by her side, whatever happened. Life was too short to waste time dancing to the tune of twisted people.

He was going home.

The End

ABOUT THE AUTHOR

Jon Mayhew lives on the Wirral with his family and has done all his life. A teacher for many years, he enjoys traditional music and plays regularly in ceilidh bands and sessions. Jon is also an award-winning author. His dark children's books are published by Bloomsbury.

Find out more at www.jemayhew.blogspot.com

Find JE Mayhew on Facebook and twitter.

Made in the USA
Las Vegas, NV
15 April 2021

21463668R00215